SKIES OF OLYMPUS

TRIALS 1, 2 & 3: HERA, ATHENA & ARTEMIS

ELIZA RAINE

Editors: Leonora Bulbeck, Anna Bowles

Cover: The Write Wrapping

For my husband. It's my magnificent octopus!

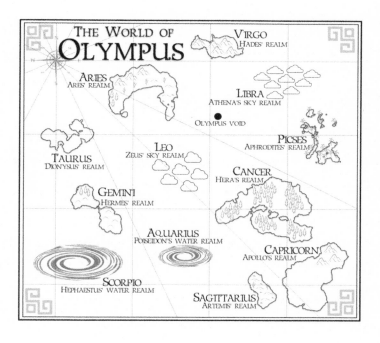

THE WORLD OF
OLYMPUS

VIRGO
HADES' REALM

ARIES
ARES' REALM

LIBRA
ATHENA'S SKY REALM

OLYMPUS VOID

PICSES
APHRODITES' REALM

LEO
ZEUS' SKY REALM

TAURUS
DIONYSUS' REALM

CANCER
HERA'S REALM

GEMINI
HERMES' REALM

AQUARIUS
POISEIDON'S WATER REALM

CAPRICORN
APOLLO'S REALM

SCORPIO
HEPHAESTUS' WATER REALM

SAGITTARIUS
ARTEMIS' REALM

HERA

SKIES OF OLYMPUS

TRIAL ONE

LYSSA

A silence fell over the crowded cargo deck as the last side of the wooden crate was crowbarred loose. Not a comfortable silence, or an amazed silence, but an unpleasant silence. The type that is never followed by anything good. Captain Lyssa of the *Alastor* stared, tight-lipped, as a being she had never seen before swam gently in wide circles around the tank that had been inside the crate.

It was the same size as a human, with a torso and head that was humanoid. It had no legs though, and Lyssa frowned at the tail-like limb that was there instead. The whole body and face were covered in iridescent white scales that glistened pale purple when the thin shafts of light fell on them. A brisk cough snapped her attention to the woman stood beyond the tank, the Lady Lamia.

'I'm sorry, my lady. Can we just have a minute alone?' Epizon said, stepping forward. The covered head he had addressed nodded curtly in response. Epizon turned and marched towards the maze of stacked crates filling the back of the ship's hull. Lyssa walked quickly to keep up with him, his stride much longer than hers. As soon as they were out of earshot, she spoke.

'Epizon, I know what you're going to say, and it's too late. We can't afford to upset these people.'

Epizon spun to face her, his dark face set and angry. 'Captain, our code isn't much, but we're not slavers!' His deep voice rose as he spoke, and she glared at him. He looked down, taking a long breath, visibly containing his emotion. 'Captain, we did not know there was a being in the cargo. We will not sell beings.'

'She's already here, with six Cyclops guards and the money. What exactly do you propose we do?' Lyssa gestured back towards where the Lady Lamia stood, surrounded by the ugly beings. They were large, stupid creatures with one amber eye in the centre of their forehead, and sharp protrusions erupting all over their hairless skulls. A nervous-looking human boy stood behind her, holding an open box of silver drachmas.

'You know exactly what I think we should do,' he said, urgency in his low voice. 'You can't seriously be suggesting we hand this creature over to her. You've heard the rumours.'

Lyssa clenched her fists and looked back towards the Lady Lamia. The daughter of a god, and clearly not all human, she was famous in Olympus for her cruelty. Some of the rumours said she only ate living flesh. Lyssa's nose scrunched up in revulsion at the thought. Her eyes flicked to the tank, and her stomach lurched. The creature's huge green eyes were fixed on her. Even from a distance, they were piercing enough to unsettle her. This thing had been alone in the dark for weeks in the hull of the *Alastor*. Lyssa looked back at Epizon. Any moral turmoil she felt was magnified plainly on her first mate's face. He looked at her beseechingly.

'Of course not,' she breathed, and Epizon's tense stance relaxed. 'But we really can't afford to fight her. That's why we took this bloody job in the first place; she was paying well,' Lyssa muttered. Her 'ask no questions' attitude suited the captain of a smugglers ship, but this wasn't the first time it had landed her somewhere she didn't want to be.

'Don't worry, Captain,' her first mate said, his huge frame filling out as he stood taller. 'Maybe we can reason with her.'

Lyssa snorted. 'Ever the diplomat,' she said, rolling her eyes. 'The woman is rumoured to be a vampire demigod. The chances of getting out of this with no damage are slim to none.'

Epizon shrugged. 'Cost of doing the right thing, Captain.'

'If that cost ends up being our lives, it's on you,' she said, turning back towards the tank.

'I can live with that. Besides, we've taken on worse things than her and her Cyclopes,' he answered, starting towards the lady.

'I'm more worried about the thing in the tank,' Lyssa muttered, and followed after him.

LYSSA KNEW she didn't look like much of a threat, a slightly shorter-than-average human woman whose only standout feature was her mass of flame-red hair. Epizon, on the other hand, was well over six foot, built like a Minotaur and had skin the colour of onyx. Remarkably, he was human too, though Lyssa was sure there must be some giant in his ancestry somewhere.

She shot another sideways glance at the tank being as they passed it. Its unnerving gaze was now, like everyone else's on the deck, on Epizon. Their intention showed in the tension of Epizon's walk, the way he seemed to grow as he approached. The guards simultaneously moved closer to the lady, protecting her on all sides.

'Lady Lamia,' Lyssa addressed her guest formally as they reached the tank.

'Do we have a problem?' The lady's silky-smooth voice came from behind a dense black veil. The red shine of her eyes and lips was all that could be seen behind it. Her head-dress and long gown glittered with gems and metals that were intricately woven into a blue fabric that looked like liquid when it moved. If you believed the rumours, the expensive and demure outfit was hiding a form nobody had ever laid eyes on. Lyssa wondered what kind of being she was. She couldn't even tell how many limbs she had.

'Yes, I'm afraid we do. You are aware, I think, that it is against code to trade in living beings. We were unaware of what was in the crate, and now that we do know, we're not going to be able to complete this job.' She tried to make eye contact through the veil and prayed that the rumours were exaggerated.

After a pause, the lady replied. 'We've already paid you half of the fee. An exceptionally generous fee.'

'Obviously, we will return the money.'

'But wouldn't you be out of pocket? You have been all the way to Leo and back.'

There was a movement under the gown, and the nervous boy stepped forward, holding out the box of silver. Now Lyssa could see him, she realised he was older than she had first thought. He was strong and fit, muscle packed across a lithe frame, and not at all bad to look at if she ignored the filthy shirt and torn black trousers. Light-brown hair was pushed back from a face that looked weather-worn, and his warm eyes sparkled with a defiance that belied his hesitant motions.

The lady spoke again, and Lyssa snapped her attention back to her. 'A ship of this poor condition would benefit from all these drachmas, would it not?' she asked softly.

The adrenaline Lyssa could feel flowing through her spiked, and she tensed involuntarily. She had felt Epizon do the same beside her. This was not going to end peacefully. Insulting a captain's ship was a sure way of indicating that. The lady moved forward. She seemed to glide rather than step. The ugly guards all moved with her.

'We will not trade with you, Lady Lamia,' Lyssa repeated, holding her ground. She'd meant what she'd said to Epizon about not wanting a fight, but now it was coming, she couldn't stop the excitement trickling through her body.

'Captain Lyssa,' the lady said quietly. 'Relax. This is not a being as you or I know it. It requires nothing to live and cannot communicate. It is barely sentient. Think of it as purely decorative.'

Epizon growled almost imperceptibly beside her. The lady had touched a nerve. Lyssa looked over at the creature's unsettlingly piercing green eyes, fixed on the blue-robed Lady Lamia. There was no way it was barely sentient.

'All the same, it is against the code. We can't help you.' Lyssa's voice betrayed her growing disgust.

The Lady Lamia let out a bark of laughter and glided back to where she had stood. This time her guards moved away from her, towards Lyssa and Epizon.

'You really don't have any choice, young lady. I am already here, as is my quarry. You cannot afford to fight this fight.' Her voice was getting louder as she continued to glide backwards. The guards advanced. 'I'm surprised you can afford anything, to be honest,' she continued. Lyssa took a deep breath, trying to concentrate. 'In fact,' Lady Lamia said, now a safe distance from the imminent violence, 'how do you afford this monster of a man?' She gestured at Epizon. 'How much do you want for him?' She laughed again.

Epizon growled loudly this time and widened his stance. Lyssa moved a few feet away from him. Her skin was beginning to throb with energy, the muscles in her face and neck twitching as she tried to keep control of herself a little longer.

'Do you know what *lyssa* means in the ancient language?' she called out to the lady as she focused on the two guards now slowly turning in her direction. The other four continued on towards Epizon. Lyssa smiled and closed her eyes.

'Of course I do. Though I don't see the relevance,' the lady replied dismissively.

'It means "rage",' Lyssa said quietly, and let the coursing energy overcome her as she opened her eyes.

THE THROBBING in her skin became a steady flow of power that she could feel surging through every part of her body. As the first Cyclops put his head down to charge at her, she dropped to a crouch. The second he was within her reach, she launched herself upwards, her fist catching the creature in its low, bent cheek. A sickening thud preceded the creature's wail, and he flew up and backwards into the air. Lyssa was aware of a roar from Epizon as she began to run towards the second guard. She found the confusion and indecision on his face grimly satisfying. He chose to stand his ground too late and had no time to brace himself for the kick she planted squarely under his chin. His face crumpled, and he sank slowly to the floor. Lyssa's momentum took her over the top of his prostrate body, and she stumbled onto her hands and knees. She looked towards Lady Lamia and jumped to her feet when she couldn't see her.

'Lady Lamia's back on her ship,' a voice sounded in her head.

'How the hell did she get there?' Lyssa shouted, turning to the tank to check the being was still there.

'Don't know; don't care. They've got serious weapons, Cap. Time to run,' replied the voice.

The tank creature was hovering, showing no emotion, staring at Epizon. Lyssa followed its stare and was relieved to see that three of the Cyclopes lay dead or unconscious behind where he stood. The last danced around Epizon, head down, moving backwards and forwards jerkily, like a boxer. It had clearly reached its goal a few times with its sharp horns, as bright trickles of blood stood out on Epizon's dark bare arms. He held them both out wide, goading the creature. It snarled and there was a loud pop. The beast crumpled to the floor, and a small whooping cheer came from high up somewhere in the shadows of the mass of stacked crates.

'About bloody time!' yelled Epizon. He turned to Lyssa. 'We need to get out of here,' he said.

'I'm not taking these ugly brutes with me,' Lyssa grunted, kicking one of the fallen guards.

'Easy, Captain,' said Epizon, his calm returning faster than hers. 'Len, get off those boxes and get up on deck.'

The ship shook violently and they both fell. Lyssa cursed loudly as her leg scraped down one of the dead Cyclopes' head spikes.

'Shouldn't have kicked it,' called Epizon, already back on

his feet and running for the hauler at the back of the deck. The ship jerked sharply again, and there was another yell from the boxes.

'Abderos, we'd better be on our way,' shouted Lyssa.

'I told you we had to go!' came the indignant response in her head. 'We're about a league high. Do you want to stay here or try to lose her closer to the ground?'

'Stay in the sky, Abderos. We're faster than her up here.'

'Aye aye, Cap.'

She leaned over to inspect the tear in her trousers over her bloody shin.

'Want me to kiss it better?'

Lyssa groaned and looked up at Len. 'Not the time, Len. It's fine. Get upstairs and help Epizon before we take any more damage,' she said.

'But, Cap, I shot a Cyclops! I need a reward.' The satyr leaned towards her, lips pursed for a kiss.

'Len!' Epizon roared from the hauler at the same time Lyssa aimed a cuff at him. He hopped out of her reach and trotted towards the back of the deck, laughing.

Satyrs were half goat, half human, but usually goat-sized, and Len was small even for his race. His bottom half was dark brown furry goat hind legs, with a small white tail. The fur reached his waist, and then, quite abruptly, his round human torso made up the rest of his three-foot stature. He had dark hair around small, pointy horns on an otherwise human-looking, mischievous face. He could get in and out of almost any space on the ship. Len had been a compromise when putting together her crew. He was an excellent medic and knew more about Olympus than anyone else she knew. Unfortunately, in every other way, he was a typical satyr. He fancied anything female, said exactly what he was thinking out loud and had no concept of personal space.

Lyssa pushed herself to her feet and started towards the hauler, testing her injured leg.

'Wait!' shouted a male voice. She spun, the voice unfamiliar to her. She pulled her slingshot from her belt as she turned, dipping into the pouch full of lead shot at her hip, and found herself aiming at the slave boy. He threw his arms above his head. 'Don't shoot! Please.'

'What are you doing on my cargo deck?' she demanded.

'I didn't mean to be here, but unless you shoot me, it's better than on her ship.' He nodded towards the dead Cyclops at his feet. 'There are lots more of them, and they smell terrible.' His voice was clear, and he was surprisingly well spoken.

'How did you end up with the Lady Lamia?' she asked, her weapon still levelled at him. He kept his hands in the air. She scanned his body, looking for weapons. She could see none. He was definitely closer to her age than she'd first thought.

'I was kidnapped,' he said. 'From Libra. Her thugs took everything I had and then put me to work on the ship. They even took my boots.' She looked down at his feet, and he wiggled his bare toes at her.

'Are you from Libra?' she asked. She didn't get the feeling he was lying, and there was something almost haughty about his demeanour.

'No.'

'Do you still have the box of silver you were carrying?'

He hesitated. Hope lifted in her. Epizon wouldn't approve of keeping the money, but gods know they needed it.

'Yes. I hid it.'

'What?'

'I hid it. Whilst you were all fighting. You're much stronger than you look, by the way.'

'You hid it? On my own cargo deck?'

'Yes. What kind of ship is this?' He looked around at the scuffed wooden walls interestedly.

Lyssa's temper spiked, and she drew the band back tight on the slingshot. She caught herself and took a deep breath.

'Let's get a couple of things straight, shall we? You are, essentially, a stowaway on my ship. Meaning I have every right to fling you overboard and watch your flailing body fall through the skies until you hit the ground. You should be kneeling at my feet with that silver and asking me to deliver you back to wherever the hell you came from, not hiding it on my own ship and asking stupid questions!' Anger danced across her skin, leaving a trail of tingling heat as her voice rose.

'Hey, I don't want to be here any more than you want me here!' he protested. 'Why would I want to be on a battered old smugglers ship when I could be—'

Lyssa didn't find out where he could be. She'd closed the gap between them in a second and had her hand around his throat before he could react. His face paled and his bright eyes widened in fear as she forced him backwards until he was pinned against the dark wooden hull. He struggled in vain, banging his head against the dull brass rim of a porthole.

'I don't think you're taking me seriously,' she hissed at him.

He stopped struggling. 'How are you so strong?' he choked.

'Where is the silver?' she said, squeezing her hand

against his neck. He pointed behind her frantically. She loosened her grip.

'In the crate with the coconuts,' he gasped. She let go of him, and he slid to the ground, clutching at his throat.

'I want to get off this ship,' he croaked as she strode towards the chest-high stack of coconut crates on the other side of the deck.

'Fine by me. We're headed to Libra, anyway.' Her face split into a broad grin, and the tingling anger began to ease as she moved a loose lid off the top crate. The ornate wooden box was there, nestled amongst the dark, hairy fruits. She flipped open the lid and was about to pick up a handful of the gleaming silver coins when there was a thunderous crack, and the ship lurched hard to the left. Crates began crashing off tall stacks onto the floor around her, and she heard the boy yell.

'She's got storm ballistas, Cap. We can't outrun them without a boost!' came the voice in her head.

'Shit,' she cursed, and shoved the lid back on the box of silver. She ran to where she'd left the boy on the ground, and dragged him up to his feet. He scowled but let her shove him towards the door to the hauler.

The ship creaked as it rocked, righting itself, and the fallen crates scraped across the already scuffed floor as they slid around. The boy stopped at the open doorway, peering into the wooden box beyond. It could fit about five people in it and was only lit by a small porthole on the far wall.

'I'm not getting in that,' he said, planting his feet.

'Yes, you are,' Lyssa said, and pushed him.

He stumbled forward, and she jumped in behind him. The box immediately began moving upwards, and she saw the panic on his face. A small stab of pity pushed through her adrenaline.

'It's just a hauler; it moves between decks. We'll be out in a second,' she told him. He glared at her, and she liked the defiance on his face better than the fear. 'What's your name?' she asked him.

'Phyleus,' he growled.

'Well, Phyleus, this "battered old smugglers ship" is about to give you quite a show,' she said, as the hauler arrived at the top deck of the *Alastor*.

2

LYSSA

Adrenaline hummed through her veins as she yanked open the hauler door and hit the deck running. The main mast of the *Alastor* stood huge and proud ahead of her, shimmering silver sails billowing as the ship flew through the sky. Brightly coloured clouds raced past the ship on either side as she ran towards the mast, anticipation building in her muscles. She threw her hands out in front of her as she reached the wide wooden pole, skidding to a stop and pressing her palms flat to the cool wood. A smile spread across her face as she felt the pent-up energy buzzing through her leap as she connected with her ship. She tipped her head back and concentrated as hard as she could on the Rage flowing through her. She got angrier and angrier as the pulsing energy built, until a torrent of power was surging and straining to be free of her control.

Just as she thought she couldn't contain the feeling any longer, she heard the sound of the sails snapping taught and was vaguely aware of the blazing red colour rippling across their surface. The ship lurched forward, and she gripped the mast hard as they sped up, soaring through the clouds faster and faster as the sails drew her magic from her. Power flowed from every part of her body into the ship, and she let out a cry of delight. Channelling her Rage magic into the ship made her feel incredible, so much more powerful than when she used it to fight. She was using her power to tear through the skies and outrun her enemies. She was using it to fuel her beloved ship and make her crew safer and stronger. She was invincible.

The clouds got brighter and deeper in colour as they shot past, which meant they were moving higher as well as faster. Her hair whipped around her face, stinging her cheeks. A wild grin split her face as she pictured the Lady Lamia's ship languishing behind them, the lady's fury at her prey escaping. Lyssa had won. She would always win.

'Captain!' Epizon yelled across her moment, jolting her attention back.

She eased her hands from the mast, the ship immediately starting to slow as she severed the flow of power. Spasms rocked though her muscles as the energy whirled, looking for an outlet. She screwed up her face as she let go completely, flexing her hands into fists as she tried to work the Rage out of her body. She took a few long breaths and turned, ready to reprimand Epizon for cutting her connection to the ship short. He knew she could go much longer than that before it became dangerous for her.

'We're a hundred and fifty leagues away already! Any further, and we'll be dangerously high!' Epizon's face was bordering on desperate.

She blinked at him, the spasms in her muscles fading. Had they been moving that fast? Pride crept through the alarm she felt.

'Lyssa, please, you need to be more careful. We don't know what will happen if we get much higher than this.'

She looked around and saw the glittering swirls of dust amongst the deep-blue and purple clouds. The higher you got above Olympus, the more the sky glittered. Light danced around the ship and reflected off the sails, now returning to their normal silver shimmer as the red Rage drained from them.

'You're crazy,' said Phyleus. 'I want to get off this ship. Now.' He was standing in front of the hauler, looking nervously at the waist-high railings running around the deck.

'Well, unless you want to take the direct route down, you're going to have to wait until we get to Libra.' Lyssa was grateful for the interruption. She didn't want to argue with Epizon. Or to think about whether what he was saying was true. Careful didn't come naturally to her. She walked past him. 'I'm going to sort out the mess on the cargo deck. Go get Len, and check if that storm ballista did any damage,' she said.

Epizon nodded. 'Yes, Captain.'

'Abderos?' she said, concentrating on an image of her navigator in her head.

'Yes, Cap?' his voice rang clearly through her mind. All ships in Olympus allowed their crew to communicate with each other mentally. They steered the ships in the same way. If any crew member concentrated hard on the *Alastor* they would be able to change her direction and position in the sky. Some were better at it than others though and strangers and visitors did not get the same privilege.

'Nice flying. I'm on my way to you,' she said, and headed towards the back of the deck. The planks rose steeply near the back and levelled off again, making the quarterdeck slightly raised.

Phyleus trotted after her. 'What am I supposed to do? And how did you make the ship go that fast?' he said.

'You're going to sit quietly with my navigator until we can drop you off. And you're going to stop asking questions.'

'You can't stop me asking questions,' he huffed.

'Where are you from? You sound like you're used to getting your own way.'

'I am, as it happens. I'm noble-born.'

Lyssa rolled her eyes. His well-spoken accent and annoying arrogance made sense. A surprising pang of nostalgia flashed through her as she thought about the big white house she had grown up in. She'd been surrounded by servants making sure she got her own way too. She squashed the memory. She didn't miss that life. And this pompous fool was only proof of that.

'Where are you from?' he asked her.

'I told you to stop asking questions,' she snapped.

'Gods, you're bad-tempered,' he muttered.

'You have no idea,' she said as she reached the big, spindly navigation wheel. 'This is Abderos, the *Alastor*'s navigator.' She gestured to the man sat in a wooden chair with two large metal wheels on each side. Although all crew members needed to use the navigation wheel to make a connection with the ship initially, Abderos had a strong enough bond to the *Alastor* now that he didn't need the boost of control the wheel provided. He always sat by it anyway. Old habits, Lyssa guessed.

'Nice to meet you. Who the hell *are* you?' asked Abderos, his sandy hair flopping back as he lifted his head to peer at Phyleus. His soft blue eyes were narrowed in a frown.

'He's a stowaway slave from Lady Lamia's ship, and we're

dropping him off on Libra. Keep an eye on him,' Lyssa answered before Phyleus could speak, and headed into the hauler at the back of the quarterdeck.

SHE GOT out on the middle deck and strode down the narrow corridor, past the living quarters and through the galley. The *Alastor* was a Crosswind-class ship, the smallest class of ship in Olympus. The galley was the only room below decks that spanned the full width of the narrow hull, and it was right in the middle, under the main mast. The rest of the rooms were either side of a central corridor running from stern to bow.

She stopped when she got to the cramped infirmary, and bent to start opening cupboards at random. This was Len's domain, so all the battered old storage cupboards were mounted a foot off the floor. Above the cupboards, there were portholes over a foot wide, ringed in dull brass, showing the swirling purple clouds colliding with sparkling dust outside. Lyssa found some gauze and tape together in a drawer and shoved them in her pocket, then took one of the big cargo haulers straight from the galley down to the cargo deck.

She looked around at the scattered bodies as she slid open the door and sighed heavily. The tank took up most of the available space in the centre of the deck. She reckoned it was at least ten feet square. The creature hovered in the middle, staring at one of the Cyclops bodies.

'Are you female?' Lyssa asked as she reached the tank and stared at the creature.

The startling eyes flicked to hers, and it moved through the liquid towards her slowly, barely causing a ripple. Lyssa guessed it was female, because of the small swell on its chest and the perfect violet braid of hair floating behind its head. There was an undeniably feminine quality to the enormous green eyes. It had a tiny mouth with deep-blue lips that had not opened once, and no ears, just long slits Lyssa assumed acted as gills.

She put one hand up to the glass. The creatures eyes flicked to her hand, then back to her face. Lyssa waited a moment more, and when the creature didn't move, she shrugged, turned around and slid down the glass tank until she was sitting on the floor. She started to roll her black cargo trouser leg up but gave up quickly, working instead through the gaping hole ripped in them. The wound wasn't deep, or even very painful, but it was seeping blood into her boots.

She found the sight of her own blood reassuring. She liked to see that it was red human blood, with no visible trace of god blood. She'd never actually seen god blood, obviously, but rumour had it that it was liquid silver. They didn't even call it blood; they called it ichor. Lyssa was only the granddaughter of a god, so hers was probably diluted, she supposed, as she taped the dressing onto her skin. She didn't know if all the descendants of the gods had powers. There were lots of them; the gods weren't fussy about sharing mortals' beds. All of the direct children had powers. Some had incredible strength or speed or wit, and others were gifted in things like music or art or beauty. Most of the best-known people in Olympus were children of the gods, and they were usually happy to use their powers to live like kings. It was the ones who wanted more, like Lady Lamia, who entertained the gods the most though.

'Where are you from?' she asked aloud, leaning her head back against the cool glass of the tank and closing her eyes. She didn't expect a reply. 'I grew up on Libra,' she told the being, delaying dealing with the mess around her. 'In case you don't know, that's Athena's realm. But I was born on Leo, Zeus's realm. In fact, Zeus is my grandfather. I have him to thank for this bloody temper.'

She opened her eyes and pushed herself to her feet. She started as she turned to the tank. The creature was directly behind her, as close as it could get through the glass. Its wide eyes fixed on hers, and she found she couldn't look away. The flecks in its eyes seemed to glitter and swirl, like the skies outside that she loved so much. Happiness began to seep into her.

'There's a fair-sized breach in the forward hull, Captain. We'll have it patched in the next half hour. Do you need help with the Cyclopes?' Epizon's voice sounded in her head, breaking the spell.

She stepped backwards, slightly dazed. The happiness vanished and she shook her head a little. 'No,' she said to Epizon, and backed further away from the tank. 'I can get them overboard.'

She tried not to put her back to the huge green eyes the whole time she was dragging the Cyclops bodies into the hauler.

3

LYSSA

Tipping bodies overboard wasn't a pleasant job, but it didn't bother Lyssa as much as it used to. She wondered if that was a good or bad thing as the last booted foot vanished over the railing.

'You were being serious? You actually throw people overboard?'

'Why aren't you where I left you!' she yelled, spinning to face Phyleus.

He shrugged. 'Ab said I could have a look at the top deck,' he said. He sounded casual, but his eyes sparkled as he spoke, and he rolled his shoulders nonchalantly. He was deliberately goading her.

She clenched her teeth. If he wanted to play games, he would lose. 'Abderos said you could call him Ab? You're friends now, are you?'

'Having lots of money buys you friends,' he said, and walked to the railing and peered over it, careful not to lean out far. 'How far down will they fall?' he asked.

She sighed and faced the sky, leaning her arms on the

railing next to him. The clouds were lighter now, and the sparkling dust only drifted around in thin wisps.

'Not that it matters, as they're already dead, but we're about a league and a half high now. In another hour we'll be level with Libra, and you can go and buy some friends there.' She heard the hauler door open and glanced towards the front of the ship. Epizon and Len stepped out onto the deck, and she smiled at Len's attempt to keep up with Epizon's giant strides as they crossed the deck.

She was about to call out to them when blinding white light filled her vision. She squeezed her eyes shut instinctively and flung her arms across her face to further shield them as Phyleus cried out in surprise.

'What's going on?' he shouted.

There was only one thing Lyssa knew of in Olympus that caused blinding white light. The arrival of one of the twelve gods. But that couldn't be it, surely. Why would a god visit her ship?

SHE CAUTIOUSLY DROPPED her arms and opened her eyes, heart racing. She gasped, then dropped to her knees.

'Athena,' she breathed, fear and excitement warring within her. What was Athena doing on the *Alastor*?

'You may stand,' the goddess said. Her voice was crisp and deep and almost musical.

Lyssa immediately did as she was told, gazing in awe at the goddess of wisdom. She was wearing a white traditional toga with a purple sash running from shoulder to waist, and she had her long blonde hair braided around her head like a wreath. Pale grey eyes, fierce with intelligence, scanned the deck of the ship. They skimmed over the rest of the crew kneeling on the wooden planks and came to rest on Lyssa. Lyssa stared back, for once at a loss for words.

'Captain Lyssa of the *Alastor*,' Athena said. Lyssa nodded dumbly. 'I'm afraid I need you to change course. You must head for the Olympian Void.'

'Of course, Athena,' Lyssa answered automatically.

'Are you not going to ask me why?' Athena said after a pause, her eyebrows raised. 'I thought you would be more difficult to persuade.' A small smile played on Athena's lips.

Lyssa blinked at her. Sense, and apprehension, began to trickle through the awe that had taken over her tongue. 'How do you know who I am?' she said slowly.

'I know all about you. I have followed you for years. Since you escaped your father and found freedom on this ship.' She gestured at the sails dancing with light. Lyssa's breath caught and her chest tightened.

'Why are you here? Why must we go to the Void?' The awe left Lyssa's voice, replaced with wariness.

'The gods have become bored.' Annoyance flickered across the goddess's pristine face. 'And when the gods get bored, mortals usually suffer. It has been agreed that we will bend one of our most sacred rules.' Athena's cool grey eyes were fixed on Lyssa's. 'We are going to grant mortals immortality.'

Lyssa gaped, wide-eyed, back at the goddess. 'I thought the gods weren't able to make people immortal,' she breathed.

'The gods are able to do anything they like,' Athena answered sharply. 'We *choose* not to do some things for prosperity. The gods tire of the same company quickly. If we all went around making our favourites immortal, it would only take a few millennia for there to be no mortals left.' Athena sighed. 'They have such short attention spans, my brethren gods.'

'Is that why you're here?' Lyssa asked as thoughts raced around her head. An eternal life? What would that be like?

'In a way, yes. Mortals need to earn this prize, Captain Lyssa. Each of the twelve gods has devised a Trial in their own realm that will kill all but the strongest of heroes. And each god is putting forward a hero to take part. Zeus has made his decision, and it is a bad choice indeed. He has chosen your father.'

Nausea rolled through Lyssa. 'No,' she whispered. 'No, he can't become immortal.' The image of her father knelt over her mother's bloody body, suppressed so well for years, sharpened in her mind.

'I agree. He is a cruel man.' Athena's face softened slightly as she spoke. 'I regret that the gods did not punish him for what he did to your family.'

Rage leapt inside Lyssa, and she opened her mouth to speak. The softness vanished from the goddess's face, and power rolled over Lyssa like a physical wave. It was power she could only dream of, and the angry words died on her lips. She stared back into Athena's now-cold glare.

'Do not forget yourself. I may be more sympathetic to you mortals than the others, but I will not tolerate lack of respect.'

Lyssa bowed her head and gritted her teeth. 'Of course, Athena,' she said. 'Forgive me. I just—'

'You are my choice of hero for the Trials.' Lyssa's head snapped back up, her eyes wide. 'I believe you are the only person who can stop him from winning.'

'Please, no,' stammered Lyssa before she could help herself. 'You can't—' This time the wave of power hit her so hard she stumbled backwards.

'You will be at the Void for the Trials ceremony at sunrise tomorrow, Captain Lyssa. You, your crew and this ship will be the strongest weapon against him.'

Before Lyssa could say another word, the goddess had vanished. She stared at the spot Athena had just stood in, her body vibrating with anger and fear. She was supposed to be free. She had beaten her past and made herself a future. How could she go back and face him? *Immortality.* The word rang through her mind. How could she *not* face him? The thought of that monster having limitless time to impose his cruelty on the world sent a shudder through her.

She stepped away from the railings, towards Epizon. He was on his feet and moving towards her, his heavy boots the only sound on the deck.

'You can do this,' he said as she reached him, and his deep voice soothed her.

She looked up at him, the only member of her crew who she would ever let see the fear in her eyes. 'Why? Why do I have to do it? I already beat him!' Her voice rose and heat prickled across her skin.

'Athena has chosen you for a reason. We'll beat him again.' He squeezed her shoulder. 'You won't be alone this time, Lyssa.'

'Immortality? Did she say immortality?'

Lyssa started at Phyleus's voice. She stepped away from Epizon and glared at Phyleus as he padded barefoot and cautiously across the deck towards her.

'Wait a minute.' He put his hands out. 'Are you *the* Lyssa? As in Lyssa, *daughter of Hercules*?' He stared at her.

She folded her arms and took a deep breath, trying to calm the raging emotions threatening to overcome her. 'Yes,' she said eventually.

'Well, that explains a lot,' Phyleus said, something like

excitement on his face. 'Although,' his face softened, 'I am sorry about your family. I remember hearing about it years ago.'

Lyssa swallowed hard and closed her eyes. The thought of others gossiping about her brutal past made her feel sick. The last thing she needed now was to lose her temper. She needed to think. 'Get off my ship, Phyleus. I don't care how; just get off my ship.'

'Are you going to compete in these Trials?' he asked, ignoring her command.

She opened her eyes and unfolded her arms. 'My father murdered my mother and brother, and instead of being punished, he became famous.' Lyssa fixed her eyes on Phyleus's. 'He claimed Hera made him do it out of jealousy, and those monsters believed him, or found him interesting enough to pretend to.' She advanced on him as she spoke. He didn't move. Roiling heat burned through her. 'Every year, he gets more power, more fame, more wealth. The more publicly cruel he is, the more he gains. He is utterly remorseless.' Her voice became a hiss, and her face was only inches from his. 'Bored gods have turned my father into the most dangerous fucking man Olympus knows. Can you imagine if he became immortal?'

Phyleus shook his head, his face pale.

'She's going to compete and she's going to win,' said Epizon quietly, stepping towards them. 'Captain.'

She glared fiercely at Phyleus a second more, then hissed and spun on her heel. She flexed her fists as she marched towards the front of the ship, gripping the railings hard when she got there. She stared out at the swirling clouds, oranges blending into soft reds and pinks as they melted together. She tightened her grip on the solid wood of the *Alastor* and drew as much reassurance as she could from its sturdiness. She wasn't the girl who could do nothing but watch as Hercules killed her mother and brother. She wasn't the girl who ran, taking as many silver drachmas as she could carry. She was a woman who would stand and fight, a woman with a ship and power. It was time to stop running. It didn't matter what the rest of Olympus made of it. All that mattered was that she stopped Hercules becoming immortal.

4

HEDONE

'Aphrodite, please, you have to help me!'

The goddess of love narrowed her eyes at Hedone, dropping the apple she was holding back into the golden dish at her side with a quiet clink.

'I have to do nothing. I don't care if you are the daughter of a god; never presume to tell me what to do.' Power rang through her calm voice, and Hedone bowed her head. Anger didn't make Aphrodite any easier to look at. Today her skin glowed pale under masses of rich dark hair. Her eyes were almost black, and her lips a deep red. She made Hedone's own dark hair and eyes look dull and boring. 'I don't understand why you need my help, anyway. You are the demigoddess of pleasure. What in Olympus can you not achieve yourself?'

'Theseus doesn't want me. I've tried everything I know to try, but he is not tempted by my flesh or my seductions. I do not have the power to make mortals fall in love. But you do.' Hedone looked up hopefully. Aphrodite straightened in her golden throne. Hedone stayed kneeling on the white marble floor, trying to ignore the ache in her knees.

'Has Theseus selected you for his crew in the Trials?'

'Yes, Aphrodite.'

'Then he wants you to become immortal with him if you win?'

'Yes, Aphrodite.'

'But he doesn't love you?'

Hearing someone else say it out loud like that was like a punch to her gut. 'No, Aphrodite,' she whispered.

'Hmm.' The goddess picked up the apple again and tossed it between her beautifully manicured hands. Hedone held her breath, hoping. 'Hedone, do you know how many times we've tried to create the perfect Olympus?'

Hedone shook her head.

'No? Nor do I. I've lost count now.' She took a bite from the apple, her full lips mesmerising as she did so. She chewed slowly, her gaze unfocused for a moment. 'The last one was the most interesting. We let them do whatever they liked. Full freedom. They began to create new things with Zeus's electricity and Hephaestus's metals.' She looked at Hedone again. Her eyes were fierce compared to her soft voice. Hedone gulped, trying not to let her nerves show. 'Things that allowed them to leave Olympus. Can you imagine? Obviously, we couldn't let that continue. Athena begged us not to destroy them all and start again, but Zeus's word is final.'

Worry began working its way through Hedone's hopefulness. Why was Aphrodite telling her all this? She knew of rumours saying as much, but she couldn't see what it had to do with what she was asking for.

'The trouble is, dear girl, every time you mortals do something interesting, it usually signals your end.' She took another bite from the apple.

'I don't understand,' Hedone mumbled. 'Do you mean the Trials?'

'Partly, yes. I am bored. So very, very bored. We have all these restrictions now in Olympus; we control everything. It's boring. But now we have the Trials.' She leaned forward in her throne, a smile starting to tug at her sensuous mouth. 'I like moral Theseus well enough; he has been an asset to my realm. But if we are to make new immortals, I would much rather share eternity with somebody more ...' She waved her empty hand in the air as she looked for the right word. 'Interesting. In fact, I think we can make this whole competition more interesting.' Her eyes flashed as she smiled properly. 'I think I will grant your request for love.'

Hedone took a sharp breath in, her concern dropping away in an instant. 'You will?' A wide smile stretched across her youthful face.

'Oh yes. But not with Theseus.'

Hedone's smile vanished. Her blood suddenly felt like ice in her veins. 'No,' she whispered, fear engulfing her.

Aphrodite gave her a cruel smile. 'Don't be sad, darling. You won't be pining over Theseus any more, and that's what you wanted. In fact, you won't even remember you ever loved him.'

Tears flooded Hedone's eyes as the horror of what Aphrodite was saying sank in.

The goddess's own eyes sparkled. 'Let's spice things up a little, shall we?'

MEGARA:

Husband, spare my life, I beg you. I am Megara. This is your son. He has your looks. See how he comes to you.

HERCULES:

This is not my son. It is the son of my enemy. Before his own mother, let this little monster die.

MEGARA:

You will shed your own blood? You are a madman.

HERCULES'S FATHER, AMPHITRYON:

Stricken with terror of his father's blazing eyes, the child died before he ever felt the blow, fear snatching his life away. Hercules now raised his heavy club against his wife and crushed her bones, her head removed from her mangled body completely.

EXCERPT FROM

HERCULES FURENS BY SENECA

Written 421–416 BC

Paraphrased by Eliza Raine

5

LYSSA

Lyssa looked down at herself with a frown. When Athena had told her she had to attend a ceremony at the Void, she had assumed the over-the-top fanfare would be reserved for the gods. She was wrong. The whole ceremony was being shown on Hermes flame dishes, and everyone in Olympus had a flame dish. They were shallow iron bowls a few feet across that held oil that permanently burned with gentle orange flames. The gods, and those wealthy enough, were able to replace the flames in the dishes with any images they liked, and this ceremony would be quite a spectacle.

Lyssa was wearing what she always wore, black laced-up boots over black trousers, a white shirt with short sleeves and her thick black belt with holster. The holster was empty though. She would have liked the comfort of her slingshot, but she had been told that when she was presented to the crowds outside as a hero of the Trials, she must be unarmed. She'd tried to protest to the harried people organising the ceremony that there were twelve gods out there and that her little weapon could hardly matter, but they had ignored her, fussing over her curly red hair. Normally, she just tied a red scarf around the tangled mess so it stayed out of her eyes, but she had been forced to sit in a tiny room for an hour whilst an equally unfortunate lady had tried to drag a comb through it. By the time she'd finished, her hair was twice the size it usually was. The lady retied the scarf across the top of her head so her hair was pulled back from her face but still tumbled over her shoulders at the back. Lyssa scowled at everyone who commented on it and refused to admit to the poor woman that she actually quite liked it.

Now she was standing in the tiny room alone, waiting for somebody to tell her where to go next. She hated waiting and was fidgeting nervously, frustrated that there wasn't enough room to pace back and forth like she could on her ship. Lyssa wasn't exactly shy, but she'd never been exposed like this before. Being notorious wasn't exactly good for business when you were a smuggler. The only time she had ever experienced any sort of fame was six years ago, when Hercules had accused Hera of forcing him to kill his wife and child.

Cold tendrils of hatred curled around her insides, and her muscles constricted. *Don't think about him. Don't think about him*, she chanted in her head. She'd had years of practice at blocking out thoughts she didn't want. Today was just the same. Except, she knew it wasn't. She was going to see him, today, for the first time since she'd fled. She'd seen his face often enough, on the flame dishes or depicted on Zeus's realm, Leo, where he had so much influence. But she hadn't seen him in the flesh since that terrible night.

She flexed her fists and took a deep breath. *I am no longer the girl who ran.* She repeated the mantra until a new blonde woman dressed in an immaculate deep-blue floor-length dress came into the cluttered little room, without knocking.

'You could have done with more make-up,' she said, moving uncomfortably close to Lyssa and peering at her.

Lyssa scowled and shuffled as far backwards as she could, stumbling over piles of clothes on the floor behind her. The woman pursed her lips and straightened up. 'Well, you are the only woman out there today.'

A shout made Lyssa shake her head in surprise.

'The *Alastor*! Where in Zeus's name is the *Alastor*? The others are going on!'

She looked at the open door, and the woman grabbed her wrist and started dragging her from the little room. She half ran down a narrow stone corridor, and Lyssa reluctantly jogged to keep up, the shouting voice increasing in volume.

The corridor opened out onto a spacious area that was almost empty. The room felt so big because the ceiling was so high, and what she had first thought was a wall opposite her was actually a series of giant royal-blue curtains that stretched up and up. She guessed the curtains opened onto the stage. A red-faced human man pounced on them.

'*Alastor*?' he shouted.

'I'm Lyssa, yes,' she stammered.

His face clouded over with a look of disappointment, and her scowl returned.

'Well, don't just stand here, get out there!' the man said, and gave her a shove towards the curtains.

Another shiver of nerves rippled down her, and she scolded herself mentally. She drew herself up to her full, if still short, height and stepped through the gap in the curtains being held open for her. She blinked in the bright light and sucked in a breath as she tried to take everything in.

·   ·   ·

UNABLE TO RESIST a chance to show off, the gods had decided to hold the ceremony on a giant marble platform floating over the centre of the Olympian Void. The Void was a huge black tear in the otherwise vivid skies of Olympus, and anything that got sucked into it was lost forever. The only reason it existed was so that the gods could demonstrate the limitless extent of their power. They could create and destroy anything. The fact that they could also sling anything that displeased them into it was a happy bonus.

White clouds drifted above them, crackling with sparkling purple energy and giving off a bright, warm light. They were the same lightning-filled clouds that surrounded Zeus's sky realm, Leo. Their stark whiteness was emphasised by the fierce purples and blues swirling beyond them in the skies. They were a long way above Olympus here, and the skies glittered everywhere she looked.

The platform had buildings at both ends, and each was in the ancient temple style, with huge white fluted stone columns holding up a triangular roof. The one she had just emerged from had deep-blue curtains hanging across the entrance that opened out onto the large marble stage area she was now stood on. Steps ran down from all three sides of the stage to the platform. The temple at the other end of the platform, opposite her, was a mirror image but had blood-red curtains, and the stage area held twelve great white stone thrones. They were empty.

She could see an ocean of creatures between the steps of the two temples. Humans, centaurs, satyrs, harpies, giants, Cyclopes; all manner of Olympian citizens had turned out for the ceremony. They were currently all facing in her direction, cheering and shouting and waving flags and banners.

A looming figure blocked some of the light to her left,

and she looked slowly around, concentrating on stopping her mounting apprehension from showing on her face. The giant stood next to her was so tall, and the light so bright, that she could not see his face. He was standing very still though, and she wondered if he was as uncomfortable as she was. She could see nothing around his huge form, and there was nobody to her right, just steps leading down from the stage.

'Citizens of Olympus!' a voice boomed out of nowhere. Lyssa jumped, her heart racing at the shock. She wasn't the only one; many in the crowd visibly jumped, and a few cried out in surprise. Lyssa hoped no one had noticed her reaction. The giant had maintained his stock-still composure. Embarrassed laughs and chatter died out as the crowd slowly began to turn to face the direction of the red temple. Tension and excitement hummed through the air, and the slow hush became a silence as the last few turned to face the other way.

'Consider yourself honoured and humbled in the presence of your gods!' the voice roared, and the red curtains lifted.

Lyssa's gasp was lost in thousands of others. Her gaze was too fixed on the red temple to notice the giant finally shift next to her.

THE TWELVE GODS of Olympus stepped out of the shadow of the temple entrance and moved to their thrones on the stage. The awed silence broke as one centaur started clapping. Within seconds the applause was deafening.

Lyssa slowly clapped along with them, trying hard to squash the awe and concentrate on the details. It wasn't easy. Until Athena had appeared on the *Alastor* the day before, Lyssa had never seen a god in real life. They were on the flame dishes all the time, so the faces they wore were familiar, but actually being this close to them felt very strange. A compulsion to kneel and wave and bow and smile washed over her. She tried to concentrate harder.

Zeus was in the middle, with Hera on his right. His bearded, handsome face was the most recognisable, given that he was king of the gods. Hera stood out next to him, her dark skin and black hair contrasting with the glittering teal and blue jewels she wore. On Hera's left was Poseidon, distinguishable by his long silver hair and beard. Next to him was Aphrodite. She was harder to recognise, as she changed her appearance regularly, but her beauty surpassed the others at any distance. Today she had dusty-pink hair flowing to her feet, merging seamlessly with her flowing dress, and warm brown skin. She was one of the few gods smiling. Lyssa assumed the stooped, broad, dark-haired god wearing a leather tabard at her side was her husband, Hephaestus. She had never seen him before, and she tried to study his scowling face and oil-covered clothes. On his right, in the last two thrones, were the twins Artemis and Apollo. Artemis was smaller than the other figures, lithe and young-looking, with blonde hair in thin braids. Apollo was as blonde as his sister but looked even more youthful, possibly due to his broad smile and regular waves to the crowd.

Back near the middle, on Zeus's left, was Athena. She was dressed the same as she was when she had visited the *Alastor*, her long braid wrapped neatly around her head like a crown. The sight of Athena reminded Lyssa why she was there, and gave her a much-needed feeling of grounding. Next to Athena was Ares. He was the largest of the gods, larger even than Zeus, rippling with muscles. He wore an

ancient-style plumed helmet that covered his face. As far as
she knew, his face had never been seen by mortals. To his
left was Dionysus. He was the antithesis of Ares's solid seri-
ousness, smiling and waving, slouched in his chair. By a
long way, he looked the most normal of the gods, wearing
human-style clothes and sporting a mop of messy dark hair.
Hermes was next to him, looking restless and bored. He had
red hair and a red beard, and Lyssa's eyes were drawn to his
famous winged boots.

Last in the row, but to Lyssa, by far the most interesting,
was Hades. This was a god whose realm, Virgo, was hidden
in the core of Olympus and almost impossible to get to.
Many images of Hades were in circulation, but even those
who lived on Virgo did not know which were accurate. It
could be all of them or none of them. And today would not
be the day Olympus found out. The being in the last throne
was a swirling mass of black smoke. The smoke was
humanoid in shape, but it never settled long enough to give
any indication of features. Lyssa's muscles tensed and her
breathing tightened as she stared. She suddenly felt like
only he and she were there. The smoke head lifted slightly.

'Your gods!' the commentator boomed, and she blinked
away the feeling, trying to look anywhere else. 'You are here
today to witness something never seen before in Olympus!
The gods have chosen to bless us with an opportunity never
before possible!' The crowd cheered and whooped. 'Of the
twelve heroes before you, only four will have the chance to
take on the deadly Trials. Today we find out who's going to
get a chance at immortality!'

Lyssa's face creased into a frown, and fervent chattering
rippled through the crowd. Only four heroes? Relief rolled
over her, and her tense stance sagged. She was a nobody.
There was no way she would be chosen over the others.

Even as she thought this, a twinge of regret pulled at her. She'd almost had a chance to become immortal. A chance to fly the skies forever.

A stab of pride followed the regret. Athena had said she was the only one who could stop Hercules. What if he was chosen as one of the four? *I am no longer the girl who ran.* The thought, repeated so often in the last day, forced its way through the others. This was her chance. She needed to be chosen. Not just to save Olympus from Hercules's unending cruelty, but to face the man who had destroyed everything she had loved. Perhaps even kill him. A shudder rippled through her, and she stood straight again. Her hands balled into fists. She was no longer the girl who ran. She would stand, and fight, and avenge her family. She had to be chosen.

6

LYSSA

'Your first hero, son of Zeus, captain of the *Hybris*, the mighty Hercules!' roared the commentator.

For a second Lyssa was sure her heart stopped beating. Her stomach lurched, and she thought she might be sick as the crowd began to scream as they swung back to face the blue temple. Hercules stepped out into view, waving. Images of her mother and brother flashed through her mind. How could they cheer a man capable of what this monster had done? She could only see his back and a little of his profile, but he was still familiar. He was more muscular now, and his beard was longer, in an effort to imitate or impress his own father, she presumed.

He turned and looked down the line towards her. His smile widened as he made eye contact with her. She glared back into his cold grey eyes. Her skin throbbed as the feeling of fire began to roll across it, and she could hear clanging in her ears. Power and adrenaline rushed through her, the Rage building in every muscle. He opened his mouth, and his smile widened further. He was laughing at her, she realised. Dark spots appeared in the corners of her eyes, and she could see nothing but his face.

'YOUR SECOND HERO, son of Poseidon, captain of the *Virtus*, the witty Theseus!'

The boom of the commentator's voice caused her to break eye contact with Hercules. A long breath escaped her, and her vision began to clear a little. She clenched her teeth and flexed her hands repeatedly into fists as Hercules turned back, waved one last time at the crowd, then stepped back out of her sight. She wanted to yell and kick and scream as frustration roiled inside her. She couldn't lose her temper now. She needed to be chosen. She needed to stop him.

She took long, deep breaths and clenched her sweaty hands as Theseus strode out into view, waving cheerfully to the screaming audience. Blood still pounding in her ears, her muscles tense, Lyssa watched as the beautiful, privileged Theseus laughed easily as the crowd cheered. Her barely contained anger surged. He lived with the favour of Aphrodite, and he had no idea how to live a difficult life; everything had come easily to him. He was outrageously good-looking, blessed with rich brown skin and dark wavy hair that fell messily to his shoulders, interspersed with braids. Warm brown eyes crinkled when his full lips smiled and his easy confidence only increased his appeal.

She tore her eyes from his perfect proportions and looked ahead to where the gods were sat, some clapping lazily and others ignoring the whole thing. She tried to make out any expression on Poseidon's face, any pride or interest in his son. If there was, she couldn't see it. He was paying more attention than some of the others, but his demeanour was unreadable.

Theseus stepped back, and Lyssa's muscles constricted again. She took a deep breath, skin prickling as she waited for the next announcement. She had to be chosen.

'YOUR THIRD HERO, son of Poseidon, captain of the *Orion*, the colossal Antaeus!' rang the voice.

The marble floor shook ever so slightly as the giant to her left took one enormous stride forward. The applause was deafening but couldn't drown out the rushing in her head. She had one more chance. She glued her eyes to the giant's back and refused to look to her left, where she knew Hercules stood in the line of other potential heroes.

Antaeus was about ten feet tall, and he was covered in muscle. He was shirtless, and he wore green canvas trousers tucked into huge black boots. She could see his back clearly, and it was covered in tattoos of snakes, all different colours and sizes. She squinted as the snakes all slithered across his skin, their long bodies entwining and curling around each other. She had seen moving tattoos many times but never with such lifelike quality. They were mesmerising.

Then the giant stepped back and turned to his left, nodding his head at the other captains. Then he turned towards her and did the same. She knew most of the crew of the *Orion* were boxers or wrestlers, so the scars on his face and chest and the clearly previously broken nose were no surprise. The bright blue eyes under heavy black eyebrows were though. There was no doubting he was a son of Poseidon. Dark hair flopped over his forehead as he nodded at her, and she inclined her head jerkily in response.

This was it. The Rage racing around her body was

making her dizzy. Her mouth was completely dry, and her fingernails were piercing the skin of her clammy palms. Her muscles were aching with tension. She had to stand and fight. She had to be chosen.

'YOUR FOURTH AND LAST HERO, granddaughter of Zeus, captain of the *Alastor*, the fiery Lyssa!' bellowed the commentator.

Light flashed behind her eyes, and for a moment she couldn't see. She took a shaking step forward and blinked hard, trying to clear her vision. Bile rose in her throat as she took another step forward, and she couldn't hear the crowd at all. She was in the Trials. She would have to face Hercules. She couldn't run.

'Enjoy this, Captain Lyssa.' Athena's voice cut across the pounding in her head. 'You are one of their heroes.'

She sought the goddess's face in the great stone throne across the platform, and instantly the pounding quietened and the flashing light stopped. She found she could breathe easier. She took another step forward. She was no longer the girl who ran. She stood taller. She would win. She raised her arm and waved it awkwardly.

'Smile,' said Athena, and she forced a smile onto her face. She thought the crowd got a little louder. She dragged her eyes from Athena and made herself look around at the faces below her. A lot of them were not looking at her, they were looking at the more impressive and famous captains behind her, or still staring in awe at the gods in the opposite direction. But more than half did have their attention on her, and to her surprise, they looked excited and encouraging. Although most of the faces she could see were human, there were more different creatures here than she'd ever seen in one place. She spotted a banner being held by a group of satyrs not far from the bottom of the steps that read 'Go Alastor', and she broke out in a real grin.

'Well done,' said Athena. 'Now go back.'

Unexpectedly reluctant, she retraced her steps backwards until she was in the shadow of the giant again.

A hush fell over the crowd, and she realised that they were all facing the gods again. Zeus stood up.

'Welcome, all.' His voice was deep and clear and lyrical, even more beautiful to hear than Athena's was. 'Each of the twelve gods of Olympus has devised a dangerous and difficult Trial in their own realm. The crew who has won the most of these events at the end of all twelve will be granted immortality.' He paused, and hundreds of wide-eyed, silent faces stared at him. 'Eternal life!' he roared with a laugh, throwing his arms up in the air. 'What a prize!' Excitement hummed through the audience. 'And of course, for a prize so unprecedented, we have had to make sure our Trials are impossible for all but the most special heroes.' He gestured at Lyssa and her fellow competitors. 'Most of them will die.' Antaeus twitched next to her. 'The captains shall receive the same information at the same time,' Zeus continued. 'Only once a Trial has been won will the next one be revealed. Heroes, tonight you will dine together, at a feast in my name. Tomorrow the first Trial will be revealed. Feast now and enjoy what might be your last. If you survive, you will be celebrated. If you win, you will live forever!'

Tumultuous applause erupted from the crowd, and Lyssa hoped his dramatic words had been for their benefit. She had a horrible feeling, though, that they were not.

7

LYSSA

Lyssa was relieved that she and the other guests had been asked to go back to their ships whilst the feast was prepared. The *Alastor* was one of a hundred or more ships docked together underneath the giant platform. Small longboats were taking passengers back and forth whenever they needed to get between their ships and the platform.

As Lyssa's longboat sank below the edge of the platform and she saw all the ships hovering together, she felt herself relax a little. Directly underneath the grand elegance of the gods' temples were the same ships she saw every day. Including her own. The thought was comforting. As the longboat rose level with the deck at the front of her ship, she grabbed the railing and pulled herself over. As soon as her feet hit the deck, she took a deep breath and closed her eyes, savouring the feeling of being in control again, and back on the *Alastor*.

'Your hair looks great, Cap.' Abderos's voice broke through her moment's peace.

She groaned and headed across the deck towards the

quarterdeck. 'Everybody on the quarterdeck in five,' she yelled, projecting the instruction to everyone on the crew.

She needn't have bothered. When she reached the back of the deck, everyone was already there, and they clapped and cheered when they saw her, Abderos bowing deeply in his wheelchair. Len threw himself to his knees, yelling about not being worthy. For a second she tensed, anger flashing instinctively at being mocked, but it drained away almost immediately, and she laughed.

'Don't go too overboard. I might get used to this,' she said, and Len jumped back to his feet, looking alarmed.

'So, what's the plan?' he asked.

'We all go to dinner later tonight.' She shrugged and headed towards her chair. 'The gods won't be there, just the four crews and a delegation from each realm.'

'Are there many satyrs?' he asked.

'Yeah, and I think they might be backing us,' she said, and told him about the banner she'd caught sight of.

Len grinned. 'How about nymphs?' he asked, his eyes getting a glint that made Lyssa uncomfortable.

'Probably, there were all sorts out there, but don't get any ideas about misbehaving.' She tried to impress this on him with as stern a stare as she could muster, but it didn't seem a match for his excitement.

'Do we need to dress formally?' asked Epizon.

She shrugged. 'It's a private event, and I couldn't care less what you're wearing. But you need to remember this. I'm not going to pretend we wouldn't all like to win, but this is going to be the most dangerous thing we've ever done. I understand if anyone wants to leave before we start.' She looked around at all of them in turn. Abderos looked resolute, Len excited, Epizon fierce. Phyleus stood behind them all, his face unreadable. She narrowed her eyes at him. 'We'll go to Libra to stock up now, and drop you off.'

'About that,' he said, and leaned back on the railings. Lyssa rolled her eyes at his attempt to look comfortable on the ship. He'd been terrified just hours before. 'I have a proposition for you.'

She raised her eyebrows. 'No.'

'You haven't even heard it yet!' he said indignantly.

'Hear him out, Cap,' said Abderos. She shot him a glare, and he wheeled his chair back half a foot. 'Or not.' Abderos shrugged.

'I have a lot more silver than what's in that little box you got from Lady Lamia. Enough to give you a decent shot at the Trials,' Phyleus said.

'No,' repeated Lyssa. 'No way.'

'In return I'd want a place on the crew of the *Alastor*.'

Lyssa pushed herself to her feet. 'Is this a bloody joke to you?' she yelled. Epizon rose to his feet beside her. 'You heard Zeus; we'll likely all be killed!'

'But if you win, we all become immortal!' Phyleus protested.

'I think you should consider his offer,' said Epizon levelly.

Lyssa shot her first mate a foul look. 'Well, I'm not interested, and I'm the captain, so he leaves.' She folded her arms and sat back in the creaky wooden chair.

'Captain, how are we supposed to compete in twelve deadly Trials with no money? We have no idea how long they'll take, and we're already dangerously low on rations.'

Lyssa narrowed her eyes and stared at the deck.

'If this is going to be as dangerous as Athena and Zeus implied, then we could definitely do with stocking up the infirmary,' said Len quietly.

Guilt washed through Lyssa. She looked at the satyr. 'Phyleus is an arrogant, glory-hunting idiot who wanted nothing to do with this ship before he had a shot at immortality. He has no place here.'

'I can hear you, you know,' Phyleus said from the railings.

'I'm well aware of that.' She looked directly at him. 'I don't care how much bloody silver you're offering us. You don't buy your way onto this crew!'

'You clearly need the money!' Phyleus protested, pushing away from the railings and turning his hands up beseechingly. 'You can buy new clothes, stock your galley to bursting, fix your broken longboat—'

'How the hell does he know our longboat is broken!' Lyssa exclaimed, looking straight at Abderos.

The navigator looked away meekly. 'He was here for ages, Cap, and he asks lots of questions. Sorry,' he mumbled.

'The point is, I've not seen your living quarters, but I bet they could do with some new blankets, your washrooms some soap ...'

A pang of longing shot through Lyssa. Soap. Gods, she'd love some soap.

'The *Alastor* needs some love, and I can fund it,' Phyleus said. He had moved closer to the crew as he spoke.

'New blankets. Imagine new blankets, Cap,' said Abderos.

'He doesn't seem so bad,' shrugged the satyr. 'Not bad enough to turn down food for.'

'We really need to fix that longboat, Captain,' said Epizon.

Lyssa sighed and closed her eyes. She didn't like that Phyleus reminded her of her past, and she hated his arrogant haughtiness, but he didn't seem dangerous. He was brave and ambitious to want to compete in the Trials, and he looked fit and strong enough to work on the ship. And, gods, they needed the money.

'Well. It seems I am outnumbered. You'd better be able to get us this silver before the feast tonight.' She stood up and looked him in the eye. 'Welcome to the *Alastor*.' Sarcasm dripped from her voice.

'You won't regret this, *Captain*,' he beamed at her, emphasising the word *Captain*.

'I doubt that,' she growled.

8

HEDONE

Hedone rolled onto her back, letting out a long breath. The plush silk sheets tangled around her legs as she turned. She ignored them, staring at the wood panelling on the ceiling. The Trials started tomorrow, and she knew she should be excited about her first day on Theseus's new ship, the *Virtus*.

He had been so proud when he unveiled the ship, excitement buzzing through him as he showed her and her fellow crew members the huge, shimmering sails and big, spindly navigation wheel. His eyes had shone as he had presented her with the luxurious living quarters she now lounged in, white silk draped over rich mahogany everywhere she looked. And while it was all beautiful, she couldn't help feeling like something was missing. She was aware, dimly, that Theseus's enthusiasm used to be infectious and that his presence in her bedroom when he was showing her the ship should have been important to her. When she thought of him and his laughing eyes, she got a fleeting rush that was instantly replaced with a bored melancholy. It was confusing her.

She sighed again and sat up in the huge bed. She hated being alone. It was one of the many drawbacks of being the demigoddess of pleasure. Every night she spent in the company of another seemed to deepen her feeling of isolation, but her power compelled her to share herself and be with others. More than anything in the world, she wanted to love somebody, and feel their love in return. Theseus flashed in her mind, but his face vanished almost immediately, and the hollow loneliness settled again.

Psyche and Bellerophon, her two crew mates, had suggested they get some sleep this afternoon so that they were ready for tonight. They had been so much more excited than her about the Trials. Everyone was competing to become immortal. There was nobody in Olympus who didn't want eternal life, surely, Hedone told herself. But it was almost too much for her to consider. She ran a finger down the side of her cheek, feeling the soft skin of her face. What would she do with a never-ending life if she had nobody to share it with? Maybe that was why she felt so unsettled. The thought of being lonely forever filled her with dread. Again a surge of emotion rose in her but was so fleeting she couldn't hold on to it. It was almost like she had forgotten something important. She reached for it mentally, scrunching her perfect face up as she tried to place it, but nothing came. She began to speak aloud.

'O Aphrodite, hear my prayer. Please send me somebody to love who will love me eternally in return. Please, end my loneliness.'

She sat for a while longer, imagining a perfect life. She pictured her beautiful home on Pisces, her children running up the beach towards her. She hugged her legs to herself as she imagined the big strong arms of a beaming man, scooping all of them up in an embrace, telling them he loved them and would always be there for them. She heard the laughter in her head as they played together, not a worry in the world. She felt the warmth on her skin as her dream man ran his hands along her shoulders, down her body, whispering his need for her. Her eyes filled with tears as the longing grew.

'Please, Aphrodite. Send me love,' she whispered.

As he passed through Pholoe, Hercules was entertained by the centaur Pholus. He roasted
meat for Hercules to eat whilst he ate his own meat raw. Hercules called for wine, but
Pholus only had sacred wine that belonged to the centaurs. Hercules told him to be brave
and not to worry and opened the wine. The centaurs smelled the wine and came to the cave,
armed with rocks and trees. Hercules killed all who fought against him, and the rest he shot
with arrows as he chased them.

EXCERPT FROM

The Library by Apollodorus
Written 300–100 BC
Paraphrased by Eliza Raine

9

LYSSA

Lyssa didn't think she had ever seen Len so excited. Admittedly, he didn't get off the ship as much as she and Epizon did, but she still marvelled at his enthusiasm. It couldn't all be down to the prospect of seeing so many members of the opposite sex, could it?

Her whole crew was crammed into the little wooden longboat, which was moving slowly with so many passengers, on its way to the feast. She felt tiny as they moved through the maze of ships hovering motionless under the platform. A gentle breeze rolled over them as the longboat drifted along, but the temperature never changed this high above Olympus.

'Is he always like this?' Phyleus asked, pointing at Len, who was sitting next to Epizon, telling him at length about the last encounter he had had with a maenad. 'And what's a maenad?'

'He's not usually quite this bad,' she answered. 'And most of what he's saying right now is untrue, anyway. A maenad is a follower of Dionysus; they're basically party girls. Always drunk and often dancing. The one he met last year did show him her bottom, but not on purpose. She just didn't know he was lying on the ground, and danced right over him in a short skirt.'

Phyleus laughed. It was a nice sound, and it annoyed Lyssa that she liked it. She had half hoped he wouldn't come through on the silver, but the *Alastor* was now, as he had promised, full to bursting with rations and a fair few luxuries to boot. They hadn't had time to get the longboat fixed, but she was sure it could wait.

'We're about to see a whole lot more than maenads,' she told him, frowning. He was staring out at the cluster of silent, hovering ships. 'I bet you know nothing about Olympus at all.'

His features sharpened as he snapped his head round to her. He wore defiance like a mask. 'I know plenty about Olympus.'

'Do you know what kind of ship that is?' She pointed to a gargantuan ship they were passing, with a full-sized pool set between masts twice the size of the *Alastor*'s, and what she assumed were fake palm trees lining the deck.

Phyleus stared at it, the muscles in his strong neck twitching. He clearly didn't. Lyssa didn't feel bad about making him look stupid. It was his own fault for being so stuck-up.

'I'll take it from here, Cap,' said Abderos. His chair was wedged between the rows of seats in the longboat, and he didn't look very comfortable, but his eyes sparkled at the talk of ships.

'You're about to get a lesson from the best,' she told Phyleus, leaning back.

'That big ship with the pool is a Zephyr,' Abderos began. 'They're the largest class of ship in Olympus. They were originally designed as cargo ships, so the cargo deck is massive, and really tall, but now they double up as luxury cruising ships, like that one. Apparently, Achilles has a Zephyr with the cargo deck turned into a show hall for all his longboats. Man, I'd love to see that.' Abderos's soft blonde hair blew up off his forehead as he let out a long sigh. 'Anyway, they have three masts and three sails on each, where we have two, 'cause they need the extra power.'

'Do the ships ever run out of power?' asked Phyleus.

'Nope. Not as long as there's light for the solar sails. And it's never dark in most of Olympus, so we're all good. Zephyrs also have a quarterdeck at both ends of the top deck, so you can steer from either end, which is pretty good. Course, the best ships ever made, that'll be the Whirlwinds.' He started swivelling in his seat, trying to find one to point out.

Lyssa coughed.

'After the *Alastor*, obviously,' he said distractedly. 'There's one!' He waved excitedly at a ship that was nowhere near as big as the Zephyr, but stood out all the same.

'Is it made of metal?' Phyleus asked, squinting at it.

'No. Just the outside is encased in metal. They're battle-ships. Those towers all along the edge are weapons turrets; they all have ballistas in them. They're basically giant cross-bows. And you see how the back of the ship is raised really high? The quarterdeck is high up so the captain can see what's happening in all the ballista towers. Three masts again, but the sails are much higher up so they don't block the view from the quarterdeck.'

'One of many reasons my Crosswind is better,' said Lyssa. 'I wouldn't trade the view of my sails for any number of weapons.'

'Then it's just as well Crosswinds can outrun ballistas, Cap,' Abderos grinned at her.

'The *Alastor* is faster than any normal Crosswind, and you know it,' she said.

'What's that long ship?' asked Phyleus.

'That's a Typhoon. A two-mast ship but much longer, and they have ballistas and a small sail on the front. You'll see how much pointier the front is when we go past in a minute.'

Lyssa stopped listening to Abderos and looked again at the Whirlwind battleship as they floated past, trying to read the name on the side. Hercules had a Whirlwind named *Hybris*, which meant 'pride'. That Hercules could take pride in anything that he had done made her feel sick. This ship was called *Pali*, meaning 'fight'. She looked back at her own ship, looking small moored between the dozens of larger ships. Small, but solid. She could just make out the word *Alastor* printed on the bow. It had been easy to name her. *Alastor* meant 'blood feud'. Lyssa gritted her teeth. She would beat Hercules.

As the longboat came up over the edge of the platform, Phyleus drew in a breath, and even Len finally stopped talking. The area between the two temples that had held the crowd earlier was now lined with long tables of all different sizes and heights. Benches ran down either side of the tables, and they were covered in food and drink. There were ornate bowls of fruit, giant platters of meat, small dishes holding olives and pastes and dips. There were vegetables Lyssa didn't even recognise on every bit of tabletop she could see from the boat, and the smell was divine.

At intervals between the tables were tall stone columns that matched the temples, and on top of each was a large, flickering flame. Nothing was holding the flames in place;

they just burned gently and impressively on top of the columns. Each of the stages in front of the temples had torches at their corners too. The temple with the blue curtains now had a band set up on the stone stage. A beautiful blonde woman in a silken white toga played an enormous golden harp, and three men sat behind her, playing a variety of stringed instruments that glittered with gold. The music was soft and pretty.

The longboat halted beside the platform, and Len hopped out quickly. Epizon stepped onto the stone platform and then leaned over to grab one side of Abderos's chair. Lyssa stood to help, but Phyleus got there before her. Together the two men lifted Abderos out of the longboat and onto the platform. Lyssa looked around as she climbed out of the boat last. They weren't the first to arrive, and there were lots of others around them, chattering excitedly as they left the boats and saw the food.

'Where shall we sit, Cap?' asked Abderos, looking up at her.

She scanned the tables and spotted what she was looking for. Hercules was sitting in the centre of the platform, positioned so that he could see everyone. He looked straight back at her. Fire surged across her skin, and she swallowed down the Rage. She looked away and pointed at a table close to the red temple. It was the furthest from him, but they would need to walk past him to reach it. Epizon laid a hand on her shoulder, and she looked up at his warm face.

'It's fine, Ep. I'm fine,' she lied, and headed towards the table.

The closer she got to him, the more the Rage flooded her body. Her muscles began to shake as she fought to contain the furious energy. Hercules held her gaze as she approached. She glared back, filling her look with as much hatred as she possibly could, trying to give the anger an outlet. His handsome eyes crinkled at the corners as he smiled.

'Daughter,' he said as she passed in front of him, and he lifted his wine glass.

She froze, her stomach lurching at the word. Epizon stopped a few paces ahead of her and turned to her slowly.

'Don't you dare call me daughter, you fucking monster,' she hissed, turning to Hercules.

He gave a bark of laughter. 'I'm glad to see you have some fight in you. You must have inherited some of my qualities.' He took a long drink from the glass. As he lowered it, she spat in his face. He leapt to his feet, his bench clattering to the marble floor behind him.

'That and your strength, Hercules. Don't underestimate me,' she growled.

The fury contorting his attractive face was hugely satisfying, and she gave her own bark of laughter as she whirled on her heel and strode towards Epizon. He turned too, and they made their way quickly down the tables.

'That wasn't smart, Captain,' said Epizon out of the side of his mouth.

'I know,' she answered, her heart pounding as adrenaline rushed around her. 'And I don't care.'

10

HERCULES

As the red-haired girl got further from him, Hercules calmed his anger. Let her run away. He wouldn't stoop to her level in front of all these staring people. They all knew he was unbeatable; he had no need to prove it here. He would save it for the Trials.

'Pick that bench up,' he barked at a servant. A small boy hurried to pick the bench up, and another offered him a piece of cloth. He wiped the girl's spit from his face and sat down.

'She's pathetic,' purred the girl to his left. He put his hand on her bare leg and felt her tense in anticipation.

'So was her mother,' he replied, a hard smile on his face at the memory. His daughter looked like her mother. He wondered if she really had inherited his strength. It seemed unlikely, given that shoddy ship she captained. He forced himself to relax. This child was no threat to him or his ends. The reluctant admiration he felt for her fierceness was just going to make it more satisfying when he made sure she didn't survive the Trials.

'Evadne, fetch me more of this wine. These are empty.'

The girl pouted. 'There are servants for—'

He cut her off by squeezing her leg hard. She stopped talking but didn't make any noise of pain.

'Go,' he said, and let go of her.

She leapt up. He watched her lithe figure move as she sashayed towards the closest servant, her shiny blue-black hair skimming her bare shoulders. It had been hard to find a gunner as young and pretty as she was. He could get any girl he liked whenever they docked, but he had wanted someone on board the *Hybris* who he could play with whenever he wanted, and there was no way he was letting more members of crew than were necessary on his ship. Not when they would all be granted immortality. The more immortals there were in Olympus, the less special they would be. And he would have to put up with them forever.

There was a buzz of noise from the other end of his table, and he looked over. Theseus was walking up the aisle between the tables and came to a stop opposite him.

'Hercules,' he said with a nod of his head.

Hercules stood up, because he knew he was the tallest of the two of them. 'Theseus,' he nodded back. He did not smile. Theseus thought he was better than him. He was younger and thought himself more popular. His eyes flicked to the woman stood behind him, and his breath caught involuntarily. His hatred for Theseus deepened further as he recognised her as Hedone, the demigoddess of pleasure.

'Allow me to introduce my crew,' Theseus grinned, having obviously noticed Hercules's reaction. 'This is Hedone, my medic.'

Hedone was wearing a draping silk toga, as most of the women here were, but somehow hers hung in a way that was much more suggestive than the others he had seen. Her long black hair framed a face that held eyes darker than any he had ever seen, and voluptuous lips that once he had looked at, he could not take his eyes off. He knew at that moment he needed to have her. If he was going to be immortal, it would be with a woman like this at his side.

He smiled at her, relaxing his shoulders and allowing an easy charm to show on his face. He reached his arm across the table to her, and she returned his smile as she put her hand in his.

'A pleasure,' he said, more huskily than usual.

She narrowed her eyes seductively, and his stomach flipped.

'And my first mate and gunner are over there,' Theseus said, gesturing to two people who had been talking to some seated guests on the next table.

Hercules blinked at them, not caring in the slightest who they were. The woman was dark skinned with braided hair, like Theseus, and was wearing a gold dress. The man was young and soft, with pale hair and pretty features. Hercules knew instantly that Hedone did not want these young, pretty male clones. She wanted a real man. Someone who looked like him, with muscles obvious through his clothes, dark hair and a beard deliberately shot through with grey in precisely a way that made him look experienced and distinguished.

'And who are your crew?' Hedone asked. Her voice made his muscles constrict. It was as sensual as she was.

'This is Asterion, my first mate,' he said. There was a loud scraping as the whole bench moved backwards as Asterion stood. A few people in the vicinity quietened as they looked over. Theseus didn't flinch, though, as the Minotaur to Hercules's right nodded gruffly at them.

Asterion was huge. He wasn't as tall as the giants, only about eight feet in height, but his bulk matched even

Hercules's. His massive torso and thighs were that of a human, but his head and his lower legs came from a bull. He was covered in short black fur and had black hooves at the bottom of his animal lower legs. Mighty horns curled out of his sturdy black skull, and cruel red eyes glinted above his bearded snout.

'Ah, and here is Evadne, my gunner,' Hercules said as Evadne returned, followed by a servant carrying a huge decanter of wine. She blushed as Theseus bowed to her, and Hercules made a mental note to address that later. It would not do to have a member of his own crew infatuated with Theseus.

'Well,' Theseus said with a wink at Evadne, 'we're having a bit of a celebration on the *Virtus* later. Feel free to join us.'

They all carried on up the table, Hedone throwing a lingering look back at Hercules over her shoulder. Hercules and Asterion sat down.

'I assume we will not be visiting the *Virtus* tonight, Captain,' said the Minotaur. His deep voice was so low it didn't carry at all. As much as Hercules wanted Hedone, there was one thing he wanted more.

'Of course not. When the first Trial is announced tomorrow, we will be ready to go. Speaking of which ... Evadne, I have a job for you.' He turned to the girl, who had just returned to her seat.

Annoyance flickered across her face, but she quickly replaced it with compliance. 'Yes, Captain?'

'I want you to go and tell one of the giant crew that we have inside information about the first event tomorrow. They have had too much attention and support. I want to crush their morale before they even get started. Do you think you can make them believe that the first Trial is going to be on Leo?' he asked her, taking a sip of wine.

'Of course I can, but how do you know the first event won't actually be on Leo? They'd have a massive head start if it is,' she said, helping herself to a handful of plump olives.

'I'm not an idiot,' he growled. 'There's only a one in twelve chance of Leo being the actual location of the first Trial. I can live with those odds. Besides, if they do get lucky and end up in the right place, I will still beat them at whatever the challenge is.' He sat back and took another long draught of wine.

'Right,' Evadne said, sucking on an olive. 'And you've picked Leo because it's more believable that Zeus would have tipped you off if it was your home realm.'

Hercules looked at her.

'Of course.' She nodded and stood up again.

11

EVADNE

I t wasn't hard to spot the crew of giants. They were surrounded by other creatures who lived on Poseidon's and Hephaestus's water worlds. Evadne found the Telkhines the most unpleasant. They looked like dogs, except that they had flippers for front legs and a squelchy finned fish tail at their back end. They were supposed to be incredible metal workers, but she couldn't see how when they were shaped like that.

The giants' ship was called *Orion*, and there were five of them on the crew. She knew Captain Antaeus by sight since the ceremony earlier that day, and she knew that he was one of three full giants. The other two were half-giants. The groaning table she was approaching seated giants of all sizes, as well as two Cyclopes. She decided to go for one of the men at the edge of the group, to draw less attention to herself. Fixing a broad smile on her face, she sat down next to a striking-looking half-giant who was examining a leg of meat closely.

'Hi,' she said.

The large man started and dropped the piece of meat. It

thudded onto a shining metal plate. He looked down at her, and she was surprised by the handsomeness of his face. He had electric-blue eyes and thick, dark hair pulled back into a knot at the nape of his neck. Like the others around him, his face bore the scars of the life of a fighter. An erratic orange scar ran from his full bottom lip all the way down to his chin, standing out against his pale skin. Also like his fellow giants, he was wearing green cargo trousers, but he was the only one with his chest covered. He wore a fitted black shirt, open at the top. He frowned at Evadne, and she decided that she couldn't tell how old he was.

'Why are you over here?' he asked her bluntly, and reached for a huge tankard. The mug was almost the size of her head.

'It's boring over there,' she said, tilting her head towards the middle of the platform, where Hercules sat. 'And that's not a very polite way of saying hello.' She pouted.

He took a long drink and then put the mug back down on the table hard enough to make her jump. She waited for him to respond, but he just picked up the bone with the meat on it again.

'I'm Evadne,' she tried. 'I'm the gunner on the *Hybris*.'

He stopped midway through tearing the meat off the joint with his teeth and looked down at her again. He spat out the meat. 'You're on Hercules's crew?'

'Yes,' she said.

He snorted and threw the bone back onto a big platter in the centre of the table. 'Then you definitely shouldn't be over here. Leave before Bergion or Albion see you.'

'Who are they?' she asked, as innocently as she could. It was hard not to feel intimidated when everyone around her was so much bigger than she was. A roar of laughter came from the centre of the group, and a number of equally huge mugs were clanged down on the table, and she suppressed a flinch. 'And who are you?' she added, trying to smile convincingly.

'I'm Eryx, and Bergion and Albion are the twins over there.' He leaned back so that she could see, and pointed to the end of the table. Two black-skinned, shirtless giants were mid-arm wrestle. They both looked to be a similar height to Captain Antaeus, but one of them was much fatter. They both had shiny bald heads, and the thinner one had a long black-and-grey beard. She couldn't see their eyes, as they were both squinting and straining as they tried to push the other's arm to the table, but she was willing to bet they were bright blue like those of the other sons of Poseidon. She tried not to gulp visibly.

'It's a party; I can sit where I like,' she said, straightening her back.

Eryx raised his eyebrows and then laughed. 'You won't last long in the Trials,' he muttered. 'Are you even old enough to take part?'

Evadne bristled and reminded herself that she was playing a game. That's what she wanted him to think of her.

'Of course I am, I'm seventeen.' She needed to make sure he was on the crew of the *Orion*. The colour of his eyes suggested he was, but she had to be sure. 'What do you do on the ship?' she said.

'Gunner,' he grunted back.

Bingo, thought Evadne. It was time to turn on her best acting skills. She sighed loudly. 'This party is so boring. I was hoping Captain Hercules was going to let us go to Theseus's party on board the *Virtus*, but he says we have to prepare for tomorrow.' She made her voice whiny and young. She needed him to think she was vacuous and impulsive for this to work. 'Are you going to the party?'

He snorted again and threw her a sideways scowl. 'Do I look like someone who goes to parties on pleasure ships?'

She fluttered her eyelashes and inched closer to him. His big hands clenched into fists.

'Sure you do,' she said. 'I could go with you.'

He turned on the bench so he could see her better. 'Why are you talking to me?'

Evadne mentally cursed. She'd overdone it, and now he was suspicious. 'I just thought you looked bored too, and you might be up for a little adventure,' she smiled up at him.

His hands relaxed a little as he laughed again. 'A little adventure!' he said incredulously. 'Do you have any idea what we're starting tomorrow?'

'Exactly!' she said. 'I don't understand why we can't have some fun tonight!' She scowled this time and folded her arms. 'I mean, it's not like Leo is far away, and we've prepped the ship every way we can. What else are we supposed to do tonight?'

He was staring at her, and she looked innocently back at him.

'What? I think I'd enjoy spending the evening with someone like you,' she said coyly, unfolding her arms and leaning towards him. It was difficult when he was so much taller. He opened his mouth to reply but said nothing. He had definitely noticed that she'd said Leo, she thought, but she didn't know if he would point out what she had just 'let slip'.

Eventually, he spoke. 'Your captain is right; you should go back to your ship and prepare yourself for tomorrow. That's what I'll be doing. You should leave this table. Now.'

She let out another big petulant sigh. 'Fine. I'll know next time not to bother coming to giants for fun.' She stood up and left him sat alone as she performed her best flounce up the long table and back towards the other guests.

'YOU'VE DONE WELL,' Hercules said as she rejoined him after mingling convincingly for a while. He raised his wine to her. She flushed. 'Ten minutes after you left him, he went to talk to his captain, and now the whole crew are leaving.'

Evadne picked up her own drink and took a gulp. Now she just hoped that the first task was not on Leo, or Hercules would not be happy.

Dealing with Hercules's temper was worth it for the most part. Since taking a place on the crew of the *Hybris*, she had lived in luxury. She wanted for nothing, and Hercules was the greatest lover she could ever hope for. He was a celebrity, and he had chosen her to be the only woman on his crew. And most importantly, she now had a very real shot at immortality.

A shiver went through her, and she tried not to think about it, for fear of overexcitement. She needed to be able to concentrate. It was most likely that the first event would be in one of the eleven other realms, and she wouldn't have to deal with his wrath at all, but if she did, she just needed to remember why she was here. She had a chance at fame, fortune and an infinite life.

12

LYSSA

Lyssa was a little concerned about Len. She knew having an entirely male crew could be a liability around some creatures, like sirens or nymphs, but she hadn't realised quite how enthralled they could all become with one woman.

Hedone, on the crew of the *Virtus*, had collected a gaggle of admirers as the evening had worn on. She was apparently the demigoddess of pleasure, and it looked to Lyssa like she had quite a bit of power. Len's short stature had helped him to push between the legs of a lot of the other adoring creatures, both male and female, so that he could sit at her feet. Lyssa could just see him through the group, gazing up at Hedone with his mouth hanging open slightly as she regaled the group with a story about a party in her home realm of Pisces. Lyssa couldn't tell whether the story was actually funny or whether everyone was just laughing uproariously because they had drunk so much fine wine. Or maybe it was because such an attractive storyteller was telling the jokes that everyone was laughing at. Abderos couldn't get through the crowd because of his chair, so he was sitting behind the group, craning his head to see round people.

Lyssa shook her head and stood up. It had become late, and many of the guests were starting to leave, having filled their bellies with the excellent food the gods had provided. She tapped Abderos on the shoulder. 'Come on, Abderos. Time we left, anyway.'

'No way, Cap. Hedone says they're carrying on the party back on their Typhoon.'

'And you think we're going?' Lyssa raised her eyebrows. 'Not a chance.'

'Cap, we might die tomorrow. You heard what Zeus said. I wanna see Theseus's Typhoon!'

'We're going back to the *Alastor*. Now.' She stared at him, one hand on her hip. They both knew Captain's orders were always followed.

Abderos rolled his eyes. 'Fine. Let's all mosey on to our deaths stone cold sober,' he grumbled, and reversed his chair away from the group. She suspected he never thought he had a chance of going in the first place and was trying his luck.

Len would be harder to dissuade. She was just about to attempt to work her way through the group to get Len's attention when a loud crash took hers. Everyone turned to look over at the source of the noise.

HERCULES WAS STANDING, the bench he had been sat on was overturned, and there was a large platter of fruit tipped over and scattered across the table. In one hand, he was holding a large jug and waving it, laughing. Opposite him, on the other side of the table, were three centaurs. Centaurs were rarely seen outside of their home realm, Artemis's Sagittarius. They were insular, unfriendly people, and Epizon had spent all night trying unsuccessfully to engage one of the delegates in conversation.

'Your wine?' boomed Hercules, and the remaining guests all fell quiet. Even the band stopped playing, their attention fully on the muscular man in the black shirt. 'I think you'll find it's my wine now!' He waved the jug at them again and took a glass from the table.

The centaur in the middle took a step forward. Lyssa guessed he was male, because his sculpted bare human chest was flat, rising out of the body of a sleek black stallion. He was taller than Hercules, at least seven feet from head to hoof. His voice was soft when he spoke, but it carried across the silent platform.

'That wine has been brought from Sagittarius. It is all we centaurs may drink, and only centaurs may drink it. I ask you again not to insult our people by indulging in something so personal to us.'

Hercules stopped pouring wine from the jug into his glass and looked at the centaur. He slowly began to tip the contents of the glass onto the marble platform at his feet. The two centaurs behind the black male began to stamp their feet, their tails flicking. Lyssa felt herself tense.

'I find it insulting that you will not share it with me,' hissed Hercules, and he put the jug to his mouth. As he began to tip the jug back to drink the wine, there was a roar, and the pale brown-and-cream-coloured centaur leaped over the table. Hercules caught the creature around his human waist before his back legs had landed and flung him backwards into the table. There was an almighty crash as the force collapsed the table, and the other two centaurs sprang forward.

The group Lyssa was standing with was suddenly

animated, some scrambling to get out of the way and back to the longboats, and some trying to get a better look at the action. She ducked under the table in front of her and stood up on the other side, unable to take her eyes from the fight.

The first centaur was lying in the wreckage of the table, unmoving. The other two were either side of Hercules, the black centaur not facing him as he was trying to land kicks from his stronger back legs on his opponent's body. Hercules's eyes were alive, a maniacal smile on his face as he swung at the horse-people, ducking their flying hooves. The jug lay broken on the platform, red liquid spilling slowly across the white marble.

There was another roar, and it was impossible to tell whether it came from Hercules or the black centaur he had managed to grab by the back left leg. Hercules pulled hard, and the powerful front legs of the centaur gave out, and his torso crashed to floor as he was dragged backwards. Hercules began to swing the creature up into the air and then carried on in an arc, around and around, like the centaur was a toy.

Lyssa's stomach lurched as she realised what he was going to do, and the silence of the crowd was broken by a number of gasps. Hercules let go as he came to face the edge of the platform. The centaur's arms and legs scrabbled as he seemed to hover in the air for a moment, and then he was falling. Lyssa saw people on the other side of the platform rush to the edge and look over. She had no desire to see. She knew what would happen. He would be sucked into the Olympus Void.

Hercules had turned to face the last centaur standing. In contrast to his easy, solid stance, the horse-man was shaking. Lyssa didn't know if it was through fear or anger. To hear about Hercules's superhuman strength was one thing, but to see it in action was quite another. She could see sweat rolling down the snow-white flanks of the centaur, his hooves clicking frantically as they faced each other. At that moment, she wanted nothing more than this magnificent creature to back down, to disgrace himself but to retain his life. There was no way he could best Hercules. But with another roar, the white horse-man reared up on his back legs and tried to bring his front hooves crashing down onto Hercules.

He was too fast though. Hercules ducked under the centaur's huge body and took hold of his front and back leg. He pulled hard as he stood up. The creature was flipped, his human chest and head hitting the ground hard. There was a sickening snap and a scream of pain. Hercules laughed as he took another leg in both hands and twisted. The centaur's screams got worse, and Lyssa turned away. She dropped back under the table, and Epizon caught her arm and pulled her up on the other side.

'The longboat is waiting,' he murmured as another snap cut through the screams.

She didn't respond but headed straight for the boat, where she could see her crew were now boarding.

Nobody spoke on the trip back to the *Alastor*. When the longboat docked and the crew filed silently onto the deck of the ship, Lyssa tried to feel the familiar sensation of relief and safety she usually got from the *Alastor*. But all she could feel was roiling disgust, fear and anticipation. She felt ashamed for doing nothing to help. But her Rage had not come. Fear had overpowered her anger. Witnessing the reality of what this man, her father, could do after so many years had left her unable to do anything but stare in horror. She turned to Epizon, quiet beside her.

'Should we have helped?' she asked, silently praying he wouldn't say yes.

'The only way we can help is by stopping him becoming immortal. If you had gotten involved tonight, you would not have lived to enter the Trials.'

She nodded. Although she knew it was true, she would never admit that she couldn't have helped if she'd wanted to. Epizon nodded meaningfully towards the rest of the crew, heading across the deck to the hauler.

'Guys,' she called, and jogged to catch up with them. 'Don't let what we saw tonight affect what we do tomorrow. It just proves how important it is that we stop him winning.' She looked at each of them. Phyleus was pale, and Abderos wouldn't meet her eye.

'He broke that poor creature's legs,' Abderos said quietly.

'Yes,' replied Lyssa. 'He is a monster who enjoys torturing as much as he does killing. And we are going to stop him.'

13

ERYX

E ryx was tense as he watched the orange flames flicker gently in the wide iron flame dish. It was raised on a sturdy wooden post next to the navigation wheel on the stern quarterdeck. He was desperate to see the flames flash white and to have their first Trial revealed.

After that idiot girl had let slip that Hercules had inside information and the first Trial would be on Leo, the crew of giants had boarded their ship, the *Orion*, and started to make plans. They didn't want to leave too early, or it would look suspicious, but a head start for a ship like theirs could make all the difference. The crew of the *Orion* needed a Zephyr, as no other ship in Olympus was large enough for three full giants and two half-giants to live aboard, but nothing they possessed could make a Zephyr fast enough to compete with the others in speed.

Eryx ran his hand through his black hair apprehensively. A thud behind him indicated Antaeus's arrival on the quarterdeck.

'Anything?' he asked gruffly.

Eryx shook his head without turning around, his eyes glued to the flames. They had left the Void a few hours after everyone had quietened down, following the end of the feast, and they were well on their way to Leo. The only ship still showing any sign of life when they had left had been the *Virtus*, and that had likely continued all night. Eryx screwed his broad face up in distaste. He couldn't understand how people could enjoy a party after the gruesome fight Hercules had caused. It wasn't that he was squeamish; he just had more respect than that. If he hadn't been fed up with the others arguing, he wouldn't have gone back to the platform for one last beer and witnessed the brutal scene. His feelings for the pretentious airhead who had sat with him last night soured further. Anyone on that crew was of no interest to him.

Antaeus spoke aloud. 'Everyone on the stern quarter-deck, now,' he barked.

Slowly the rest of the crew arrived on the deck. Busiris was first. His skin was the colour of gold, and he had thick black liner around his onyx eyes. He was a half-giant, like Eryx, but the similarities stopped there. Busiris was the only son of Poseidon on the ship without the bright blue eyes. He was also the only member who hadn't made his living as a fighter. He was a ruler of a small settlement on Aries called Egypt. Busiris had been more than happy to leave his people under the charge of his deputy for a place on the crew of Poseidon's sons, in return for funding the ship. He had bought the *Orion*, kitted it out to accommodate the giants and used everything else he was willing to part with to attempt improvements. Eryx thought they would have been better off spending money on supplies, as they had no idea where they would have to go or when, but nobody on board listened to Eryx.

Albion and Bergion stumbled up not long after Busiris, having clearly just woken. Bergion pulled at his beard as he yawned, and Albion tried to squish his huge, fat stomach past his brother to get nearer to the flame dish.

'Have we heard anything?' he asked, excitement tinging his groggy voice.

Right on cue the flames jumped to life, flashing white. They flickered for a second, then died right down. A pretty blonde man in a deep-blue toga appeared.

'Good day, Olympians!' he beamed. 'Are you all ready to find out what the first Trial is?' He didn't wait for an answer. 'I'm sure you are, so without further delay, let it be revealed!'

Eryx rolled his eyes. Trust the gods to turn this into some sort of cheesy entertainment.

'Here's the god hosting the first Trial.' His eyes were gleaming and his excitement was infectious, even through the flame message.

Eryx silently prayed they were about to see Zeus's face. The image faded for a moment, and Antaeus growled with impatience. Eryx's stomach sank as Hera's striking figure materialised. She was standing in front of a huge, glittering lake, the banks of which were lined with pale stone buildings.

'Good day, heroes of Olympus.' Her voice was deep and clear and calm. Eryx tried to look at his captain without moving his head too obviously. Nobody made a sound. 'The first of your many deadly, near-impossible Trials will be to slaughter a long-standing threat to my peaceful realm. There is a lion stalking my people.' She spread her arms, gesturing at the settlements behind her as she spoke. She was wearing a traditional, conservative toga with a vivid turquoise sash over the shoulder that shone next to her dark skin. 'It eats living creatures and is a source of constant terror. The death toll stands at fifty-two as we speak. This monster has skin that is impervious to all weapons, and as such, it has evaded the attempts of the citizens of Cancer to kill it. Whichever crew kills the beast wins the task. Good luck.' The image vanished and the flames flickered red and orange again.

There was a silence that lasted another moment, then the booming roar of an angry giant.

14

HEDONE

Normally, Hedone loved a good party, and Theseus's ship, the *Virtus*, was made for parties. She sat on the empty quarterdeck alone, watching the few guests still up on deck, gorging on the expensive food and wine they had brought from their home realm of Pisces. Theseus visited with Aphrodite regularly, and she gave him a constant supply of exquisite culinary treats. Hedone wasn't quite sure what Theseus was giving her in return, but she could make a good guess. She didn't really care what Theseus got up to.

She listened absently as an old satyr berated a drunk human for wasting good opportunities. She held a glass of her favourite rich red wine, but it was barely touched. She had tried drinking last night, at the start of the party, hoping to clear her head of the beautiful man she had met, but the wine had made it worse. She had tried dancing with the others, but it felt pointless without him there, and the attention she got was unwanted. When the guests had started to leave, or head down to the numerous living quarters, she had come up to the quarterdeck and sat alone, trying to work out her feelings for Hercules.

The more she had thought about him, the more desperate she had become. His intense grey eyes and his fierce power made her shiver. She longed to touch him, to feel him, to kiss him. She wanted him to need her too, to fill with passion when he saw her and claim her as his own. She needed him to notice her, and the best way she could think of doing that was to help him win the first Trial. But she couldn't do that if it meant putting her own crew at risk. She didn't care if they won or lost, but she didn't want to hurt them. She had sat for hours, trying to come up with a way to help him.

The low orange flames in the flame dish suddenly crackled to life. She jumped and watched as the excitable man introduced Hera. The first Trial was to kill a flesh-eating lion. No doubt Theseus would come up with some clever strategy before they even arrived on Cancer. As she got up to go and wake him, it occurred to her that she was the only crew member who had seen the message. A smile spread across her beautiful face. Maybe she could keep the *Virtus* safe and help Hercules have one less competitor to worry about after all. She took a long drink from her glass and sat back down.

15

LYSSA

Time was dragging as Lyssa waited to find out what the first Trial was. She'd given up trying to sleep in her plush new blankets, and headed to the cargo deck to check on the tank creature. She wasn't surprised to find Epizon already there. He was sitting on a crate that had been dragged over to the tank. The creature looked exactly as Lyssa had last seen it. It was hovering, facing Epizon, unblinking, and he stared back at it.

'I think she's female,' he said as Lyssa pulled herself up to sit next to him.

'Me too,' she said. 'Any idea what she eats yet?'

He shook his head. 'She shimmers though. Do you think she might need light?'

'If she does, she can go a while without it. She was inside the crate for weeks,' Lyssa replied.

'You did well at the ceremony,' Epizon said, looking at her.

She felt a surge of pride at the compliment. 'I nearly lost it,' she told him, looking down at her lap. 'Athena spoke to me. She calmed me down.'

Epizon raised his eyebrows. 'She may be the only one of the gods that isn't a sadistic lunatic,' he muttered.

'I wouldn't be so rude about them now they're paying attention to us,' she warned him with a smile. 'Even I can't rescue you from the wrath of a god.'

He smiled back at her. 'Sure you could,' he said.

They both looked back at the tank creature.

'We should name her,' said Epizon.

'We should work out how to ask her what her name is,' Lyssa replied.

They sat silently for a while. The creature alternated her gaze, looking between them, only blinking once.

'I think you should trust Phyleus. He's on the crew now,' said Epizon.

Her face creased into a grimace, her green eyes narrowing. 'He's a jumped-up idiot, and he doesn't care for any of us.'

'Lyssa, do you remember when we first met?'

'Of course I do,' she said. She thought about the night she'd met Epizon, his huge frame squished into the cramped metal lean-to he was living in. 'I thought you were after my stolen drachmas.'

He smiled. 'It took you a long time to trust me. I'd never known anybody as desperate for freedom as I was.' He put his huge, callused hand on her leg, dwarfing her thigh. 'That freedom is at real risk now. We need to accept all the help we can get.'

'Guys, the flames are white! Get up here!' Abderos's voice rang in their minds simultaneously. They leapt off the crate together.

'Showtime,' breathed Lyssa as she ran to the hauler.

.   .   .

Lyssa was relieved the first event was on Cancer. Hera was a merciful god to those who had never crossed her. With any luck, the event would be exactly as she had described, with no hidden surprises. Also, Cancer was not far from the Void. The sky realm of Leo was regarded as being the centre of Olympus, as it belonged to the lord of the gods, Zeus himself. It was over two hundred feet above the surface, but only empty ocean existed beneath it. Most navigation was done using Zeus's realm as a starting point. The Void was a little to the north-east, about fifty leagues away from Leo, and Cancer was south-east of Leo, about a hundred and fifty leagues. It wouldn't take the *Alastor* more than a day to get there.

'If she wants the lion gone, she could just remove it, right?' Lyssa mused, aloud.

'Of course she could. But what fun would that be?' answered Epizon. He was leaning against the back of the quarterdeck, watching the orange clouds swirl past the ship. The flickering edges of the clouds shimmered, greens and purples glimmering through the bright umber.

'Any ideas yet?' Lyssa asked him.

'No. If its skin is impervious, then we can't use traditional weapons, like slingshots or arrows.'

'Poison?' Abderos suggested.

Epizon scowled. 'That seems a cowardly way to kill anything.'

Abderos shrugged, looking over his shoulder at Epizon's unimpressed face. 'That's how you'd get rid of pests on Libra,' he pointed out.

'Who's a pest?' said Len, his hooves clicking on the floor as he stepped out of the hauler and onto the quarterdeck.

'That depends,' Lyssa said. 'Has anyone ever tried to poison you?'

Len grunted. 'Never accept berries from angry wood nymphs, that's all I'm saying,' he muttered as he pulled himself up onto one of the benches that lined the right side of the deck, next to Phyleus. He turned to face Lyssa. 'So.' He clapped his small, hairy hands together, looking hopeful. 'What's the plan?'

'Poison it,' Abderos said.

Len guffawed as he looked at him. 'You volunteering as bait? Or have you forgotten that it only eats living things?'

Abderos stared back at the satyr a moment, then turned to Lyssa. 'Captain, I propose we use Len as bait. We could pick up a new medic on Cancer. They can't be worse than him.'

Lyssa laughed aloud at Len's outraged face.

'Stars, I'm only joking,' Abderos said with a big smile at the satyr. Len continued to scowl.

'Well, it seems pretty obvious,' said Epizon. He straightened and turned away from the hypnotic skies. 'If we can't kill it from a distance, we're going to need to get close to it. And one of us will need to be strong and quick enough to fight it and win.' He looked at Lyssa. Phyleus and Abderos followed his gaze. She swallowed.

'Do we know how big it is?' asked Abderos.

'No,' replied Epizon. 'We only know what was in Hera's message.'

'But we know where it is, right?'

'Ab, you watched the same message we all did. We have no idea where it is.' Lyssa could hear the strained patience in Epizon's voice. She thought he might be more nervous about the Trials actually starting than he had let on.

'Someone on Cancer must know where we can find it,' she said. It was easier to think about the less fatal parts of the plan, like finding the creature, than what she was expected to do with it.

'Where are we landing then, Cap?' asked Abderos.

'I don't know. The largest settlement on Cancer is Corinthia. All the towns there have docks big enough for the *Alastor*, so I guess we'll pick a port and start there. We moor up and start asking questions.' She shrugged.

'Can I suggest Port Galatas?' Phyleus had stood up.

Lyssa felt a stab of annoyance. He had no right to offer opinions. She also couldn't help noticing how tight his new shirt was across his muscular shoulders. She blinked the thought away. 'No, you can't. I don't know anything about Galatas.'

'Then I know more than you do, Captain,' he said, stepping forward, brown eyes sparkling. He was ready for a fight.

'Gods, you're irritating. Why Galatas? Have you been before?' She had visited a number of ports on Cancer before, but never that one.

'Yes, years ago. And there are a few reasons. It's close to Port Nemea and a couple of other large docks, so we have a higher chance of being closer to the lion. It has the busiest docks, which means we have a larger number of people to talk to. And if any other crews dock there, they'll see our ship and be disheartened that we've beaten them to it.'

Lyssa cocked her head, considering. Phyleus looked pleased with himself.

'Shouldn't we be going all stealthy?' Len asked.

Epizon answered. 'Stealth is pointless. We'll give ourselves away as soon as we start talking to people to find out where the lion is.'

'Added to which, we've been on every flame message in Olympus,' Lyssa said.

Len grinned. 'I know! I'm finally famous!'

Lyssa rolled her eyes. 'You won't be leaving the ship this time,' she told him.

'You're damn right I won't!' he shot back, suppressing a small shudder. 'The place is littered with peacocks. I don't get on with peacocks.'

The corner of Phyleus's mouth quirked up in a smile. 'Why don't you like peacocks?' he asked.

Len turned and looked up at him. 'The same reason I imagine you don't like harpies. Enormous, pecking, stupid animals larger than yourself are unnerving. At least you can reason with a harpy.'

Phyleus raised an eyebrow, still smiling. 'Fair enough,' he said.

'Abderos, we'll likely need you to stay on the ship too, in case we need a quick getaway, or a lift out,' said Lyssa.

'No problem, Cap.'

Lyssa never knew if Abderos was really happy staying on board all the time, or if he longed to be off the ship. The practicalities of his being chair-bound meant that it would be nearly impossible on a challenge like this though, so she was relieved when, as usual, he didn't argue. She had asked him once if he had considered mechanical legs, and he had told her that one day his own would work just fine again and he wasn't about to 'lop them off, thank you very much'. She didn't ask how he planned to go about this. Maybe, one day, she should.

'Land ahoy, Captain,' said Epizon, and all four crew members looked past the sails in front of them.

Directly ahead, rising from the deep blue ocean they were soaring over, lay Cancer. It was mostly flat, and its surface was covered in rich green forests broken up by sprawling turquoise lakes. They looked to her like hundreds

of green and blue interlocked fingers. As the *Alastor* sped
closer, Lyssa could make out settlements in clusters all along
the banks of the lakes. The buildings were all made from
white stone, and the roads were white too. The forest was
densest around the outer edge of the whole island, so that it
was much harder to approach from the ocean. The ports
that the ships were allowed to dock in could only be
approached from above, and they fringed a massive lake in
the centre of Cancer.

ABDEROS SET a course for Port Galatas, and half an hour
later, they sailed into the docks. The docks were a replica of
the wooden piers that jutted out from the banks of the lake
into the water, except that they were fifty feet higher up.
Haulers ran between the pier platforms and the ground.

Lyssa, Epizon and Phyleus were stood on the deck at the
bow of the ship, watching the white stone buildings get
larger as they glided to a stop next to an empty raised pier.
They were not the only large ship in the docks, but there
was no sign of the *Hybris*, *Orion* or *Virtus*. Either they had
beaten them all there, or their competition had docked
elsewhere.

As soon as the ship was totally still, Epizon stepped
easily from the edge of the deck onto the pier and began to
walk towards the hauler at the end. Phyleus followed, his
footsteps sounding lighter on the wood than Epizon's heavy
boots. Lyssa half stepped onto the pier and faltered. She was
trying hard to ignore the fact that she was terrified. Epizon
clearly expected her to fight this beast, and in normal
circumstances, she would agree. When the Rage was
flowing though her, she had a god's strength. But last time
her Rage should have been boiling beneath her skin, she

had felt nothing but fear and revulsion. If she had to face Hercules, she didn't know if she could depend on her power, and without it she had nothing. Lyssa took a long look up at the shimmering sails, picturing them flooded with red as her power flowed through them. The Rage would come. She had to believe it would. She took a deep breath, stepped fully off her ship and set off up the pier after her crew mates.

'I doubt we've got much time before the others get here,' said Epizon as she stepped into the hauler with them. 'If they're not here already. So we need to move quickly.'

She nodded.

'Even if we find the lion first, how are you going to kill it?' asked Phyleus.

'That's not your problem. You're only here because I don't want to leave you on the ship.' That was only partly true. Lyssa wanted to test his cocky defiance, to see if he was able to back up his smooth talking with half-decent actions.

'Gods, you talk to me like a child,' he said, glowering at her.

She ignored him. 'We need to find the lion first. Epizon, you take the tavernas nearest the docks, as you have the advantage of looking imposing,' she said. He looked offended and she laughed aloud, despite her nerves. He was wearing his favourite floor-length black coat, which in theory hid his weapons but in reality made it look like he had an arsenal stored about himself. 'Well, you really didn't need the coat,' she said, smiling. 'The weather doesn't change on Cancer.'

He looked sceptically at her and pulled open one side of the offending garment. 'How else would I hide this?' he asked. He had a huge knife strapped to his right thigh.

'There you go; you've proven my point,' she answered.

'You are the most intimidating. Let me know if you find anything out. Phyleus, you stay with me.'

They stepped out of the hauler into the bright light. The huge bulk of the *Alastor*'s hull loomed over them, hovering a foot above the crystal-clear water of the lake.

'Good day to you, travellers,' came a cheery voice. They all turned to see an older man in a traditional toga coming across the sandy shore to them.

Hera was the most traditional of the gods, and the goddess of family and marriage. In theory Cancer should have been a world full of happy families. But Hera was also the goddess of revenge. Lyssa had not spent much time in Cancer's pristine towns, but she knew enough not to trust the smiling front the folk all put on.

'Good day,' she replied, walking to meet him. 'You're the dockmaster?'

'I certainly am,' he beamed.

'Great. How much do we owe?'

'Oh, but for you, my dear girl, it will be nothing. You are here to slay this evil creature!'

Lyssa shifted uncomfortably. It had been naive to believe for a moment that the people here wouldn't know who they were.

'Have you heard of any of the other crews arriving on Cancer yet?' Phyleus asked.

'No, no, and news travels fast here. You are the first.' He clapped his wrinkled hands together excitedly. 'Just wait until I tell my wife I met you all! You're her favourite, you see. You're everyone's favourite here!'

'Us? Why?' exclaimed Lyssa, genuinely surprised.

'Dear girl! The very name of your ship epitomises what we Cancerians stand for. You seek revenge on the man who destroyed your family.' He continued to grin cheerfully, and a flicker of anger shot through her. These people knew what she had been through and how dangerous Hercules was, but they saw it as a game. 'We'll be sure to do everything we can to help you, and we'll make things as difficult for that father of yours as we can!'

She felt sick when she heard the word *father*, and opened her mouth to tell this man he was deluded, but Phyleus and Epizon stepped forward at the same time.

'You're very kind, thank you,' said Epizon.

The dockmaster's grin slipped momentarily and was replaced by a look of alarm at being addressed by the huge black man, and Lyssa got some satisfaction from imagining him greeting the giants when they got here.

'Do you know where we can find this lion Hera speaks of?'

'Oh, yes, of course. The Nemean Lion. She lives in the forest just north-west of Port Nemea, south of the nymph settlement.'

Epizon and Lyssa looked at each other.

'She? The lion is female?' asked Phyleus.

'When she wants to be,' answered the man with a scowl.

'Right,' said Lyssa. 'Well, we won't use up any more of your time. We'll take the *Alastor* to Port Nemea right away. Thank you.'

'No, no, no!' he exclaimed. 'The lion's lair is not much further from Port Galatas than it is from Port Nemea, and we can give you directions from here.' He beamed at them all in turn, though still slightly nervously at Epizon.

'That would be very helpful,' said Epizon. 'We just need a minute to talk through our plan?' Though he worded it as a polite question, it was clear there was only one answer.

'Of course, of course. I'll just be over there.' The old man gestured at a small white stone hut further up the shore, where white roads began to run up the gentle slope towards the town of Port Galatas. Lyssa nodded at him, and with one last smile, he turned and made his way up the beach, leather sandals crunching across the stony sand.

When she was sure he was out of earshot, she turned to the others. 'Well?' she asked.

'I like him,' said Epizon.

'You like everyone,' retorted Lyssa. 'He's either telling the truth and he wants to help, or he's in the pay of one of our competitors and it's a trap.'

'I think it's very likely that we're the first here. Isn't the *Alastor* the fastest ship in the Trials?' Phyleus said.

The compliment to her ship made the retort die on Lyssa's lips. She eyed Phyleus.

'Len, did you learn anything last night about who the Cancerians are supporting in the Trials?' she said, picturing the satyr and projecting the question to him.

'Who do you think, Cap?' came the reply. 'Blood feud and all that? Hera hates Hercules. They're probably the most likely to back us out of all the realms.'

'Thanks, Len. Talk soon.' She looked at Epizon and Phyleus. 'It seems he's telling the truth. Let's go.' She pulled the red scarf keeping her hair out of her face tighter and set off up the beach.

After coming to Nemea and tracking the lion, Hercules tried shooting him with an arrow. When he realised the skin was impenetrable, he took his club and chased him. The lion hid in a cave with two openings, and Hercules blocked one off and entered through the other. When he caught the beast, he tightened his arms around its neck until he had strangled it.

EXCERPT FROM

THE LIBRARY BY APOLLODORUS

Written 300–100 BC

Paraphrased by Eliza Raine

16

HERCULES

The *Hybris* made no noise as it sailed into the busy port of Nemea. Hercules always landed and took off himself where possible, in order to remind his crew that they were there by his good graces and not because they could do anything he couldn't.

His Whirlwind-class ship was the best that drachmas could buy, and Hercules had filled the towering pillars along the deck with rows and rows of storm ballistas. They had more range than any of his rivals' weapons, and Zeus had made sure that he had limitless shot. He smiled as he thought about testing them out on that girl's miserable Crosswind.

Asterion and Evadne were waiting for him, close to the tall dock he had moored perfectly next to. Asterion wore the black tabard he only wore when going ashore. When on ship the bull creature hated to wear the awkward clothes that had been made for him, so he usually went without. Hercules couldn't care less what he did or didn't wear, as long as he could fight. Evadne looked young and pretty, in black leather trousers and boots, and a blood-red shirt that clung to her body. Her blue hair was tied up in a high tail, and she looked serious. He had made sure that she knew Theseus was not to be admired, and she had regrettably lost some of her youthful enthusiasm since. They both nodded to him as he marched past, then fell in behind him as he stepped off the *Hybris*.

'Let's go kill a lion,' he smirked.

HERCULES KNEW CANCER WELL. He visited often to flaunt the fact that he had Zeus's protection. Hera had hated him since his fateful clash with her six years ago. She denied it, but he knew it was her who had sent the madness to him. The madness that led him to kill his wife, Megara, and his son. He felt no ill will towards her though. In fact, he felt indebted to her. He may never have taken his temper that far, never have felt the incredible power that came with taking a life. The day she sent that madness to him was the day he unlocked his true strength. He looked up into the bright blue sky and smiled his thanks.

He had chosen Port Nemea because it was the busiest of the port towns. If any of the locals knew where this lion laired, then they would have passed through Port Nemea at some point. There were at least twenty more docks jutting out from the beach, on either side of theirs, and almost all had ships moored up. Many were longboats, with two or three to a pier, and none were as impressive as the *Hybris*, but there were a couple of Typhoons and one pleasure Zephyr. Hercules took a moment to find the names of the Typhoons, stencilled across the top of their hulls at the bow. Neither were Theseus's *Virtus* and he was unsurprised. The *Virtus* was nowhere near as fast as his ship was.

As he reached the end of the dock, a small, harried-looking human woman in what might once have been a white toga stopped in front of them. He paused.

'Good day, sir,' she squeaked, looking up at him. Her thin, wispy hair was pinned to her head, and he guessed she was middle-aged. Her eyes darted to Asterion, stood stock-still behind him, and widened.

'It will be, yes,' he replied.

'Yes, yes.' She looked nervously at the sheets of parchment she was holding. 'I just need to collect your docking fee, and I'll be out of your way.'

Hercules grunted and gestured at Evadne. She stepped forward and handed the woman a few drachmas.

'Thank you, dear,' said the woman, making a note on her ledger. 'I'll be off then. Enjoy Port Nemea,' she said, starting off towards the next dock.

'Wait,' called Hercules, and she froze.

'I'm really very busy,' she said as she turned back towards them.

'I won't keep you long. I assume you know who I am and why I'm here.'

She looked down at her leather sandals. 'Yes, of course,' she mumbled.

'Good. Have any of the other ships in the Trials docked yet?' he asked.

'I really shouldn't—' she started to reply, and Hercules took a step towards her. His chest expanded as he stood straighter, and when he spoke, his voice was soft but deeper.

'Just answer the question, and you can go about your business,' he said.

She only hesitated a second longer. 'You are the first I know of,' she said, looking down at her feet to avoid meeting his eyes.

Satisfied, Hercules swept past her and into the hauler at the end of the pier.

His two crew members stayed a few feet behind him as he made his way up the beach. A long white promenade ran between the beach and scores of bright white stone buildings. Many had white tarpaulin covers jutting out from the building fronts, shielding fruit and vegetables in crates from the bright light. Many others had large arching doorways and enticing smells wafting from inside. Hercules knew that the further away from the beach he got, the more residential the buildings became. Tall white columns contained homes stacked one on top of the other for the treasured Cancerian families to live in. They lined the streets beyond the bustling port area he was currently in. Only the wealthy families on the edges of the settlements had houses that were detached from other buildings. They also had gardens bordering the dense forest surrounding the town.

Hercules made for one of the larger tavernas on the busy promenade, facing the beach. Some only served food, but most served wine too, and he decided these would be where he would find the loosest tongues. He stopped outside an establishment called Orexi, which was flanked by an open-fronted shop selling purple vegetables on the right and a leather beater on the left. An old man was sitting outside on a stool, lazily stroking a soft-looking piece of brown hide. He squinted at Hercules as he strode through the stone arch of the taverna.

Hercules looked around, eyes sharp, and sat at an empty table near the centre of the room. The inside of the building was white like the outside, except the ceiling, which had been painted ocean blue. The taverna was about half full, with clusters of people around blue tables painted to match the ceiling. There had been a dip in the buzz of conversation as Hercules had entered, followed by his crew, but as he had sat down, the chat resumed restlessly.

A boy of about eleven came to the table and asked what they would like.

'Wine,' answered Hercules without looking at him. He was scanning the room, assessing the clientele.

'Which wine, sir?' asked the boy, and Hercules looked at him with a flash of annoyance.

'Red,' said Evadne quickly, and gave the child a look. He hurried off.

Hercules looked at her and then noticed the absence of his Minotaur. 'Where's Asterion?'

'He can't use these,' she answered, gesturing at the small wooden chair that was creaking under Hercules's own considerable weight.

He thought for a moment. 'Go and tell him to scout the harpy settlement west of here. They might know something.'

'You can tell him,' she protested.

He clenched his teeth and fixed her with a stare. Her pout vanished. 'How many times must I tell you to do something,' he said, so low and quiet that only she could hear him. It was not a question.

She dropped her eyes and stood, her chair scraping on the tiled floor. Hercules let out a slow breath, trying not to get angry with the girl in public. He needed the locals to warm to him. It had never taken him this long to instil obedience into his admirers though. If she didn't fall into line soon, he would have to get rid of her. He supposed he would take her punishments a little further. He relaxed and his anger ebbed away as he thought about that. A small smile played on his lips, and the boy returned with the wine in a glass decanter.

'That's a lot of wine for one,' said a distinctly feminine voice.

He looked up and his smile broadened. He had always loved women with red hair. His traitorous wife had been a redhead. A scowl flickered across his face at the thought.

'Oh, am I bothering you?' the girl said, misreading his frown.

'Not at all,' said Hercules, sitting back in the too-small chair. 'Take a seat.'

She beamed and sat down opposite him, where Evadne had been sitting. She was petite and slim, with a strong square jaw, freckles and bright, lively green eyes. Her red hair fell about her shoulders in long waves.

'You're Hercules,' she said excitedly.

He nodded and took a sip of wine. It was sharp and fresh.

'You're here to kill the Nemean Lion!' She clapped her hands together, and it made her look younger than she had before.

A cough behind her made the girl turn quickly. Evadne was stepping up to her now-occupied chair. 'Hi,' she said. 'I'm Evadne.'

As the girl started to speak, Hercules cut her off. 'Leave. Now.' He was looking at his gunner.

Evadne opened her mouth, and Hercules drew breath sharply. She closed it again. He caught a glimpse of the fury on her face as she wheeled around and stormed back through the taverna arch.

'Oh dear,' said the pretty girl coyly. 'Have I caused an issue with your girlfriend?'

'She's my gunner. I don't have girlfriends,' replied Hercules.

'Do you like girls though?' she asked.

He smiled. 'Yes. Very much.'

She beamed again, her eyes raking over his handsome face.

'Did you say Nemean Lion?' he asked her.

'Yes. That's why you're here, isn't it? To kill the lion?'

'It is. Does it lair in Nemea?'

'Just outside Nemea, to the north. Not far east of the harpy settlement. May I?' She pointed at the wine.

Hercules couldn't help admiring her boldness. The casual naivety of youth. He nodded. 'Does everyone in Nemea know where it lairs?'

'Yes, of course. Everyone on Cancer. Or how would we know to avoid it!' She laughed as she poured herself wine into what would have been Evadne's glass.

'What's your name?'

'Gata.' She sat back with the glass and fluttered her eyelashes at him.

Hercules had known hundreds of girls like Gata, on every constellation in Olympus. He knew he should be moving on, using the information she had given him. But her childish adoration was what he wanted after Evadne's impertinence. He had hours before any of the other ships arrived on Cancer. Even when they did arrive, he couldn't see how any of them would be able to kill a monster with impervious skin. He was the only one who could do it.

'Gata, I'm in a bit of a hurry. Do you think you can help me?' He leaned towards her and smiled his most charming smile. Not that he needed it; he already knew the girl would throw herself at him. He saw her arms tremble and her lips part slightly, and knew she was his.

17

LYSSA

The walk through Galatas had taken longer than Lyssa had expected, because all the locals they passed had wanted to wish them luck and shake their hands. They were stopped constantly as they walked through the crowded area of tavernas and shops, and only a little less so as they made their way to the east of the settlement through the big white housing blocks. By the time they had reached the quiet, greener houses on the edge of Galatas, most of the well-wishers had dissipated, much to her relief. The peacocks, however, had increased in number. She was starting to understand Len's issue with them; she hadn't seen one smaller than he was. The birds ambled around them as they walked, the bright blue of their bodies standing out against their green fanned tails. The eyes in their plumage kept drawing her gaze as she walked down the immaculate shiny white streets.

'Len's right; they are kind of creepy,' she said.

'They're beautiful,' said Epizon.

'You would say that.' She rolled her eyes. Epizon saw the best in everything. 'Well, I s'pose they're better than those sycophantic idiots we've spent all morning pushing our way through.'

'You don't enjoy the attention?' Phyleus asked her.

She snorted. 'Do you?'

'I don't mind it,' he answered mildly. 'But I wouldn't want it every day.'

'We should appreciate the support for our cause,' said Epizon.

'They think it's a game!' Lyssa protested, stopping on the path and throwing her hands up in the air. 'That my past and these stakes are entertainment!'

Epizon stopped too, and he looked at her levelly. 'You knew that before we started this,' he said softly.

'I know,' she muttered, kicking at a few dry twigs on the ground. A peacock made an alarmed clicking sound as a twig landed near it, and scuttled away. 'It's just hard not to get mad when they're all parading around, talking about him like it's a show for their entertainment.'

'It is to them. It's not their fault. Save your anger,' said Epizon.

She glared at the ground a few seconds more and then resumed her trudge down the path towards the settlement edge. Epizon sighed, smiled reassuringly at Phyleus and followed after her.

After a few more minutes, they had reached a gap in the houses, just as the old dockmaster had told them they would. Through the gap was an impenetrable-looking forest. A dark tangle of trees, roots, plants and mossy rocks faced them. They were on higher ground now, and Lyssa turned and looked back past the shiny towers to where the *Alastor* was moored. She could only just see it in the distance, dark against the glittering blue lake, gold light rippling across her solar sails.

She turned back to the thick forest, a slight sense of foreboding creeping over her. The dockmaster had told them they needed to go east, but directly between them and the lion's lair was a harpy settlement. If they wanted to give the harpies a wide berth, they would lose time, so they had decided to skirt as close to the settlement as they could. Lyssa thought they would have been better off taking the *Alastor* to Port Nemea, but Epizon insisted that as long as they lost no time moving through the forest, this was the quickest way.

He looked at her as he began unstrapping the knife from his thigh.

'Let's go,' she said, and they pushed their way into the thick foliage.

IT WAS clear folk didn't often enter the forests on Cancer, as there were no paths or accommodations made for travellers. It was much darker than in the town, the tall tree canopies blocking most of the bright Cancer light.

Epizon went ahead, his long coat protecting him from branches, his big knife hacking a way through the thick lower branches that blocked the way. 'I knew I'd need my coat,' he told Lyssa.

She rolled her eyes again, wiping sweat from under her headscarf. It was warmer in the forest, a thick humidity seeming to make everything damp. Huge plants growing from amongst the tangle of roots on the ground sprouted leaves almost as big as she was, and she squeezed around the ones Epizon hadn't hacked away, unwilling to disturb them more than she had to. The forest was alive with noises, birds calling and twigs cracking and insects buzzing. She was fairly sure there was nothing too dangerous native to

Cancer's forests, but she didn't want to take any chances. After all, they knew there was a man-eating lion around somewhere.

She had been following in Epizon's wake, leafy green debris from his knife littering the compact dirt around her, when the smell in the air changed from damp and earthy to something much less pleasant. Epizon slowed to a stop, and Lyssa heaved herself over a mossy tree trunk lying between them to join him. She wiped her slimy hands on the back of her trousers as they all looked up at the dark canopy of trees.

'Harpies,' muttered Epizon.

'What happens if they see us?' whispered Phyleus loudly, stepping over the bark much more easily than she had.

'It depends if we're on their land or not. If we're not, then they'll probably just throw faeces at us,' Lyssa answered quietly.

Phyleus screwed up his face in disgust. 'And if we are?'

'They'll kill us,' she said.

They moved more quietly through the woodland, swearing less when they tripped over roots, and carefully checking the canopy above them for signs of flying creatures. The stench got stronger. To Lyssa, it smelled like rotting fish, and she was sure it was made worse by the now-oppressive heat.

'It's getting lighter, Captain,' said Epizon quietly. 'That means there's probably a clearing ahead.'

He was right. The thickness of the undergrowth was lessening, and the wall of green trees ahead of them was brighter.

'We need to try and go around it. Get to the clearing;

then we'll follow the edge of it until we're around the other side,' she said.

Epizon strapped his knife back to his thigh, and they carefully and quietly climbed through the tangle of vegetation until they reached the edge of the clearing. The smell was now almost overwhelming. The rotting-fish stench mixed with the smell of excrement, and she felt Phyleus heaving silently behind her. She ignored him, assessing the scene in the clearing.

In the middle was a cluster of very tall trees that had had all their leaves removed, leaving bare branches. Lyssa guessed the trees were at least sixty feet tall, and she struggled to see the top from her hiding place. The branches started about ten feet up from the ground, and harpies lined them, some asleep, some chattering to each other. Up to the neck, they looked like overgrown birds with disproportionately large clawed feet, but from the neck up, they were human. They all had wrinkled necks and heads with the distorted features of a woman's face. They were not tall, only around four feet, but Lyssa knew their folded wings could span double that.

Under the trees, surrounding them in a ring, were bits of wood hung together clumsily to make cages. Voles and squirrels ran backwards and forwards inside, trying to squeeze through the gaps in the wood. Littering the forest floor around the rudimental cages were small bones, and Lyssa felt slightly sorry for the scrabbling little creatures. There couldn't be many things worse than ending up as a harpy's dinner.

Lyssa caught her breath as one of the harpies shrieked and expanded her leathery wings as she dived from a branch. The bird creature landed silently in front of the cages, facing the opposite side of the clearing from their hiding place. She shook her wings out, hissing. Epizon tensed beside her as the harpy turned and began stalking around the group of trees, coming closer to where they were hidden. The quiet buzz of chatter increased sharply, and then all the bird-women began dropping from the branches, stretching and shrieking single words repeatedly.

'Fresh!' one nearby yelled in an ugly, high-pitched voice.

'Flesh,' replied another, its wings folding behind it.

'Ripe,' called another.

Lyssa's leg muscles were tensed, ready to run, and she hoped the other two were ready as well. She never had time to give the signal though. She jumped violently, barely containing a scream, as a reeking harpy dropped down right in front of her.

'Strangers,' it hissed.

'Run!' she yelled, and turned back to the forest, her legs already moving. She had time to register that Epizon and Phyleus had already started running before pain shot through her left shoulder, and she was being dragged backwards. She struggled and kicked, anger surging through her. There was nothing like pain to get the Rage going. Vice-like claws dug into her right shoulder, and then she was off the ground, being lifted out of the forest and into the clearing.

As the harpy moved higher, she could see the mass of leathery creatures below, shrieking and chittering excitedly. She tried to reach her arms up, but the clawed grip on her shoulder stopped her. Power was flooding her body, and her vision narrowed as the harpy brought her towards a massive branch on one of the central trees. She tensed as the bird-woman dropped her, flinging her arms and legs around the branch to stop herself from falling. The impact thumped through her chest, and she took a huge breath. Her Rage overtook the pain, and she hauled herself up to a sitting position quickly as the harpy landed expertly next to her. The branch shook.

'Strangers,' it hissed again. Other harpies took off from the ground, landing on the branches around them, staring and chittering.

'We mean no disrespect,' said Lyssa slowly, trying to calm her racing pulse. She had nothing to lose by trying to reason with the creature. She didn't want to fight. And there were a lot of them. 'We're just passing by.'

'So close?' the harpy said, cocking her head. She had one red eye much lower than the other, and slits for nostrils. Her lips were thin and parched, and lank hair hung in patchy threads from her scalp.

'Yes. We didn't mean to. We'll leave now.' Lyssa rolled her shoulders as she spoke, her legs wrapped tightly around the branch. She looked down, relieved when she couldn't see the others. Heat prickled across her skin in anticipation.

'Payment,' said the harpy.

'I have drachmas,' she answered hopefully, but suspecting it wouldn't be any good. Harpies had no need for silver.

'Payment,' the ugly creature repeated, lifting a clawed foot towards her.

'What do you want?' Lyssa asked, leaning away from the sharp claw, every muscle tense and ready.

'A finger,' the harpy said, eyes shining.

As the hooked claw lunged for her, Lyssa threw herself sideways. Her strong legs gripped the branch for a moment; then she was falling towards the ground. She tumbled in the air, trying to right herself, and closed her eyes, feeling power flow through her body. Her Rage-fuelled strength took over her limbs, and her feet hit the ground with a thud. Her momentum sprang her back up, smashing through the cages as she took off running towards the dense forest.

Deafening shrieks were catching up with her, and she didn't slow or stop to look. She crashed through the forest edge, hardly slowing, stumbling and leaping over boulders and roots in her way. The further she got into the forest, the weaker the shrieks became, but she didn't slow. Only when she was sure they had given up following did she stop, taking huge gulps of warm, sticky air. She had no idea which direction she had taken, and she swore loudly, kicking at a boulder.

'Epizon?' she panted, picturing him vividly in her mind.

'We saw which way you went, Captain. We'll be there soon.'

Epizon found her a short while later, sitting on the boulder, her breathing back to normal, an angry scowl on her face.

'Which way?' she asked, jumping off the rock as soon as she saw him. He pointed and she began moving immediately.

'How did you do that?' asked Phyleus, scrabbling to keep up with her.

'Do what? Get caught by stinking harpies?' She yanked a leafy branch out of her way viciously.

'No. Fall ten feet and not break both your legs,' he said warily, falling back a little.

'Zeus's granddaughter, remember? If you're stronger than the ground, it can't hurt you.'

'Right,' he said after a pause. 'How—?' he started to ask, but she cut him off.

'Be quiet. They're still nearby.'

Phyleus fell silent as he followed her through the trees. The disgusting smell was just starting to clear from the air, and Epizon had decided they were far enough away from the clearing to take up his knife again, when a voice in her head made her jump.

'Cap, you there?'

'Gods! Yes, Ab, I'm here.'

'Did I make you jump?' He sounded triumphant.

'What is it?' she asked, shaking her head.

'You were right about going to that party on the *Virtus*,' Abderos said. 'They just sent out a message. It looked like a hell of a night. I could see some nymphs asleep behind Theseus, and if they were wearing anything—'

'Abderos! Get to the point, please,' Lyssa cut him off.

'Sorry, Cap. Basically, they overdid it and never set off this morning. They apologise profusely to their fans and will try harder next time, blah, blah, blah.'

Anger welled inside Lyssa, and she kicked the tree closest to her. Leaves rustled as it shuddered.

'Captain?' said Epizon, stepping over a root towards her.

'That moron Theseus never left this morning. They're still on their idiotic party boat at the Black Hole,' she hissed.

'Why do we care? Surely one less crew is a good thing,' said Abderos.

'Theseus is Hercules's biggest competition. Without Theseus involved, Hercules will win!' She half shouted the last few words, and Epizon put his hand on her shoulder.

'It's anyone's game,' he said quietly.

She glared back at him. They didn't understand. 'The *Hybris* is here. Try to find out where it's docked,' she said to Abderos, ending the conversation. She shrugged out of Epizon's attempt at reassurance and set off again. He sighed and followed her, Phyleus close behind.

18

EVADNE

E vadne was furious. She knew she'd pay for letting it show, but she couldn't help it. She couldn't believe he'd picked today, now, at a moment this important, to decide to cast her off to play with some girl he'd just met. Asterion had already left to find the harpies when she exited the taverna, so she had picked a direction and started marching down the paved road. She was so angry she wasn't paying any attention to where she was going or what was around her. *Why couldn't he have just asked the redhead a few questions and moved on?* she seethed.

Though she didn't want to admit it, she knew why Hercules had asked her to leave. There was only one reason he would want to be alone with the girl. She growled aloud, drawing the alarmed attention of a woman buying fruit at the stall she was passing. He was an idiot! Was he so cocky, so arrogant, that he thought he had time for this sort of thing? She knew the answer to that too. An overwhelming feeling of uselessness washed over her, and she slowed down, almost reaching a stop.

'Whoa!' a man exclaimed as her sudden slowing caused

him to almost crash into her. He skirted around her, his arms full of bags, and shot a glare back at her.

She looked around herself. She was in a square with many more food stalls than there had been on the promenade with the taverna. Cancer was a world of marriage and family, and it didn't do for young women to roam around the residential areas alone. She knew she could only stay in the market and port areas of Nemea.

She took a deep breath and tried to calm down. She considered her options. She needed to prove that she was useful, or Hercules might decide he didn't need her. Or worse, keep the redhead. Anger surged again inside her at the thought. She'd gone through too many of his sordid punishments to be dumped now. She wouldn't let the humiliation be for nothing. She would be on the winning team at the end of all this, and she would be immortal. She would prove to him that she was the only woman strong enough to be with him. He had to see that eventually.

They had come here for information, so she supposed that must be her first course of action. She might be able to find out where the lion was before he did, or, as a backup plan, where to find Hercules if he got there first. Evadne turned, looking for someone who might talk to her among the busy shoppers. A woman with golden-coloured hair tied up in a complicated knot was pulling a clean white tarpaulin down over the front of a vegetable stall a few feet away. Evadne walked towards her, concentrating on masking the fury still pulsing through her.

'Excuse me,' she said as timidly as she could.

The woman turned towards her, still holding the heavy tarp. 'Hang on,' she said, and wrestled the sheet down to the ground, where she began tucking the weighted ends under the wooden feet of the stall. When she had finished, she stood and faced Evadne, dusting her hands off on her long skirt. 'What do you need?' she asked.

'Well, you see, I've heard that the first of the events is being held here,' she started. She was trying to sound innocent and young.

The woman cocked her head at her. 'Yes,' she replied. 'To rid us of the Nemean Lion.'

'Exactly. And I would so love to get a glimpse of the heroes. Do you know where they might end up?'

The woman frowned. 'Are you asking me where the lion is?' she said.

'Erm, well, I guess that is where they'll all end up, so, yes,' Evadne smiled.

'Girl, you take us for fools. I know who you are.' Evadne's smile vanished. 'You're on the crew of the *Hybris*. And I'll be damned if I'm helping that murderous captain of yours. I hope she eats him,' spat the woman. 'Now you'll excuse me.' And she swept away from her closed-up stall and into the throng of people in the market square.

Evadne clenched her fists and took a breath. Well, she reasoned, she had learned two things. Hercules was not as popular as he thought he was, and the lion was female. She resolutely schooled her face into a calm expression. She'd keep talking to people until she had enough information to take to her distracted captain, and then she'd make him listen.

The fourth person she stopped to talk to was a harried-looking male satyr. He was the only one of his race she had seen so far, and she knew satyrs had a reputation for succumbing to flirtation, so she had high hopes as she stepped in front of him. He looked up in annoyance and she smiled. He looked less annoyed.

'Is there a reason you're in my way?' he said to her gruffly.

'Oh, yes. I hoped you might help me.' She made her voice sound girlish and grinned.

'What do you want?' He sounded cautious, and his horns twitched as looked her up and down.

'Well, I wondered if you knew where I might find the heroes of the tournament. I just want a glimpse of them,' she said hopefully.

He snorted. 'They'll all be eaten, girl, just as everyone else who's tried their hand at slaying her has. You don't want to see that.' He tilted his head up to see her face better. She was at least a foot taller than he was.

'The lion is female then?' she asked.

'Usually. But she can be anything she wants to be. That's why pretty young things like you shouldn't be sniffing around this sort of thing. She's dangerous.' Evadne pretended to look shy at the compliment. The goat-man shifted the bag on his back. 'Why don't you come along to my friend's taverna, down by the docks. Maybe you can see the heroes from there, if they dock at Port Nemea. I hear Hercules already has.'

'He has?' She sounded delighted. 'What if he's already found the lion?' Now she tried to look worried.

'Pah! She'll have found him more like. I heard he's just her type, womanising and immoral.'

'What do you mean?' asked Evadne, the youthful innocence slipping from her voice slightly.

'The Nemean Lion is a creature of Hera's. Sure, she says she's out of control, but that's nonsense. Hera created her, and she does her bidding. The lion lures single young men with no intention of marrying to their deaths. Does that sound like something the god of marriage would want to put a stop to?'

Evadne shook her head slowly.

'I shan't be on Cancer any longer than I can help it, I tell you,' the satyr ranted on. 'No fun at all. You're the only girl I've seen on her own in three days! Not that I'm desperate or anything, you know. Just would be nice to have some female company.' He stopped, and Evadne realised he was waiting for her to agree.

'Er, I'm sorry, but I have a friend that I really should find.'

The satyr's face fell. 'A male friend?' he asked.

She gave him an apologetic smile. Not just a male friend, she thought, as she began to hurry back towards the docks, but a single one with no intention of marrying. Evadne had a horrible feeling that Hercules may have come across the Nemean Lion sooner than he had intended.

19

LYSSA

For the second time, Lyssa noticed that the earthy smell of the forest was changing. It was nowhere near as nasty as the rotten smell of the harpies, but she wouldn't go so far as to say it was pleasant. They were well past the harpy camp now, and if the dockmaster had been right, then they would find the lion's lair soon. Lyssa was fed up with the claustrophobic feel of the gloomy forest, and like the bad smells, the humidity only made the feeling worse. Sinewy roots pushed their way through the moist earth, winding their way across the forest floor. They looked like veins. She thought about the cool, open space of the deck of the *Alastor*, flying through the skies, and clung to the memory.

'What are we looking for?' asked Phyleus as he wrestled with a low bough covered in prickly leaves.

'A cave or big tree hollow, I assume,' answered Epizon.

'How do you know we won't miss it?'

'I'm guessing that a flesh-eating lion will leave some fairly obvious traces of its existence,' said Lyssa, throwing him a look. 'Can't you smell it?'

Phyleus took an obvious sniff, and Lyssa shook her head.

'We've got some work to do on this one, Epizon,' she said.

Epizon smiled. 'You don't say. Seriously though, Captain, we're close. The smell is stronger now, and—' Epizon cut off abruptly. He gestured for them to get down, urgency on his now-serious face.

All three of them ducked down, hidden easily by the haphazard boulders, mouldy trunks and enormous plants that made up the forest floor. Lyssa's heart started to pound as she heard the distinct sound of someone else forcing their way through the unrelenting trees. They crouched silently, time stretching as the sounds grew closer. She could hear a slight muttering now, and it sounded female. That meant it was a local, or Evadne from Hercules's crew. There were no women on the *Orion*, and the *Virtus* wasn't here. Her throat restricted slightly. If it was Evadne, Hercules wouldn't be far away.

The woman's voice became clearer, and they all crouched even lower as the trees to their right began to move a little, then a lot, as a figure pushed through. The figure was still ten feet away from them, but they could see well enough. Lyssa's mouth fell open in surprise.

A girl no older than herself, with flaming-red hair, was dragging a huge, muscular man dressed in black across the forest floor. The man must have been unconscious or dead, because when she couldn't pull him through the undergrowth, she was lifting him by the waist of his trousers and heaving him over obstacles like a ragdoll, all the while cursing him for being so heavy. Lyssa stared, agape, at the man's lifeless form. It was Hercules.

20

HERCULES

Hercules moaned softly as he woke. His head hurt, a lot. He didn't usually get headaches. His vision was blurry as his eyes adjusted to the dim light. A tingle of panic crept over him as he realised that he didn't know where he was. He swallowed down the panic before it formed fully, and reassured himself that he was in control of himself, wherever he was.

Where had he been? He closed his eyes again, the blackness easier to deal with. He had been in the taverna with the pretty redhead. He had told her he would spend an hour alone with her if she would show him where she thought the lion's lair was, and she had agreed, enthusiastically. It was hard for an unmarried couple to be alone on Cancer, so she had told him to meet her near one of the larger estates near the forest edge, on the far side of the residential region, and then she had slipped away. He had waited long enough to finish his wine and gone after her.

He screwed his eyes shut tighter, willing what happened next to present itself. His head throbbed again and he suppressed a groan. All he could remember was a peacock's face, alarmingly close to his, as he lay on the ground. He took a long breath and opened his eyes again. They cleared quicker this time. He started to sit up and found he was in a very large, very comfortable bed. The bed was in the centre of a stone room with no windows, lit by candles on shelves all around the edge of the circular space. It was clearly set up for romance and he relaxed. It was obvious that he was in a room used for secret trysts, so it was highly likely he was where he was supposed to meet Gata. He couldn't understand how he had gotten there though, or what had happened to him on the way.

'Gata!' he called loudly.

'Hercules!' He heard her before he saw her, and twisted to look back at an archway to the left of the bedhead. His eyes widened momentarily when he saw her, and he let out a long breath. She was completely naked as she stepped through the doorway towards him. Her red hair fell about her freckled shoulders, and she was beaming at him. 'I was worried about you,' she said, reaching him.

'You were?' he muttered, his gaze fixed on her body.

'When that awful man attacked you, I didn't know what to do. I'm just glad you were already so close to my home.'

'Attacked me?' said Hercules, his eyes snapping to hers. 'Who attacked me?' He sat up straighter and noticed absently that he had no clothes on under the sheets either.

'Just some man, shouting about you not winning the Trials.' She shrugged. 'But you're here now.'

Hercules frowned and moved his hand to his head. 'How did I end up unconscious?' he asked, feeling for a wound. It took a lot to knock him out. In fact, he'd only ever known one man to do it. Suspicion and anger surged inside him.

'That doesn't matter now,' said Gata, and she took his other hand, guiding it to her.

Hercules was distracted by the feel of her soft skin for only a few seconds. His being rendered unconscious by an unknown assailant was more than he could bear. He pulled his hand away from her.

'I must know who did this, and how!' he demanded.

She threw her hands in the air and gave a shout of annoyance. 'Gods, I did! I drugged your wine, you imbecile!' Hercules stared at her. 'You may be pretty, but there's not a lot going on up there is there?' She tapped the side of her head mockingly. Her girlish tones had fallen away, replaced by the harsher tone of a much older-sounding woman.

SHOCK WAS SLOWLY GIVING way to anger, and Hercules's hands clenched into fists. The muscles in his legs and chest tightened as he prepared himself for violence. Excitement began to rush through him.

'Who are you?' he asked quietly.

She stepped back from the bed and raised her eyebrows at him. 'Surely you've guessed by now,' she said. As she spoke, her red hair grew around her, both in length and volume. Hercules growled and sprang to a crouch in the huge bed. 'It's a shame I'm going to have to kill you so soon. You're the nicest-looking man I've had here for years. I really did want to have some fun with you first.' She smiled, and it was no longer the giddy beam that the young Gata had been giving him before. It was a cruel smile, under hungry, narrowed eyes.

Adrenaline coursed through Hercules, and his muscles twitched as he maintained his rigid crouch on the soft mattress. He needed to be ready for anything. Her red mane had grown down over her shoulders and around her neck and stopped changing, but now her chest was morphing, along with her arms. Hercules watched, transfixed, as the beautiful girl's body distorted and transformed, finally followed by her face. Her petite, freckled nose lengthened, and her eyes widened and spread. Her mouth merged with the growing snout, and sharp white teeth flashed as she flexed her morphing jaw. As her front legs thudded onto the floor, she shook her head, the fiery mane now framing the head of the most magnificent lion Hercules had ever seen. She must have been five feet tall at the shoulder, her head probably level with his own if he was standing, and she pawed the stone ground with claws almost the size of his hands. He looked into her golden eyes, and though the colour had changed, he recognised the girl he had been with in their flashing excitement. She roared, an earth-shaking sound that sent shivers through his taught body, and he smiled.

'You're still beautiful,' he told her. She dropped into a tight crouch. 'And this is going to be my greatest victory yet.'

She pounced at the same time that he leapt from the bed.

21

LYSSA

Lyssa didn't know what to do next. They had let the girl get as far ahead of them as they dared, then followed the sounds of her dragging the heavy body across the crackly forest floor. She had reached a decent-sized clearing and crossed it, Hercules's body leaving a smear though the muddy, leaf-ridden ground. She had reached a big boulder on the other side of the clearing and crouched down. The rock had a gaping mouth extending a few feet off the ground, and Lyssa had guessed it was the entrance to underground caves. They had watched, hidden behind a mossy fallen trunk, as the girl had hauled her dead-weight burden down into the tunnel. When they hadn't seen her emerge and they could no longer hear her, they had crept out from their hiding place and moved cautiously into the clearing.

'Could she really be the lion?' asked Phyleus. His usually impassive face looked conflicted as he eyed the tunnel entrance.

'Phyleus, come on. The dockmaster said the lion was female when she wanted to be. It seems pretty obvious, doesn't it?' Lyssa said. He still looked doubtful. 'What? You think because she was small and pretty, she can't be dangerous?' Lyssa's eyes flashed as she spoke accusingly. 'How do you think she was dragging around a guy the size of Hercules? More to the point, *why* was she dragging around Hercules?' She put her hands on her hips and took a deep breath. 'Gods, I hope she's killed him.'

Epizon appeared from around the other side of the boulder. 'There's no other way out that I can see, Captain,' he reported as he rejoined them.

'If she is the lion, shouldn't we hide until we know how to, well, kill her?' said Phyleus. He stumbled slightly when he said *kill her*.

'Probably. Any ideas? On how we kill her?' said Lyssa, making her way back to the fallen trunk. She had barely touched the tree when the sky above them darkened.

All three of them looked up, instinctively fearing harpies. The last thing they needed was to be given away by those gross flying brutes. Worse still, if they ended up fighting, they would waste valuable time and energy. She wasn't even sure Phyleus could fight a harpy. It would certainly be a good test of his skills. But the cause of the sudden block in light shining through the forest canopy was not harpies. It was the enormous hull of a Zephyr-class ship.

'Shit,' said Lyssa. She reached for her slingshot at the exact same time Epizon slipped off his heavy coat. 'Phyleus,' she began, but as she looked at him, she realised he already had his own slingshot out. She had expected him to look panicked, but his face was focused, his bright eyes fierce.

The three of them moved closer together until they were back to back, weapons ready. Lyssa's heart pounded as the ship hovered for a few moments more, then soared away, letting the light stream back into the forest.

'They were just dropping off,' muttered Epizon.

'How did they find the lair?' hissed back Lyssa.

'Same way we did, I imagine. Asking people,' he answered.

'Why didn't we just hover over the forest and drop off?' asked Phyleus.

'Our longboat is barely usable; we'd never have made it down in one piece.' Lyssa was worried. If the giants were here, and Hercules was alive down in the lair, then they no longer had the advantage of time.

The trees opposite the cave entrance began to shake, and the crew of the *Alastor* turned as one and pointed their weapons at the disturbance.

One by one, three giants stepped into the forest clearing.

22

ERYX

Eryx had a lot of respect for his captain, but diplomacy was not one of his strong suits. The tiny girl who captained the *Alastor* had dropped her weapon and had her arms out in a gesture for her crew mates to do the same. Eryx thought that if they knew what was good for them, they would keep their weapons exactly where they were. The black-skinned man on her left looked like he could do some damage with the glinting knife that he was holding in both hands.

'We know that the lion is in her lair and that Hercules is in there with her, probably unconscious or dead,' Lyssa was saying. 'We think it would be best to let her kill him first. One less competitor to worry about.' She tried to smile.

Antaeus gave a deep growl. 'That man and his whole crew should be dead,' he snarled. 'They tricked us!'

Eryx winced. He'd hoped that wouldn't be shared, especially not with a crew they were competing against. Eryx was in the line of trees at the clearing edge, out of sight. He had been told he was not to come out unless he was told to. He was being punished for falling for the girl's trick. The stupid, sweaty brothers Albion and Bergion were flanking his captain and, to be fair, doing a good job of looking threatening.

'They're not good people,' Captain Lyssa was agreeing.

Antaeus folded his arms. 'How do we know when she has killed him?' he asked. He was twice her height and only a few feet in front of her. She was craning to look up at him. Neither of her crew members had put down their weapons. Eryx stayed poised in the trees, ready to defend his crew mates if they needed him.

'I don't know,' the girl admitted.

Antaeus snarled again and took one long stride to the edge of the clearing. He bent his knees and wrapped his arms around the wide tree in front of him. He bellowed as he stood again, tearing the tree from the ground. He could barely fit his arms around it as he carried it to the cave entrance. He threw it down and the ground shook, leaves and branches cracking under its weight. Laid on its side, the trunk of the tree was nearly five feet tall, much taller than the cave mouth. As he began to shove the tree against the tunnel entrance, Eryx realised what Antaeus was doing. He was trapping both the lion and Hercules in the cave.

EVERYONE'S HEADS snapped round suddenly as a roar blared from the trees behind Lyssa and her crew. She and the two men spun quickly and began to back up, towards the giants. The sound of pounding hooves could be heard crashing through the forest, thundering across the woody ground. Albion and Bergion stamped their feet, bending their knees and shifting their weight like the trained boxers that they were. Antaeus gave the trunk one final push and stood straight, just as Asterion, the Minotaur, burst into the clearing. He gave a guttural howl and launched himself at the biggest threat there, Antaeus. The creature's bull head struck Antaeus in the abdomen, and the giant went flying backwards. Albion and Bergion looked at each other, roared in unison, and swung towards the Minotaur.

'He's mine!' bellowed Antaeus, already getting back to his feet. 'Disarm the humans!'

The giant brothers halted mid-swing and turned back towards the human crew of the *Alastor*. Lyssa was holding her ground, her slingshot back in her hands. Eryx couldn't help being impressed with her resolve against such a huge opponent. He had heard she was a fighter. He knew Antaeus could handle the Minotaur, and he knew he couldn't disobey orders, but he itched to join the fight. He gripped the tree next to him, watching enviously.

Albion was squaring up to the black man with the knife. He must have only been about three feet shorter than the giant, a similar size to Eryx himself. He was managing to look both fierce and calm as he raised the big knife level with his head and spun it slowly. Albion laughed.

Lyssa and the other human man were backing away from Bergion, who was smiling as he advanced on them. Lyssa was still trying to talk to the giant, but Eryx couldn't hear what she was saying over the grunts and yells of the Minotaur. He looked over just as Antaeus threw the bull into a vast tree at the edge of the clearing. Asterion hit it with a grunt and slid unceremoniously down the rough bark. The giant shouted with glee, and the Minotaur's hooves scrabbled for purchase on the forest floor as he shook his dazed head.

Eryx was so focused on the fights in the clearing that he did not hear Evadne as she crept up to him. When she touched him on the shoulder, he whipped round, hands balled into fists and ready to attack.

'Stars!' she shouted, ducking under his punch. 'It's only me.'

'Only you?' His voice was furious. 'I should kill you! You're the reason I'm stood in this bloody forest instead of out there! You sly witch, you tricked me!'

'Well, it is a competition. And besides, Hercules made me do it.' She pouted a bit. He didn't unclench his fists.

'You're in luck then. Your captain's likely dead already, so you needn't worry about him making you do anything else,' he said maliciously. Pain flashed across her face, and he was annoyed at the guilt it made him feel. *She's a liar*, he told himself.

'Do you know where he is?' she asked, her voice low.

'In the lion's lair, under that rock.' He nodded at the clearing.

She pushed past him and looked towards the blocked cave. He followed her gaze and saw that Lyssa and the other human had gone. Bergion had joined Antaeus, and they had trapped the bull between them. He was pawing the ground and snorting hard. Albion and the black man were dancing around each other, the human jabbing with the knife and Albion throwing punches. He thought they both looked like they were having a good time, under the circumstances.

'Under the rock?' Evadne asked him. 'How?'

'There's a passage down there in the boulder. I guess there are caves under us or something.' He shrugged. 'I shouldn't be talking to you. Go and help your bull friend.'

She snorted. 'Asterion is no friend of mine. I just share a ship with him. How do we get down there?' She looked up at him, her face resolute.

'We?' He goggled at her. 'Why would we go down there?'

'To kill the lion. What else are you here for?'

'To serve my captain,' he snapped.

She wrinkled her nose and frowned. 'Then what are you doing hiding in here?' He shifted uncomfortably and looked away. 'Is it because you're not a proper giant like them? They don't let you fight?'

He snapped out a hand and grabbed her arm. She barely flinched.

'Don't push it, girl,' he threatened her.

She stared back at him. 'Why are you hiding in the trees?' she asked again.

He gave a bark of frustration and let her go, making her stumble. 'Because of you! I'm being punished because I believed you, you snake!' He thought she might look triumphant or mocking, but her face softened.

'I'm punished for things all the time on the *Hybris*,' she said quietly.

'Then why do you stay?' he snarled. He didn't want to empathise with this girl. She had tricked him. But her eyes lit up when she answered him.

'Immortality,' she breathed. 'What a prize! Just imagine, having forever to get whatever you wanted.' He grunted. 'And we're going to win it, starting right now. Come on, we'll prove to your captain that he needs you by slaying this lion.' She said it so matter-of-factly that he almost followed her into the clearing.

'Wait!' he said, and grabbed her arm a second time. She turned to him. 'Why would you want me to kill the lion?'

'Because I can't do it by myself, and you can take me with you on board the *Orion* when I help you win. Apparently, I'm looking for a new captain.' She smiled at him and he hesitated. If her motivation was truly to win immortality, then she could be telling the truth. But the pain he had seen when he'd told her Hercules was dead was at odds with this indifference.

'Fine,' she said, pulling out of his grip. 'You stay hidden in the forest. I'll go and talk to Antaeus myself.'

'He'll kill you,' Eryx said.

'Then you'd better come and help me,' she said, and strolled away from him.

'What do you want me to do?' he asked as he caught up with Evadne, halfway across the clearing to the tree. The black man had vanished now too, and Eryx found himself hoping Albion hadn't killed him. He should like to fight him himself one day. All three of his crew mates were engaged in tying the Minotaur, by his ankles, to one of the highest branches they could reach on the massive tree. None of them noticed him and Evadne.

'Just move this out the way first so we can get down into the caves.' She gestured at the trunk Antaeus had laid across the cave entrance. If she was nervous about being spotted by the giants, she hid it well.

'Fine,' he grumbled, and fell in beside her.

They reached the trunk, and Eryx crouched in front of it, curling his arms as far underneath it as he could. When he tried to lift, it barely moved. Embarrassment washed over him. Only his mother was a giant, he was half human. Antaeus was much stronger than him, but he didn't want Evadne to think that. Again he felt angry with himself for caring what she thought or felt. What was wrong with him? He stood up straight and wrapped his arms over the top of the fallen trunk instead.

'It'll be easier if we roll it away,' he told her, as assertively as he could. She nodded and he heaved the huge trunk towards him. It creaked as it slowly yielded, revealing the darkness behind.

HERCULES

Hercules was lost in a maze of caves. For a while he had been following the lion's snarls and snorts, but now she had fallen silent. Although her hide was impervious to weapons and his skin was not, he was stronger than she was. He was sure of it. She had landed some lucky swipes with her monstrous claws, and blood dripped down his chest from a wound in his shoulder, but he could barely feel it. They had torn through the living rooms of her caves, rolling and wrestling, snarling and slashing, but he had not been able to pin her down long enough to end her. Now he had lost her, in this godsforsaken, pitch-dark hellhole.

No sooner had he thought this than the end of the tunnel he was padding silently down seemed lighter. He sped up, and as he reached the forked end, he could see clearly that one of the stone passageways was lighter than the other. He continued to follow the light until his path opened out into a larger cavern that slanted upwards. On the other side of the cavern was the lion, scratching ferociously at a blocked opening. He could make out large chunks of wood coming away from her claws. There was a gap at the top of the opening, and it was getting slightly wider by the second.

He thought fast. Someone else must have blocked that opening, as she clearly hadn't. That meant there was either friend or foe on the other side. And now they were opening it again. They would only do that if they meant to harm the lion or help him. He had to act quickly, or he risked losing his chance to kill the creature before someone else did.

As soon as he judged the opening wide enough, he ran at the clawing beast. He threw himself at her as he reached her back, and their combined weight forced the heavy blockage back far enough for them both to roll out of the cave.

HE HEARD a male-sounding roar but had no time to see what had caused it. The lion was trying to turn under him as they rolled, so that he would not end up on her back. He wrapped his arms tightly around her, and she struggled harder. There was shouting all around him and he risked a look up. Evadne was standing a few feet to his left, beside a black-haired giant who had been knocked to the ground. The idiot girl was firing lead from her slingshot uselessly at the beast.

'Stop!' he yelled, sure the fool would hit him instead.

She looked shocked and pulled her weapon up immediately. The lion thrashed under him as they stopped rolling. He threw his weight forward to make sure he ended up on top and squeezed his mighty arms around her tighter. Her snarls turned to whimpers. More lead shot began zinging around him, but he couldn't risk looking behind him. He heard another roar and pounding steps getting louder. It was now or never.

With lightning speed, he let go of the beast's chest and threw himself up her back, wrapping his arms around her throat. He crushed his arms together with all the strength he had and heard her neck snap. Her thrashing and whimpering stopped immediately, and he felt her go limp beneath him. A blissful feeling of power poured through him in waves. He was invincible. He loosened his arms, and the pounding footsteps came to a halt. As he stood slowly, naked and glistening with blood, he held his arms out.

'I will be immortal!' he cried, adrenaline and pride coursing through him. There was a scream behind him, and his leg buckled suddenly. He dropped to one knee, still stood over the huge lion. Pain forced its way through the elation, and he bellowed in anger.

'Stop.'

The voice was so commanding, everything stilled. Even the breeze through the trees seemed to freeze. He gritted his teeth through the pain and confusion, and looked around him.

Hera was standing in the clearing, no more than a few feet from the fallen lion. He bowed his head to her. When he looked up, he saw that three giants, including Antaeus, were also in the clearing and were bowing low to the god. He turned as far as he could on one knee to look behind him. Lyssa and two of her crew stood at the edge of the clearing, also bowed low. Even from here he could see that his pathetic daughter was shaking.

Hera took a step towards him. Pride swelled in him again, and he tried to stand back up. He stumbled but managed.

'You have been wounded, victor,' said the unsmiling goddess. 'By your own daughter, no less.'

'What?' Rage contorted his face. Now Hera smiled. He struggled around to look at Lyssa.

She stood slowly from her bow, eyes locked on his. Defiance radiated from her, and for a moment he felt he was staring into his wife's green eyes. An unexpected bolt of pain ran up his leg, causing his core to constrict, and he dropped her triumphant gaze, his mind still filled with the image of Megara's face. He clenched his teeth against the memory and the pain, briefly unable to differentiate between the two.

'Citizens of Olympus,' said Hera. He snapped his head back to her. 'The first Trial is complete. Hercules of the *Hybris* is your champion. The next Trial will be announced tomorrow morning at sunrise.' She put her arms down again and vanished with a small fizzing sound.

When Hercules turned again to his daughter, all he could see of her was her auburn hair disappearing into the forest. The giants, too, were lumbering out of the clearing into the foliage, the smallest one throwing back a dark look over his shoulder.

'Asterion!' he barked.

'Captain,' came the Minotaur's response.

Hercules looked around for him as Evadne approached the dead lion cautiously. 'Where are you, you damn fool?' The pain in his leg was causing his temper to flare, and he tried to cling to the glow of his victory.

'He's up there, Captain,' said Evadne, gesturing upwards towards a massive tree. Asterion was swinging by his heavy haunches from a branch more than ten feet off the ground.

Hercules growled. 'Go and get him down,' he barked at

her. 'I need him to help me get this –' he kicked the lion as he stepped awkwardly over her body '– back to the *Hybris*.'

Evadne wrinkled her nose. 'Back to the ship? Why?'

'I'm not wasting a trophy like this.' His eyes gleamed as he stared down at the lifeless beast, remembering the beautiful young girl she had been. 'All will know I won the first task. And all will watch while I win the others.'

ATHENA

SKIES OF OLYMPUS

TRIAL TWO

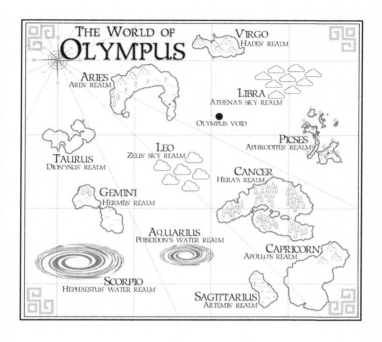

1

LYSSA

Epizon knocked on Lyssa's door again. It was the third time he'd come below deck to try to talk to her. They had left Port Galatas straight after making it back on board and were now floating just east of Cancer.

She knew how petulant she looked, hiding in her quarters, but she couldn't face the crew. Not only had Hercules won, but they hadn't even got close to the lion. They'd never had a chance of winning. All the lies she'd told herself about the *Alastor* making a difference in the Trials, all the desperate fantasies of stopping or even killing Hercules before he became immortal... They were all crashing down around her and she felt like she was drowning in doubt and anger. Worst of all, though, was the fear that simmered under all the chaos, becoming harder and harder to contain, moving ever further out of her control. Images of the broken and twisted centaur on the white marble platform swam before her, his shrieks as Hercules tormented him battering at her ears. If Hercules had become this bold in his cruelty over the four years since he killed her mother and sister, what kind of monster would he become if he lived forever? She put her head in her hands and rocked backwards and forwards on the edge of her bunk, aware of how close she was to allowing the memories of that terrible day to overcome her.

'You shot him, Lyssa.' Epizon's low voice carried though the wooden door. She lifted her head. 'Nobody has ever shot Hercules before.' She swallowed hard. That was true. 'And Hera made sure the whole of Olympus knows.' He paused. 'They all know, Lyssa. You proved to everyone he can be harmed. That's a win in my eyes.'

She tried to process his words through the grisly thoughts ricocheting around her head. Everyone knew. Everyone knew that she had shot him. Little Lyssa in her shoddy ship harmed the mighty Hercules. Epizon was right.

Lyssa looked at the locked door and realised she was sitting up straight. It was as though his words had formed a rod down her spine. Maybe the first Trial hadn't been such a loss after all. She took a deep breath and blew it out hard, trying to dispel the shreds of doubt. She couldn't be like this. She needed to be the girl Athena had seen, who was brave enough to face Hercules. She touched her cheeks. They were damp, so she wiped her sleeve across them fiercely. She was no longer the girl who ran. She was the captain of her own ship and crew, and they had another Trial to face tomorrow. She stood up and moved to the door, unlocking it slowly, gathering her confidence and trying to piece it back together into the protective barrier she relied on so heavily.

'Epizon,' she said as she swung her cabin door open.

'Captain,' he replied with a nod. His huge coat was gone and he had changed into clean black cargo trousers that were tight across his hips with a grey shirt tucked into them.

His hands were clasped together behind his back and he stood straight, to attention.

'I...' She paused and looked at the scuffed wooden floor. 'I'm sorry.'

His rigid stance melted and he stepped towards her.

'Hey,' he said. She looked up at him. 'The crew are having a party up there. You're their bloody hero right now! You made the mighty Hercules bleed, in front of the world.' He lifted his hand and for a moment she thought he was going to touch her cheek but he clasped her shoulder instead.

'I know,' she said, drawing as much strength from him as she could. 'That's not what I'm sorry about. I'm sorry about taking so long to...' She paused, trying to think of a good reason for being shut in her cabin for almost an hour.

'Get changed?' offered Epizon.

She looked down at her muddy clothes. 'Yes. Exactly. Give me two minutes. Tell the crew I was having a long bath.' Lyssa backed into the room.

'Will do, Captain,' he said and pulled her door shut. She hurried over to the large wood and iron chest at the foot of her bunk and pulled out clean brown trousers and a white shirt. She pulled off the filthy clothes she was wearing. There was no blood on them. That in itself was a good thing, she supposed. Nobody on her crew got hurt in the scrap with the giants. Just mucky. And if she wanted the crew to believe she really had been in the bath she would have to get some of the dirt off.

Lyssa had the best cabin on the *Alastor*. As well as a much bigger bunk, she had her own copper bath-tub and a porcelain wash-basin, which were right under the portholes in her bathroom. She watched the green-and-blue clouds swirling outside as she untied her scarf from round her head and started to scrub the mud from her face and hair.

Lyssa closed her eyes and dunked her face fully in the warm water. She hoped the lingering doubt and fear would wash away with the dirt.

I started to wonder how I might remove the skin from the creature's dead body. 'It would be impossible!' I thought, because I could not cut it with any mortal weapon. It was then I was advised that I could cut the lion's skin with one of the lion's own claws. This I did, and had the job done quickly. I was then able to wear the skin as a defence against war.

EXCERPT FROM

IDYLLS BY THEOCRITUS

Written 300–100 B.C.

Paraphrased by Eliza Raine

2

EVADNE

E vadne stared down at the pool of gore. She was perched on the edge of a steel container on the cargo deck of the *Hybris*, her nose wrinkling as Hercules peeled the last bit of hide from the lion's great body. An unexpected wave of nausea rolled through her at the thought of the vibrant-haired young woman the beast used to be.

Hercules had let Evadne tend to the shot wound on his leg in the longboat on the way back to the ship. If she had caused him any pain then he masked it perfectly. She tried to dress the wound but he would not allow her to put a bandage or gauze around it.

She admired his determination to avoid looking weak. As soon as they got back to the *Hybris* he had carried the lifeless creature into the biggest hauler and taken it down to the cargo deck, limping ever so slightly, before setting to work removing its impervious skin. The sight of Hercules's bulging arms and rippling chest as he effortlessly tossed the giant beast over his shoulders had sent a thrill through her. She had followed him down and stayed as silent as she could as his frustration with trying to pierce the lion's skin grew. Eventually, she had quietly suggested he try one of the beast's own claws or teeth. When the yellowing ivory claw ripped silently through the animal's belly Hercules had roared in triumph. He had then meticulously severed the skin from flesh, ignoring the innards and mess spilling out onto the cargo deck floor. He stood up straight, covered in blood, pulling the flayed hide with him. It was larger than he was. She could only guess how much it weighed.

'I need to have this cleaned and beaten,' he said.

'You're going to wear it?' she asked, struggling not to pull a face.

'I'm not immortal yet, girl. This hide is impenetrable. Let's see that bitch shoot me through this.' The last words came out as a vicious growl. Evadne pushed herself off the container, landing lightly on her feet as far from the gore as possible.

'You need a bath. And watching you work has made me feel like one too,' she said boldly. She knew what he'd want next. He'd want to celebrate. His eyes glinted as he smiled hungrily at her.

'Evadne, I knew you had your uses. I'll be in my cabin shortly. Get it ready.' She nodded coyly and made her way to the smallest hauler. She heard Hercules say behind her, 'Asterion, get down here now. I need you to take this hide to town and have it prepared for me. Then clear up this mess.' They were still in port. There was no need to leave in a hurry and Evadne wondered if Hercules would go back into town himself later tonight to parade his victory to the locals.

She stepped into the hauler and it began to move slowly towards the middle deck. She wouldn't let on to her captain how relieved she was he had won the first Trial, or how close she had come to believing he was dead. She let out a long sigh as she pictured his powerful naked body, wrestling with the lion as he'd burst from the cave. He hadn't acknowledged her part in opening the cave mouth, but she wouldn't push it. Asterion would be receiving punishment for days and she didn't envy him. She figured it was better to stay quiet and enjoy his victory with him. And right now, she knew exactly how to make to him happy.

HERCULES HAD his rooms at the back of the ship, under the quarterdeck. They took up a third of the living quarters on the *Hybris*. The cabin door opened onto a grand lounge, with walls lined in deep-mahogany wood panelling. Plush cushions softened expensive sofas that sat in a semicircle around a low wooden table. A bar, well stocked with wine and ouzo, stood against the right wall and three huge bookshelves lined the other. They were packed with books, from fictional adventures to encyclopedias.

Evadne looked at the books as she poured ouzo into two crystal glasses and set them on the table. She doubted Hercules had read a single one. They were there to impress, not to be used. She loved them, though. As a child she had spent any time she could spare escaping into the adventures of someone more fortunate than herself by reading her favourite stories. Everything she had learned in her life had been taught to her through books, not real people. And they were no poor substitute. She raised her chin, proud, as she thought about how far she had come and where she stood now. And how close she was to the ultimate prize.

She opened the wide wooden doors at the back of the living room and the space flooded with light. Hercules's bedroom was at the back of the ship and instead of having portholes to let in light, like the rest of the ship, her captain had ten-foot-tall arched windows cut into the hull. Framed in front of the bright windows was his obnoxiously lavish bed with the ship's cat, Ati, stretched across the sheets. She lifted her head lazily to look at Evadne, her green eyes gleaming. Evadne bared her teeth at the wrinkly cat and flapped the edge of the sheet to shoo her away. Ati hissed softly and leaped from the bed. Evadne couldn't understand her captain's love for the miserable animal. It was an ugly thing, with a hairless body that made her nose wrinkle in distaste.

She busied herself tucking in sheets and draping scarlet blankets artfully about until she thought Hercules would be happy. When she was done she started setting up the wash-room, a curved white marble room off the bedroom to the left. She stripped off her clothes as hot water ran loudly into the copper bath. She smiled to herself the whole time. She loved the luxury of these quarters. It was what she had dreamed of her whole life. And her captain's success today meant that she got to spend the rest of the day in them, with him. Her core tensed involuntarily as she thought about it. When things were going his way Hercules was an incredible lover. His touch took her breath away, his power and masculinity leaving her giddily defenceless. She didn't dwell on being with him when he wasn't getting what he wanted. Tonight he was happy, and that meant she soon would be too. An anticipatory shiver ran through her as she dipped one small foot in the hot water and heard the door to Hercules's chambers open.

3

LYSSA

Epizon had been right; the crew were having a party. When Lyssa entered the cramped galley a noisy cheer went up and she didn't have to fake her smile. They were all sat around the long table that ran through the middle of the galley and everybody was drinking ouzo. Len hopped off his chair and trotted over to her, handing her a glass of the milky liquid.

'To the captain!' he called, and everyone raised their glasses.

She looked at each them in turn. Epizon's eyes were warm and shining, while Len's were bright and eager. Abderos was smiling triumphantly and Phyleus... He looked back at her with something new. Maybe respect, she thought. He tilted his glass at her.

'Rude not to drink a toast,' he said. 'Especially one to yourself.' She put the glass to her lips and tipped the whole drink down her throat. It burned and she relished the feeling. Fire moving through her was what she needed. Not fear, or doubt. Fire.

. . .

'I'VE COOKED STEW. YOU HUNGRY?'

Lyssa looked gratefully at Epizon as he spoke. 'Starving,' she said.

The huge man turned from her and began pulling bowls from one of the many cupboards and setting them on the counter. The galley was a functional area, one wall lined with everything they needed to cook and eat their meals while next to the other sat a table with space for eight to eat. Cupboards and worktops filled half the first wall and the other half was lined with metal and housed the sink and ovens. Epizon moved to the taller oven and heaved a battered metal pot off one of the four burner rings that topped it. The shorter oven, installed for Abderos and Len, barely crested his knee.

Lyssa made her way to her usual seat at the head of the table, her eyes lingering on the pictures taped to the opposite wall. Not long after they had hired him, Abderos had insisted on putting up pictures of his dream ships. The long bare wall in the galley had been the perfect place for them, he had said. Len had protested that he should be able to put up some of his pictures too and nobody was surprised when a picture of a topless nymph lounging against an apple tree appeared at waist height the next day. More images began to cover the wall over the years, and Lyssa regularly added to them herself. The first she had ever put up was a picture of Libra, the first place she had felt safe after fleeing Hercules on Leo. And the place she had found Epizon. Len's questionable taste in art aside, seeing all the things that were important to her crew in one place always made her feel good, and this was no exception. They needed the *Alastor* as much as she did. And the *Alastor* needed her. The thought gave her strength and her fear receded a little more.

．　．　．

'GRUB'S UP.' Epizon turned from the worktop and began passing the bowls out to everyone around the table. Lyssa watched Phyleus as he nodded his thanks and moved his spoon in and out of the thin liquid unenthusiastically. Annoyance spiked in her and she made a point of keenly shovelling her own stew into her mouth, as if it would defend Epizon's cooking. Although, if she was being honest, it wasn't his best effort.

'CAP, I'VE GOT AN IDEA,' Len announced across the galley table. She looked up from her bowl and nodded at him.

'Fire away,' she said, trying not to let the apprehension show on her face. She didn't want to talk about the next Trial. In fact, she didn't want to talk at all. Len put down his spoon and stood up on the elevated chair he used. He wasn't much taller than when he was sitting down. Abderos, Epizon and Phyleus stopped eating and looked at him too.

'I think we need to give her access to sunlight,' he said. Lyssa blinked, unsure what he was talking about. 'The thing in the tank. I've been studying her, and reading about races from the water realms, and I think she needs sunlight.'

'You think she's female too, then?' Lyssa asked, relieved he wasn't talking about the Trials.

'Yeah, definitely,' he said. Abderos snorted.

'If Len says it's female, then it's female. Nobody quite like him at sniffing out the opposite sex,' he said with an eyebrow raised. Rather than annoyed, Len looked worryingly proud.

'We need to get her up on deck. If we're not heading off until tomorrow I think we should do it now, while we have a breather.'

Lyssa nodded slowly. 'If that's what you think. Do you want to leave her up there permanently?'

'No, no, no.' Len shook his head emphatically as he answered. 'No living creature wants constant exposure to light. Maybe let's start with a few hours and see what happens.'

'OK. We'll get her tank up top. After I've finished eating.'

Len sat back down and spooned hot stew into his mouth more enthusiastically than he had before. Phyleus looked at Lyssa, but she ignored him, concentrating on her stew. She was happy to think about the tank creature instead of the next Trial, and grateful to Len for giving her something to do.

'Are we not going to talk about the fact that we lost, or that Hercules won?' Phyleus said eventually. Lyssa dropped her spoon with a clank into her bowl.

'I'm done,' she said, standing up. 'Let's go.'

Epizon stood up immediately, while a fleeting look of panic crossed Abderos's face and he frantically spooned his stew in faster, desperately trying to finish it.

'Oh, come on, you can't just ignore this!' Phyleus threw his hands in the air.

'She's the captain. She can do exactly as she pleases,' said Epizon quietly before Lyssa had a chance to answer. She threw him a grateful look and strode out of the galley.

'Gods, it'll be a miracle if we survive this,' she heard Phyleus mutter over the sound of his chair scraping back.

4

LYSSA

Since they began smuggling goods on the *Alastor* they had accrued a number of things to help move large crates around, including low steel bases with small wheels at each corner. A reasonably sophisticated pulley system designed by Abderos and Epizon helped them haul heavy crates onto these bases so they could be moved around easily.

It still took the combined strength of Epizon, Phyleus and Lyssa to roll the heavy tank into the big hauler on the side of the ship, and the task was made more awkward by the creature hovering directly in front of Lyssa as she pushed, her unblinking face inches from Lyssa's straining one. When the creature moved the water barely rippled, making Lyssa wonder if it wasn't water at all, but a thicker viscous substance. But she was sure she could hear it sloshing about whenever the tank moved.

The creature looked exactly as she had since they brought her on board, an iridescent shimmer across thousands of tiny scales and wide green eyes that looked eerily intelligent. Once the tank was in the hauler the three of them all crammed in around it and they began to move up towards the open deck. Phyleus was out of breath and panting slightly, but when he noticed Lyssa looking at him he stood up straighter and tried to shorten his deep breaths. She couldn't deny the satisfaction she got from knowing he wanted to impress her.

The hauler stopped moving and the doors slid open. The tank creature's gaze snapped immediately to the open deck. She moved, quicker than they had seen her do before, so that she was at the front of the tank. Then she looked from Lyssa to Epizon and began swimming in wide circles, the water hardly moving around her but her speed increasing. Lyssa shrugged, unable to quell the nerves the creature gave her.

'Let's hope she thinks this is a good idea too,' she said, and Epizon and Phyleus got behind the tank with her to start pushing.

LEN AND ABDEROS were topside to meet them, but neither said anything as the tank was heaved out of the hauler and onto the deck. The further into the brightly coloured light of the sky she got, the slower the creature's circles became. When the whole tank was out and exposed, Lyssa stepped back and Epizon and Phyleus followed her lead. The creature was now totally still, in the centre of the tank. Her face was tilted towards the sky and for the first time Lyssa couldn't see the vivid green of her eyes because they were closed. For a few minutes nothing happened. The only movement visible on the deck of the motionless ship was the gentle swirl of the clouds, pinks and purples rolling past them. Phyleus shifted impatiently, drawing her attention.

Len suddenly took a sharp breath and she snapped her head towards him.

'Look,' he whispered, pointing to the tank. The creature's scales were starting to change colour. Lyssa raised her eyebrows.

'Looks like you were right...' she started to say, but before she could finish, pain lanced through her skull. She dropped to one knee as she threw her hands to her head, screwing her eyes shut against the pain. She was dimly aware of shouts around her, then, abruptly, the pain was gone.

She was no longer on the *Alastor*.

From her position kneeling on the floor, Lyssa looked around at an opulent room. It was a large open area, with white stone columns spaced at regular intervals all around. She stood up cautiously and turned around on the spot. All she could see, stretching in every direction, were the columns. The room was endless.

'Hello?' she called. Her voice echoed back at her but she heard nothing else. She took a tentative step forward. When nothing happened she tried another. A figure stepped out from behind the closest pillar, and she gasped. It was Hercules, holding a fireplace poker dripping with blood. Her breath caught. The poker... Involuntarily she looked to floor at his feet, already knowing the source of the blood on the weapon. A body lay shimmering at his feet, its red hair flashing in and out of focus. Tears filled Lyssa's eyes as she stared down at her mother's body.

'You're next,' Hercules said. He grinned maniacally at her.

'Murderer!' she screamed, as the Rage exploded through her, replacing every other conscious thought. Unarmed and barely aware of her actions, she threw herself at him. But she never made contact with his huge frame. Instead she kept falling, the pain seeping back into her head. She shut her eyes again, trying desperately to make sense of what was going on.

'Captain!' she heard somebody shout, and then felt hands on her shoulders. She opened her eyes and looked up. She was back, kneeling on the deck of the *Alastor*, the gentle clouds swirling about on either side of her. She took a huge, gasping breath, her body shaking with anger. The hand on her shoulder tightened. She turned, expecting to see Epizon, and to her surprise saw Phyleus's worried face instead.

'What happened? Are you all right?' he asked her urgently.

'I don't know what happened,' she said dazedly. 'Where's Epizon?'

'He shouted and fell too, but...' Phyleus paused and stepped to the side so Lyssa could see the huge black man sprawled on the deck. 'He's unconscious,' Phyleus finished.

Lyssa leaped to her feet. The quick movement caused a wave of dizziness to roll over her, but she ignored it as she ran to Epizon. She crouched beside him and put her hand on his hot face. His eyes were screwed shut and his breathing was shallow.

'Len!' she called.

'He's gone to the infirmary to get something to help,' said Phyleus.

'Abderos?'

'I'm fine, Cap. Only you and Epizon were affected,' Abderos wheeled his chair around the tank so she could see him as he spoke.

'Affected?' Lyssa mumbled, and focused on the tank being. She was glowing blue, her shimmering scales dazzling if you looked at them too long, and her eyes still hidden behind closed lids.

'It seems likely she has something to with this,' Len said, trotting across the deck from the back of the ship, carrying a small black pouch. Lyssa moved quickly out of his way. 'This should do it,' he said, and brought out a small vial. He pulled out the tiny cork and waved the bottle slowly under Epizon's nose. Lyssa watched anxiously as his eyelids twitched. Then he took a huge, heaving breath and Lyssa let hers out in relief as his eyelids fluttered open.

'Ep, are you all right?' she asked, leaning close over him.

'Tenebrae,' he said, as dazed as she had been.

'What?'

'Tenebrae. That's her name,' he said and eased himself onto his elbows as he started to sit up.

'Whose name?'

Epizon pointed at the tank. The creature's scales were dimming, her tail was swishing back and forth, and her brilliant eyes were fixed on Epizon's.

'Hers. She's called Tenebrae.'

5

LYSSA

'I ...' Epizon paused, looking meaningfully at Lyssa. 'I know this might sound crazy. But I was back where I grew up. As a child.'

Lyssa blinked. 'What do you mean?'

'There was a massive pain in my head, and then I was a child again. And I...' He looked away. 'I saw things I haven't remembered in a long time.'

Lyssa's heart lurched. She knew little of his past, as he rarely spoke of it, but if he had seen anything as unpleasant as she had, then she felt for him.

'Me too,' she said quietly. 'I saw Hercules, right after...' She shrugged. 'You know.'

'I started yelling *stop!*' Lyssa flinched at the thought of him in pain. He was a good man. The best she'd ever met. Len and Abderos looked away as he spoke, clearly uncomfortable seeing Epizon vulnerable. 'And then I was in a room full of columns and she was there.'

'I was in a room full of columns too!' Lyssa cut in.

'I asked who she was and she said the word *Tenebrae*.'

Lyssa turned to the satyr. 'Len, have you ever heard of

telepathic creatures like this before? Do you think it's connected to exposing her to light?' Len looked at the creature, who was still staring at Epizon.

'No, Captain. I've never heard of anything like this before. But it does seem that she gets her power from light. Surely she would have communicated earlier if she could.'

'Why just you two?' asked Abderos. Lyssa shrugged.

'She didn't speak to me,' she said. 'I think we should get her below decks again, at least until we know she isn't dangerous.'

'I agree, Captain,' said Epizon and stood up. He put his massive hand on the tank and Tenebrae's eyes flicked towards it momentarily, then settled on his face again.

NOBODY SPOKE as they wheeled the tank back into the hauler and down to the cargo deck. Epizon announced he was retiring to his cabin early, and Len and Abderos quickly followed. Lyssa was relieved to be by herself as she sat in her chair on the quarterdeck. With the Alastor motionless there was no breeze. The huge skies rolled and tumbled softly around her, though, limitless. The feeling of freedom washed over her.

'I knew this was a mistake. I should have let you drop me off on Libra,' Phyleus said as he stepped up onto the quarterdeck in front of her.

'The option is still there,' Lyssa scowled at him.

'It's one thing after another.' He shook his head as he spoke. 'I knew the Trials would be dangerous, sure, but that lion was massive. And those giants, they're idiots! They don't listen to anything you say! How can you reason with them? And now, just to add some more danger to this endeavour, we have a telepathic creature nobody knows anything about who is able to knock out the best fighter on the ship.'

.'Are you sure about that?' she said quietly. He looked at her.

'About what? You were there; Epizon was completely out,' he answered, walking to the railings.

'Are you sure about him being the best fighter on the ship?' Phyleus raised his eyebrows.

'Oh. Sorry, *Captain*. That's probably you, is it?' His tone confirmed that he didn't believe it. She sighed. Epizon was wrong; this guy was not worth it.

'You chose to be here, Phyleus. If you back out now, you get none of your drachmas back.'

'Whoa, whoa. I'm not quitting.' His chest was puffed out and he was wearing the defiant expression she didn't mind so much as his arrogant one. The one that made him look like he had a backbone. She leaned back in the wooden chair.

'Then why are you up here, whining to me?' He scowled.

'I'm not whining. I'm...' he fixed his eyes on hers, really looking at her. 'I'm trying to work some things out.'

She raised her eyebrows. 'Sounds like whining to me. Go to bed.' She stood up and made for the hauler at the back of the ship.

'I can help you win, Lyssa. There are things you don't know about me. Things that could help,' he said.

She stopped. She knew she should reprimand him for calling her Lyssa instead of Captain. She knew she should be annoyed by his arrogance. But she wasn't. She wanted to believe him.

She turned around slowly. Phyleus was wearing clean clothes now, dark leather trousers tucked into supple boots and a tight white shirt open halfway down his chest. His caramel hair was pushed back from his tanned face and his lips looked soft and full even from where she was standing. She didn't want his help, but why did she want him? She scolded herself mentally. She was just having a bad few days. Sharing her bed with an arrogant noble who thought he was better than her and her ship was not the answer.

'Good night, Phyleus,' she said firmly and turned back to the hauler.

'Night, Captain,' he answered softly.

6

HEDONE

Hedone had worked hard not to let the smile show as they watched Hera in the flame dish. Joy had spread through her like warm liquid when she had seen Hercules, bloody, naked and victorious. She felt like his passion and fierceness was just for her. She was desperate to see him again.

'It's not ideal that he won. Not surprising, but not ideal,' Theseus was saying. They were all on the quarterdeck, waiting for the next Trial announcement. Theseus wasn't taking any chances this time. He had believed her, without question, when she told him she had fallen asleep and missed the last announcement. He hadn't even been angry with her. It wasn't in his nature to be angry. She looked at his soft dark hair and perfectly proportioned face. Was he as beautiful as Hercules? She felt a pull in her gut. No, she decided. He was too pretty, too gentle. She needed a man who could take care of her, fight for her, set her soul alight with passion.

'We'll just have to make sure he doesn't win the next one,' said Bellerephon. He was sharpening arrowheads on his lap, sparks flying across his leather-clad thighs. Bellerephon was bigger and more muscular than Theseus, but his eyes were not as warm and his smile not so easy. She felt the tug inside her again and focused on the thought of Hercules. She needed to help him win. She needed him to know how she felt.

'Where do you think the next Trial will be?' she asked Theseus. He shrugged.

'The only thing we know for sure is that it won't be on Cancer.'

'Captain,' said Psyche. They all turned. The flames in the dish were white and a foot high. Bellerephon stood up quickly, his arrows clattering to the ground. He ignored them and moved closer to the dish. Hedone stood too, moving around him for a better view. The man in the blue toga materialised in the dish.

'Good day, Olympus!' he beamed. 'Are you ready for the second Trial?' Hedone held her breath. The smiling man faded slowly, then Athena appeared in the bowl. She was wearing white, as she always did, and her blond hair was braided in a crown around her head. The goddess smiled.

'Good day. Congratulations to the previous victors, the crew of the *Hybris*.' She nodded her head. 'The next Trial will be somewhat more difficult, I believe. Deep in the centre of my sky realm lurks a monster with three heads and a voracious appetite. It is as tall as a building and cannot listen to reason. It will kill indiscriminately and without remorse. Please, heroes of Olympus, kill this monster, the Hydra.' She bowed her head again, and vanished.

. . .

THESEUS RUBBED his hands together as he turned and looked at his crew.

'Excellent,' he said.

Psyche frowned at him.

'How is a massive, violent, three-headed monster excellent, Captain?'

'First, we made the right choice staying at the Void. We're closer to Libra than the other ships. Second, Hercules will get cocky because this is another brute strength challenge. And people make mistakes when they get cocky.'

7

HERCULES

Hercules watched the cat stretch languidly, then curl up at the end of the chair, carefully tucking its small paws beneath itself. Evadne thought the hairless cat ugly, with its triangular face and massive ears. He didn't care what she thought. He looked at the soft folds of skin on its neck thoughtfully. So different to the hide he had removed from Gata. He had been testing it since having a tanner on Cancer fashion it into a long cloak, with everything he had at his disposal on the ship. He had so far found nothing that could penetrate it. It would serve him well against a three-headed beast, he thought, lifting a glass of ouzo to his lips and leaning back into his seat.

'Captain?' A gruff voice rang in his head.

'I asked not to be disturbed until we reach Libra,' he said quietly.

'Right. We're one hour away.'

'Asterion, if you value all parts of your anatomy, don't bother me again until we are ten minutes away,' he growled to the minotaur.

'Yes, Captain.' His first mate was trying too hard to

recover his standing after making such a fool of himself on Cancer. A minotaur should not be so thoroughly beaten by a bunch of dim-witted giants, and Hercules was in no hurry to let him forget that. As he raised his glass once more, intense light filled his vision. He swore and turned his face away, closing his eyes tight.

'You won't be the first one there, you know,' boomed a voice. Hercules turned back.

'Hello, Father. I thought I'd see you sooner after my victory. Ouzo?' He gestured at Zeus with his glass.

'Your victory?' the lord of the gods replied. His brows knitted together and purple energy crackled in his eyes. He was a foot taller than Hercules, only just able to stand straight in his living quarters. 'You call being shot by a girl half your size a victory?'

Indignation filled Hercules and he slammed his glass down on the table.

'I won! I won the first Trial! How is that not a victory?'

The purple energy rolling off Zeus crackled out loud, and Hercules smelled the tang of electricity in the air. Zeus's eyes locked on his and he was unable to look away.

'You know as well as I do the risks in me coming here. Do not test me. You put on a pitiful display in the last Trial. You were blindly seduced by the beast herself, lost in a cave until that girl of yours freed you, and then shot by your own daughter. You may have won the Trial but you have not won anybody's respect.' Zeus words smashed into Hercules one after the other, causing his face to heat with anger.

'What do you mean, freed me? I had everything under control the entire time! Lyssa shot me after I had killed the beast, in an act of cowardice,' he spat.

'She shouldn't have shot you at all. If you were a better hero, she would not have been able to. And the girl on your crew, Evadne, convinced one of the giants to remove the tree blocking the cave for you.'

'I could have done that myself,' he snorted.

'While fighting a man-eating lion? I doubt that very much. Listen to me. As I don't trust you to cope without it, I am bringing you something to help.' The god held his arm out in front of him. Purple lightning began to roll and race around his forearm. It built, crackling and pulsing, racing faster and faster until Zeus flicked his wrist hard. The lightning shot down his arm to his hand, instantly solidifying in the form of a massive sword.

Hercules stared. It was the most beautiful thing he had ever seen. Other than Hedone, perhaps. Zeus held it out to him and he stood up to take it. It was as tall as most men, the handle cold smooth glass and the blade gleaming silver. A lightning bolt was carved into the hilt.

'She is called *Keravnos*. You must tell nobody I gave her to you, though most will guess. Say you found it somewhere on Leo before the Trials began.' Hercules swung the sword slowly, testing its weight. 'The handle is made from diamond. It will never break or shatter. And she has the same magic as your ship. She will respond to your thoughts and absorb your power. With her, you should be unstoppable.'

'Thank you, Father,' Hercules breathed.

'Thank me by not making such a mess this time. And wear that lion skin,' Zeus said, and vanished.

Hercules's bitterness at Zeus's harsh words warred with the delight of wielding the incredible weapon in his hands. He tentatively reached out with his strength, in the same way he controlled the *Hybris*. The blade thrummed to life, a deep red glow forming around it. It felt lighter and he swung it easily towards the cushions on the opposite armchair. Without a hint of resistance *Keravnos* cleaved the entire chair in two. Hercules pulled the blade up in surprise, then began to laugh. With this, he really would be unstoppable. And he would prove to his father that he could win the respect of all of Olympus, without any help at all.

8

HERCULES

'But, Captain—'

Hercules cut Evadne off with a wave of his hand.

'I have made my decision. Go and get Ati.' He looked at the girl expectantly. She was clenching her teeth. 'I said, go and get the cat. She is in my cabin.'

'I don't think she likes being up on deck much,' Evadne answered quietly.

'Nonsense. Go and get her. I want her with me when we arrive on Libra.'

'Captain, I don't think you realise how much Asterion and I can help you,' Evadne said. She held out her hands as she spoke. Annoyance began to prick at Hercules. Evadne had been so helpful, so compliant, so... young last night. He didn't want to get angry with her now but she was choosing to ignore him.

'I will not tell you again. I am doing this Trial alone. That is final. Go and get my cat.' He spoke slowly, his voice low and the menace clear. Evadne dropped her gaze to the floor and took a long breath.

'I think you are making a mistake,' she said.

Hercules tensed. 'What did you say?'

She looked up at him. 'I said I think you are making a mistake. Athena is the goddess of warfare and strategy; she would never design a Trial that could be beaten by one person alone. It's not how she works.'

Anger rolled though Hercules. This girl thought so much of herself and so little of him? He stepped towards her but she held both her ground and his gaze. That angered him even more than her words.

'You saw what I did to the lion, yes?' he hissed. Evadne nodded.

'You are aware that I am imbued with the strength of the lord of the gods, yes?'

'A Trial set by Athena will require more than str...'

He struck her across the face and she stumbled backwards with a yelp.

'Do you see my control?' he roared. 'I could knock your head from your shoulders if I wished! This is the perfect Trial to prove to the world that I am their true hero, and that the mighty Hercules needs nobody.' Evadne stared up at him, her hand across her cheek. He could see the anger in her eyes but now it excited him. He wanted her to defy him. He wanted to push her further. He stepped towards her and bent down so his face was in front of hers. 'Do you wish to challenge me?' he breathed. Her eyes narrowed and he smiled.

'No, Captain,' she muttered. Slight disappointment mingled with satisfaction as he stepped back.

'Go and get my cat,' he said and sat down in the captain's chair behind him. Evadne walked slowly past him, towards the hauler at the back of the ship.

Hercules liked to think of the captain's chair on the

Hybris as a throne. It was upholstered in red and was nothing like those wooden spindly things most ships had. The thought gave him an idea. 'Bring her a cushion,' he said, without turning around. If Evadne was right about the cat not liking it on deck, maybe a cushion would help.

'Yes, Captain,' the girl replied sullenly.

9

ERYX

'I'm not staying here!' roared Eryx, banging his fist against the rear mast of the Zephyr.

'You'll do whatever the captain tells you to do.' Busiris smirked.

Eryx widened his stance, his heavy boots thudding on the deck, and felt some grim satisfaction as the smirk fell away. When the scrawny idiot thought it was going to come down to a fight he was a lot less smug. 'Look, Libra is less than an hour away. I'm sure the captain will have made his decision by then,' he said.

Eryx looked over Busiris's shoulder, past the railings of the Zephyr, at Libra. It was one of his favourite realms in Olympus. It was made up of hundreds of flat floating islands, clustered together in a loose sphere. Even from a distance he could make out some of the larger platform-like islands that hung together around its edge.

'You're all coming.' Antaeus's booming voice carried across the massive deck of the Zephyr. 'We don't need anybody on the ship.'

Busiris gave Eryx a slimy smile, the black ink that lined

his eyes cracking as his face moved. 'That settles that, then,' he said.

Eryx snarled and stamped towards the railings. The gold half-giant wound him up so much more than the loud, simple brothers on the ship. He was sly, and Eryx didn't trust him. But his beloved captain did, so he would just have to do as he was told. As usual. He leaned on the reinforced metal railings and watched as Libra slowly got bigger. They would likely be the last to arrive, something he was sure would continue to be an issue if they survived to take part in more Trials. The sky around him became greyer, streaks of blue and purple rolling like corkscrews around the giant ship as it chugged towards its destination. A heavy hand fell on his shoulder.

'You'll get your chance this time, Brother. Just don't let that girl anywhere near you.' Antaeus spoke quietly and Eryx felt his back straighten. This would be his chance. He'd show Busiris, and Evadne. This was their Trial. Who better to defeat a giant three-headed monster than a crew of giants?

10

LYSSA

Thrills of excitement rippled through Lyssa as the *Alastor* sailed gracefully to a stop next to the long metal pier. Confidence surged through her charged body. She knew this place, and Athena was backing her. Libra would be where she would win.

THE PLATFORM SHUDDERED as Epizon leaped down from the deck of the ship first. He was wearing his big coat and had his giant knife strapped to his leg. She hadn't argued about his attire this time. Lyssa rubbed the back of her neck as she watched Len scramble over the railing, his hooves clicking on the metal as he landed. He had insisted on coming since their worrying incident with the tank creature but she really hoped they wouldn't need a medic.

'Captain,' said Phyleus, and offered his hand to help her over the railing. She rolled her eyes, put one hand on the wooden bar and vaulted easily over it. She barely made a sound as her boots landed on the pier. 'Right,' he said, and threw his own leg over the railing. 'I won't try to be civil again, then.'

'I'm a woman, not an invalid,' she muttered.

'And I'm just trying to be well-mannered, unlike you.' Phyleus dropped down beside her.

'You're ruining my homecoming,' she snapped, and turned away from him.

THE PIER PLATFORM jutted out a long way from the mass of islands that made up Libra, and Lyssa loved how surreal standing at the end felt. Ahead of her was a churning mass of activity: glass haulers zipping up and down between the islands, figures hurrying across the intricate glass bridges that linked them, the thin, flat islands themselves filled with curved buildings and tall trees. But behind her and the ship, there was only sky. Just blue and violet streaks breaking up the gentle grey clouds. There was a serenity in it that calmed the constant hum of energy simmering inside her.

'Here we go again, then,' Phyleus said.

'DO you know where we have to go?' Len asked as they reached him, standing at the other end of the pier. A breath-takingly delicate glass bridge with railings carved in intri-cate patterns connected the end of the pier platform to an island that housed three single-storey buildings. They were made from white stone and were decorated in swirling metal fingers that wrapped around the buildings completely, making odd geometric shapes. One of the build-ings looked like a tavern, with people sat at small angular tables in front of the windows. Lyssa knew not all the build-ings on Libra were so beautiful. The islands around the outside of the realm had the most extravagant architecture, to go with the incredible views of the skies. But the further into the cluster of islands you got, the thicker the mist grew and the less wealthy the residents became.

'Athena said the monster was deep in the centre of Libra. I've been in pretty far, but never to the core. How about you, Epizon?'

Her first mate had lived in the homeless shanty towns on the inner islands of Athena's realm far longer than she had, building luxurious homes on the outer islands in return for food. Athena was the only goddess in Olympus who would feed anybody who worked.

'Nope, I just went in as far in as the missionaries took food.'

'I guess we go as far in as we can and work it out from there. We must be the first ones here.'

'I don't think so, Cap. Theseus and the *Virtus* will have been closer if they stayed at the Void,' said Len, almost jogging to keep up.

'Huh. Let's hope they didn't.'

11

LYSSA

There was no way you could spend time on Libra if you had a fear of heights. It was impossible to move between islands without looking down to see the rest of Olympus a distant smudge below. They crossed the first bridge and made their way between the buildings to where a glass hauler stood open, attached to a long thin metal rod that ran up to the island above them. Nobody paid them any attention, to Lyssa's relief. They needed to move quickly and Len would not be good with any distractions. Especially not ones that would inflate his ego. Phyleus hesitated before stepping into the hauler but Lyssa gave him a small shove and he got in without a word. They moved quickly up to the island and he was the first out.

'I thought we were going in, not up?' he said, pointing into the centre of the mass of islands disappearing into the mist.

'We are,' she replied. 'Do you see any more bridges? We need to go up to find an island with a bridge heading inwards.' Phyleus groaned. 'Go back to the *Alastor* if you

can't handle it,' she said without looking at him. He snorted
and fell in behind her. They walked past a long white stone
building three or four times the size of the shops on the
previous island. It had a huge image of a serpent twisted
around a staff painted by every doorway and Lyssa could
smell the sharp tang of alcohol as they passed.

'I worked in a medical practice once,' said Len. 'But it
wasn't as big as that one.'

'Oh yeah? How'd you like it?' asked Phyleus.

'Too busy. Too many people. Too much work,' the satyr
answered, shaking his head slightly. 'Nobody was very
grateful.'

'Was it here on Libra?' said Lyssa.

'No. No, Libra would be even busier.'

'Well, personally, I'm glad you don't get much work on
the *Alastor*,' said Epizon, glancing back.

'That makes two of us,' Phyleus said.

THEY TOOK three more haulers up before they found a
bridge heading towards the inner islands. The homes on
each island had become progressively bigger as they had
moved up. On one island Lyssa gaped at a three-storey
building with long balconies that wrapped around all the
floors. It had a satisfying mix of angles and curves everywhere she looked. The iron fingers curled around the
stone and the windows, making the building look as
though it was trying to protect itself. Immaculate gardens
with tall tidy trees surrounded the house, running all the
way to the island's edge on the rear side of the house
where a longboat with a sail that looked almost too white
was docked.

'Fancy living there, do you?' said Phyleus, coming to a

stop beside her as she breathed in the smell of the tiny
yellow flowers lining the garden fence.

'Not a chance,' she snorted. When she first came to
Libra, Lyssa had been jealous of the people who lived in
these lavish homes, with a view of the unending skies and a
way out whenever they liked. Now, though, she knew she
was the lucky one. Nothing compared to living on the
Alastor.

'Yeah, right,' he said.

'Shut up. The bridge is over there.' She pointed at the
glass bridge that led the next island.

'Thank the gods,' muttered Phyleus.

'So you prefer glass bridges showing everything beneath
you, to less than a minute in a hauler? You make no sense,'
she said to him, shaking her head.

'The glass bridges have been here ages, and I can't fall
through glass,' he replied, giving her a sidelong glance.

The clear bridges had seemed insane to Lyssa when she
first got to Libra. She wasn't really scared of heights but who
wanted to see that they were walking over thin air?

'The haulers have been here ages too,' she said.

'Yeah, and I bet people get stuck in them all the time.'

'No, they don't. I thought you said you've been to Libra
before?'

'I've always had a longboat,' he replied. Lyssa pulled a
face. She'd forgotten for a moment he was wealthy. Of
course he wouldn't have gotten around with haulers and
bridges.

'Where did you say you were from?' she said, unable to
keep the edge off her voice. He looked at her.

'I'm not going to tell you if you're just going to get mad at
me for being rich,' he said.

'Gods, you're arrogant,' she snapped.

'And you're judgmental,' he slung back at her. She growled and increased her pace, catching up with Epizon.

THE ISLANDS BEGAN to change as they moved further into Libra. There were fewer white stone buildings and more temporary-looking metal ones. The green grass and luscious plants were sparser and the mist thickened. It was as if the colour was slowly draining from their surroundings. The only constants were the beautiful bridges and the glass haulers. There were more people, too, of many different races. Most moved busily and purposefully between islands and in and out of buildings, but a few looked bored and mean. A minotaur leaning on the side of a long low building that might once have been white called gruffly to them and Phyleus jumped. A woman with long blond hair wearing a very short toga stepped out from behind him.

'Dice? We've got a great prize today,' she said, her voice low and sultry. Len slowed. 'Today only. Strawberries.' The satyr stopped completely.

'Captain, she said strawberries,' he said.

'Len, no way. We don't have time for dice,' Lyssa replied, looking back at him without stopping.

'Well, you probably don't need me. I could stay here and win some strawberries.'

Lyssa sighed and stopped walking.

'Len, you know we don't have time to stop. And we wouldn't be stopping to gamble even if we weren't in a hurry. Come on!'

'Satyrs were created by the god Pan, and he is famous for his luck! If Pan can gamble, I can too.' He nodded and turned towards the woman. 'I'm in,' he said.

'Len! Seriously? I can't leave you here!' Anger coursed

through her. What did the idiot think he was doing, playing dice now?

'Epizon, get him,' she said, turning to her first mate.

'Well, we could just play one quick game,' he shrugged. She gaped at him.

'Yeah, one game can't hurt,' said Phyleus and they both followed Len towards the wide-open door of the building.

'Sorry, sweetheart. Some boys just can't resist a good deal,' said the blonde with a wink. 'Are you sure you don't fancy one game?' she said temptingly.

Lyssa felt a pull in her gut and took a step towards the building. They probably did have time for one game. How long did it take to throw a couple of dice? And she did love strawberries, all juicy and red and sweet. She couldn't remember the last time she'd eaten one. For a moment she thought she could smell them and her lips parted a little in anticipation. The blond woman's smile widened and the minotaur grunted a laugh. The laugh filtered slowly through the haze of strawberries.

'Shit,' she said, her anger redoubling and replacing the desire to play. 'You're a bloody siren!' Of course her crew had done exactly what the woman had told them to do.

The woman smiled back. 'They didn't stand a chance, love. Few and far between are those who can resist the call of a siren.'

Lyssa growled and ran after her hapless crew.

LYSSA

L yssa almost choked as she ran into the building. The smell of smoke nearly overwhelmed the smell of unwashed bodies, but not quite. She skidded to a halt and looked around her. The building was one long room, packed with tables and people. At both ends of the room she could see wooden counters covered with bottles, and scantily clad girls moving around carrying trays laden with wine and ouzo. There was a hum of sound, people talking, laughing and shouting everywhere she looked. A roar went up somewhere to her left. A lucky winner, she assumed.

She scanned the room, looking for Epizon as he would stand out the most. But there were lots of different races on Libra, and many were represented in this small area. Figures much taller than Epizon were everywhere. Eventually she spotted him, standing by a small table surrounded by people. Breathing a sigh of relief, she jogged over to him. Len was standing on a high stool next to him, holding a black leather shaker over a dice bowl. He kissed the shaker and emptied it over the bowl. The dice clattered and came to a stop. Two Typhoons. Len roared in triumph.

Lyssa had dice like these on her ship. They had six sides, showing four different ship classes and two lightning bolts. The best ship class won and the lightning bolts were bad news. The satyr's opponent, a shabbily dressed griffin descendant from the looks of his hooked beak and straggly black wings, snatched the shaker from Len and gathered up the dice. He shook them hard and tossed them into the bowl. Two Whirlwinds. Everybody knew Whirlwinds beat everything. Lyssa rolled her eyes as Len and Epizon groaned.

'Come on, Len. Nice try,' she said, and reached past Epizon to grab the satyr's shoulder.

'Not so fast,' growled the griffin. 'I believe you owe me my winnings.' He held out his hand, showing fingernails that ended in sharp talons.

Len looked at Lyssa. Her stomach tightened.

'What did you bet him?'

'Erm,' said Len.

'He bet him three drachma,' said Phyleus. Lyssa hadn't noticed him standing the other side of Epizon. She closed her eyes.

'Satyrs are always lucky! It should have been easy silver,' protested Len.

'Just pay him,' said Phyleus.

'With what?' Lyssa exploded. 'I only let you on my damn ship because of our lack of drachma! Where do you think he's hiding that much silver?'

'Are you saying you're not good for the bet?' said the griffin. Nobody missed the menace in his voice.

'Of course he is,' said Phyleus coolly. 'Double or nothing. I'll roll this time,' and he held out his hand for the shaker.

'Phyleus, you'd better be able to cover this,' she hissed. He ignored her, shook the dice and rolled. A lightning bolt and a Crosswind. The only thing worse would have been two lightning bolts. The griffin laughed and Len slowly got down from his stool.

'Time to go, Cap,' he muttered.

'No kidding.' The griffin shook the dice and they clattered into the bowl. Two Zephyrs. He had won.

'Six drachma.' He glared at Phyleus.

'Fine. Me and my buddies, we've got some business to take care of, but when that's done you can meet us at our ship and I'll give you the silver.' Phyleus stood up. Lyssa's stomach sank. Even if Phyleus really did have the silver, if he didn't have it with him there was no way they would be allowed to leave.

'That's not how this works.' The griffin's beak clacked as he spat the words. 'You pay now, or you won't have a ship to come back to.'

'I swear to Zeus, if anything happens to my ship you will die,' Lyssa flared. Her muscles were tensing, her vision narrowing as her body channelled her Rage, preparing for a fight. The griffin looked at her.

'Would you rather work the debt off here?' he gestured at one of the serving girls with his clawed hand. A mangy-looking human was groping her rear. Lyssa's face screwed up involuntarily.

'He told you, you'll get paid. Just not right now.'

'Not good enough.' The griffin stepped around the table towards them. In a flash he had moved past Epizon and lifted Len by his furry ankle. The satyr yelped as he dangled in the air. Lyssa darted towards the griffin but he was faster than her. She could see now that his legs were those of a big cat and he sprang towards the wide door, his tatty wings helping him cover a huge amount of ground. She sprinted after him, aware that Epizon was right behind her. She burst though the doors and faltered. The griffin was at the edge of the island, holding Len out over leagues of empty air below. The satyr was stock still, his eyes squeezed tightly shut. Rage flooded Lyssa. Fear and anger pulsed through her so strongly her body hurt.

'Captain, wait, don't do anything. If he drops him...' Epizon didn't finish his sentence. He didn't need to.

'We'll get you the silver. Now. I'll go and get it now,' Phyleus panted as he caught up with them.

'Good. I'll be here. Waiting with your friend.'

'Bring him back in,' said Lyssa quietly, her few words laced with menace. The griffin looked at her.

'So much hatred for such a tiny girl.' She took a step forward.

'I'll get the drachma!' shouted Phyleus. 'I'm going, now. Just don't do anything stupid in the meantime.'

Lyssa didn't know if he was talking to her or the griffin, and she didn't care. Her fear for Len was completely absorbed by her anger. Boiling Rage was flowing through her now, and her aching body pushed her towards the griffin.

13

HEDONE

'Theseus, please let's do something,' Hedone half-pleaded, the sight of the tiny satyr being dangled over the edge of the island ahead of them making her stomach churn.

Psyche rolled her eyes.

'We don't have time to stop. We should be far ahead of them by now. And why would we help our rivals?' she muttered.

Hedone scowled at her. 'It's just a game, we don't need to watch people die.'

It was true that they should have been further ahead, but Theseus had been recognised on one of the outlying islands, and they had been mobbed by supporters. More and more people had arrived to wave and shout and cheer and their progress had been slowed significantly. Hedone pointed at the fierce red-haired girl advancing on the griffin twice her height. 'That is not sporting. The brute should be stopped.'

'I agree,' said Theseus quietly. Triumph washed over Hedone. She had been desperately trying to think of ways to slow her crew down since the mob had lessened, and this was perfect. In any case, she really didn't want to see anything bad happen to the little satyr.

'I'll PAY,' Theseus bellowed. Hedone jumped, and everyone's attention snapped to her captain. The red-haired girl stopped moving.

Theseus began to walk slowly towards the group. 'How much does the satyr owe you?'

'Six drachma,' the griffin growled.

'I'll buy the debt. He turned to the girl. 'Captain Lyssa. You will owe me the drachma instead.' She hesitated a moment, looking at the satyr, then nodded. Hedone was surprised by the fire in the girl's hard eyes. She was so young to be so angry; surely no older than her own eighteen years. But Lyssa was Hercules's daughter. A shiver rippled though Hedone as she wondered what that fire would be like turned to passion, instead of anger.

'Show me,' barked the griffin, his lion legs stamping the ground impatiently. The satyr wasn't moving. Theseus dug in the leather bag slung across his chest and pulled out a coin pouch. He waved it at the griffin.

'Bring him in.' Authority rang though his voice and Hedone felt a small surge of admiration, but it melted away quickly, replaced by a surge of hope that all this was giving Hercules a chance to get ahead of them.

'THIS IS NOT JUST A GAME, HEDONE,' Psyche said beside her as they watched the griffin reluctantly dump the satyr on the ground. Captain Lyssa rushed towards the little creature and the griffin stalked towards Theseus.

'Immortality!' Psyche continued. 'We'll never have a second chance at this, and you are not helping. Stay on the ship next time.' She hissed and strode after Theseus.

Hedone sighed. As long as Psyche didn't suspect her real reason for being so unhelpful she would be fine. Psyche thought she was weak, and why wouldn't she? Hedone was the demi-goddess of pleasure. Not a quality associated with strength. Only Theseus knew what she was really capable of, who she had nearly become when they released her from the temple she was raised in. He had patiently shown her the value of a moral way of life. What if he hadn't, she wondered, staring at her captain counting out silver coins for the impatient beaked creature. Was she weak? Or was she strong, for controlling herself? For the first time in years, a desire to prove herself crept over her.

'Hedone,' rumbled a deep voice behind her, and all her thoughts fled in an instant.

14

HERCULES

Hercules knew he was taking a risk talking to the girl but he couldn't help it. He had watched patiently, waiting for an ideal time to make it past the gathered crowd without being noticed, and then the older woman had walked away, leaving the beautiful Hedone alone.

He had arrived on Libra after Theseus and seen them a few islands in, surrounded by people. He had immediately bought a big dark cloak to wear over his distinctive lion skin one, and followed the crew at a distance. Let them do the hard work of finding the Hydra for him. It meant he could watch Hedone.

'I know we are supposed to be enemies in this, but I wanted you to know I mean you well,' he said as she turned to him. Her eyes widened and longing shot through him. She was breath-taking.

'I...' she said, staring at him. He smiled.

'I must go now,' he said, and put his hand on her shoulder. He felt her shudder and frowned. 'I didn't mean to startle you,' he said as gently as he could.

'No, you didn't,' she said quickly. 'I mean, you did, but it's OK.' She smiled and his chest expanded. Her smile... It wasn't the sultry, sexy smile he had seen when he first met her. It was real and warm and beautiful. And it was for him. Confidence poured through him and he touched his other hand to her cheek. Her skin felt like silk and she drew a quick breath.

'We should meet. After I have won this Trial.' She nodded. 'Expect me, Hedone,' he said, unable to keep his hunger from his voice. Her eyes darkened and a thrill ran through him. She wanted him.

'Good luck,' she said as he withdrew his hand and turned back to the crowd. He knew he didn't need luck. But by Zeus, he did need her. He had never met anybody like her. She belonged with him. He ducked against the wall as the griffin pushed past a small crowd of humans trying to get back into the gambling hall. Hercules looked over at Theseus and Lyssa shaking hands and snorted. They had no idea what was at stake. Helping one another when they were supposed to be rivals. It was weak and idiotic. Lyssa gestured at the glass bridge and Theseus set off towards it, Hedone and the other woman behind him. It looked like Lyssa was giving him the head start. Hercules pulled his hood further down his face and waited, ready to follow.

15

LYSSA

'I'm sorry, Captain,' said Len for the twentieth time as they made their way across the bridge ten minutes after Theseus had departed.

'Len, stop. Not another word.'

'I'll pay Theseus as soon as we—' started Phyleus.

'I said stop!' Lyssa whirled to face him. 'Both of you. I am not having this conversation now. We need to focus.'

'Yes, Captain,' Phyleus said quietly. She noted with some small satisfaction the lack of sarcasm in the way he said *Captain*. She couldn't berate them, though. They had followed the call of a siren. She had been about to let her Rage outstrip her sense. If she had attacked that griffin and he had let go of Len... Nausea burned in her stomach. Epizon, and Phyleus, had been right. She should have waited for Phyleus to get the drachma. She had to control the Rage better. She *would* control it better, she resolved.

THEY CARRIED on further and further, much deeper into Libra than Lyssa had ever been before. Even less of the light from the pale grey skies filtered through the mist and the islands they travelled across grew darker. Len looked around nervously as he trotted ahead of her, at the metal lean-tos, discarded rubbish and people hunched around small fires. Epizon's languid strides had become stiffer. The trickle of adrenaline though her body quickened. Phyleus seemed unaware of any danger. He was looking around in the dark, frowning at the heaps of rags and the pitiful clusters of belongings people were defending. He looked genuinely troubled. She felt a pang of guilt as she remembered how she had lived before she came to Libra. She thought about how she had felt when she'd seen how Epizon lived and her involuntary distaste when she realised she would have to do the same. She hadn't been aware of poverty in Olympus until she had seen it herself. She swallowed hard. If she was being honest, there was a lot she hadn't been aware of until she sailed the skies on the *Alastor*. She'd be damned if she would admit that to Phyleus, though.

'CAPTAIN, THERE ARE NO MORE BRIDGES,' said Epizon. He had stopped at the end of the island and was staring into the empty blackness ahead. The darkness had even seemed to swallow the mist.

'There must be,' she said.

'Nope. Just dark,' said Len.

'Well, how the hell do we get into the middle, then?' she put her hands on her hips, anger simmering. She hadn't thought Athena would make things complicated.

'Longboat?' said Phyleus. She spun around to face him.

'Do you see a longboat here?' She flung out her arm, the movement feeling good. 'And you know bloody well that our longboat is unusable.'

'Wait, Cap, there is a bridge here,' called Len. They all turned to him. He was crouched by the edge of the island. 'It's got no rail, and it's not very big, but it is there.' He stood up and hesitantly put one foot over the edge of the island. Epizon moved quickly, his hand hovering above the satyr. Lyssa heard Len's hoof make contact with glass. He smiled. 'Yep, it's here.' He stepped out with his other leg. It looked like he was suspended over nothingness.

'I can't see it,' said Phyleus, peering hard at Len's feet. Lyssa walked to the edge and kneeled. She put her hands out, feeling for the glass where Len was now standing. Her hands ran over the cool surface.

'You must have different eyesight to humans,' she said.

'Course I do,' he replied. 'Humans can hardly see anything.'

'Hey,' Phyleus protested.

'Don't take it personally,' Epizon advised.

'How do we know we won't walk off the side?' asked Lyssa standing back up.

'I'll go first.' Len shrugged and began walking into the abyss. Epizon stepped onto the invisible bridge without hesitation and followed him. Phyleus looked at Lyssa.

'Well. He's brave for three feet tall. Captains first.' He gestured at the bridge.

'Huh,' she said. It was one thing not to be scared of heights. It was quite another to step onto an invisible bridge leagues high, leading into pitch blackness, in pursuit of a giant three-headed monster. Her skin fizzed with adrenaline. She flexed her hands. *I am no longer the girl who ran.* The thought buoyed her.

Phyleus raised his eyebrows as she took a step onto the bridge. Her breath caught as she lowered her boot, sure it would just keep moving through the empty sky. But it didn't. There was a reassuring tap as she made contact with the bridge. She looked up to where Epizon's bulk was just visible ahead and stepped forward with her other leg. Once she was moving, she didn't dare stop. And she didn't look down. Nor backwards to see if Phyleus had followed. She kept her eyes on Epizon and kept walking steadily forward, breathing slowly.

'Captain, it's getting lighter,' called Epizon after a few minutes.

'Good,' she yelled back. Ahead of her a swirling grey fog was starting to take shape, framing Epizon's figure.

'There's a new island,' he called. Relief washed through her and she squashed the urge to thank the gods.

'Good,' she called again instead. A few seconds later she could see the edges of a new island forming through the fog, and the inky darkness didn't feel so crushing. As she reached the island she risked a look down and sagged when she saw soil beneath her feet. She sped up, spurred by the hard, safe ground.

'Epizon, Len, wait for us there,' she shouted, only just able to see the big black man ahead of her now through the thickening fog. She waved her arm through the gently swirling haze and something crashed into her. She cried out in surprise and stumbled to her knees.

'Shit, what have I hit?' came Phyleus's panicked voice. She pushed herself to her feet quickly and grabbed him as he stumbled about.

'You're a bloody idiot,' she hissed, spinning him around to face her.

'Oh, thank the gods it's just you,' he replied with a relieved grin. She glared at him, then looked back to where she had last seen Epizon. She could just make out his large form next to Len's much smaller one and she pulled Phyleus along with her to catch him up.

'I think we're in some sort of canyon,' whispered Len when she reached them. She looked around and realised he was right. If she watched for long enough she could see high rock faces through the gaps in the swirling fog a few feet away on either side.

'How high do you think they go?' She was whispering too. Speaking normally didn't seem appropriate in the eerily silent fog.

'No idea, Cap,' he shrugged. 'I can't see through the fog any better than you.'

'Then we carry on though the canyon, I guess.'

The rocky banks stretched up endlessly as they walked cautiously between them. Sparse trees dotted their path, coming into view only as they were right beside them, until the path opened out suddenly. Lyssa looked from side to side, squinting to see the banks but they were gone. They had come out of the other side of the canyon.

'There's movement ahead of us,' Len whispered. Epizon silently pulled his knife from its sheath. They crept forward.

Lyssa could make out a red light, dancing high in the mist. As she approached, more lights appeared, six in total, all floating high ahead. Fireflies perhaps? The fog was lifting from the ground as they got further from the canyon and she realised they were approaching the edge of a swamp. Something huge and dark moved and she stopped abruptly. In her peripheral vision she saw the others do the same. A long low rumble began and the hair on her arms stood up.

'Captain?' said Len. The low rumble grew and grew, and in seconds it had become a screeching roar.

'Get back,' she ordered, as the dark object approached them. The smell of sulphur wafted towards her. 'Everyone, get back from the swamp.' She'd barely finished speaking when the screeching cut off and a serpent head the size of Epizon shot through the mist towards them.

Lyssa dropped to the ground before rolling to one side and springing back to her feet. She looked around wildly, registering Phyleus and Epizon sprinting away from the swamp, Len clinging to Epizon's back. The serpent thing swung towards her, its long neck disappearing into the swamp behind it, and she froze. It hissed and moved its head slowly from side to side. Lyssa stayed still, praying to Athena that it couldn't see her if she didn't move. It opened gigantic jaws, exactly like a snake would, and a massive black tongue flicked between rows of lethally sharp teeth almost as tall as she was. She took a deep breath and held it.

A mane of black, spiky horns framed the back of the creature's head, and long writhing tendrils hung under its jaw, skimming the ground, tickling the earth. Lyssa eased back a step, her skin crackling with energy. The creature froze, then in a flash it turned to face her, scarlet eyes aflame. Those red lights hadn't been fireflies, she realised with a shock. They were eyes. Six eyes. The monster screeched and lunged for her.

LYSSA RAN STRAIGHT TOWARDS IT, ducking under its jaw and racing though the slimy tentacles, guessing that the serpent would expect her to go in the opposite direction. The smell of sulphur was so strong it almost knocked her off balance as she skimmed near the edge of the swamp. She swerved, heading inland as she burst out of the mass of tendrils. She could see the Hydra's massive body now and her heart raced. Rising from its bulk were two more winding necks, their flashing red eyes visible in the mist above.

The Hydra's body was huge and it had numerous heads, most mortal but one immortal. Hercules found the Hydra on a hill near the springs of the Amymone. He forced it to show itself and grabbed it but the Hydra was able to wind itself around him. Hercules tried to smash its heads with his club but every head he killed was replaced by two more. A huge crab came up from the swamp to aid the Hydra and bit Hercules's foot.

EXCERPT FROM

THE LIBRARY BY APOLLODORUS
Written 300–100 B.C.
Paraphrased by Eliza Raine

16

HERCULES

H ercules breathed out slowly as he approached the swamp. The Hydra was a magnificent beast. Its huge body was mostly submerged in the inky black pool, but three necks the size of tree trunks wound up out of the water. They were covered in interlocking scales that shone like metal when they moved. One snakelike head, with a ring of fierce horns projecting from behind the skull, was low to ground at the edge of the swamp. Hercules guessed the Hydra had found his daughter.

HE WONDERED briefly what his father would think of him following Lyssa and her crew to the Hydra. It had been tactical, not a necessity. If that pathetic little satyr had found the bridge, he would have too, he was sure. And being behind them meant that he had all the distractions he needed for the monster, with the added bonus that it might finish off his interfering daughter for him. He ran for the opposite side of the swamp, keeping low to the ground, watching the two unoccupied heads. They were only discernible in the thicker mist above him by their shining red eyes.

He slowed as he reached the bank, excitement rolling through him. He needed no time to get his breath back; he was used to exerting himself. Without taking his eyes off the red eyes he moved his hands to the scabbard at his belt. A crystal clear ring sounded as he pulled the shining silver sword from its sheath. Instantly the two heads moving slowly in the mist above him froze.

Hercules smiled and held the mighty weapon in front of him in both hands. He flexed his wrists to the right, then left, testing the weight of the sword. It was perfect. The heads were descending from the mist. Two gaping maws lowered themselves one on each side of him, brutal teeth gnashing the air above writhing tentacles. Hercules's god-given strength surged through him and he gripped the sword harder, channelling his power. *Keravnos* began to glow red and a bark of laughter escaped Hercules's mouth. The Hydra heads hissed, and he felt he could feel the sound in his bones.

This was going to be fun.

17

HEDONE

Hedone was transfixed. Even the acrid smell of sulphur barely registered with her as she watched Hercules. He looked like a god, holding the colossal glowing red sword in front of him as the monsters approached. His perfect frame was clad in black, making the glowing sword and fierce eyes of the Hydra stand out all the more. Her breath caught as the beast hissed and Hercules raised the sword. The head on the right darted down, as the one on the left moved higher over him. He swung the sword in an arc high over his head, warding off the tongue that shot out from above him and coming down on the other neck hard. There was a loud clank as the weapon made contact. Hercules faltered and Theseus drew in breath next to her.

'Was that...?' he murmured.

'Metal?' finished Psyche, who was standing on his other side. They were far enough out of the canyon that the mist had lifted, but still well away from the swamp. Theseus was not the type to rush into a situation without a plan. 'He's doing well,' observed Psyche. Pride welled in Hedone, though she knew she had no right to it.

'Yes,' answered Theseus, still quiet. 'That's quite a weapon. It's called *Keravnos* and Aphrodite was worried that Zeus had handed it over.'

Hedone watched the glowing sword as it moved with Hercules, rolling and swiping and clashing as the two serpentine heads drew back and snapped forward again and again. He was magnificent. Suddenly, he was still, crouched low to the ground. Cold clutched at Hedone. Was he injured? She craned her neck forward, trying to see more. One of the horn-rimmed heads lowered fast, the strange tendrils hanging from its jaw writhing around as they neared the ground.

'I think the tendrils are like a cat's whiskers. They feel for things its eyes cannot see,' Theseus mused. 'Interesting.' With a burst of energy that made Hedone jump, Hercules launched himself upwards, higher than the creature's head. As he leaped over its shining neck he brought his blade down. The red glow intensified as it made contact with the scales, and an even louder clang rang across the swamp. Then the blade was sinking through the beast's neck and she could just hear the triumphant roar coming from Hercules as he landed hard on the ground. The sword had gone clean through, and the totally severed head rolled towards him. She could make out his smile as he lifted a booted foot and kicked the head towards the swamp. The red light in its eyes was fading as it rolled towards the inky liquid.

'It is metal!' exclaimed Psyche, pointing. The exposed stump of the creature's neck was flailing around, bashing into the roaring second head, and Hedone could clearly see that there was no blood, just metal that glowed ice blue. The third head, previously out of sight on the other side of the swamp, appeared high above Hercules. He raised *Keravnos* in challenge.

BUT NEITHER OF the other two heads attacked. They both rose high into the mist, the necks extended. The red eyes glowed and the roaring quietened as the flailing neck slowed down. The blue glow didn't dim, though. If anything it was getting brighter.

'I don't like this,' said Theseus. Hedone was standing shoulder to shoulder with him, and she could feel him tensing up. 'That light should be dying, not getting brighter. If this is one of Hephaestus's automatons, given life by Athena, then this will not be so simple.' Anxiety gripped her as Hercules bellowed.

'Do you fear me?' He shook his great sword at the two remaining heads.

The blue light was suddenly so bright that Hedone had to look away. When she turned back, the metal scales on the severed neck were multiplying. They were building on themselves, clinking as they interlocked, rebuilding the neck that had been removed. She gasped. They weren't just rebuilding, they were multiplying. The neck was splitting into two as it grew. Horns were forming before her eyes, shiny liquid metal hardening into brutal points as she watched. The snakelike head was next, the slimy-looking tendrils growing from its jaw as the vicious teeth took shape. In under a minute two fully formed Hydra heads rose to meet their siblings in the mist, red eyes glowing bright.

'Shit,' breathed Psyche.

'Yeah,' said Theseus.

Hedone couldn't speak. She had to help Hercules.

18

ERYX

E ryx had never been more relieved in his life than when he stepped off the invisible bridge onto solid ground. He didn't care that he could barely see through the thick white fog, or that he could still hear Albion whimpering behind him. He was off that infernal bridge and anything else would be easy. The only part of this Trial he had enjoyed so far was seeing Busiris forced to part with some silver. It had been the only way to encourage a boy who had seen the other crews make it to the centre of Libra to tell them how to do it. Eryx walked forward, his eyes fixed on his captain ahead of him. Tall rocky banks rose up on either side of them, funnelling them through the mist.

He didn't like that anything could be waiting for them at the end of the path they were walking, and that they had no way out. The unforgiving rock walls looked un-scalable. His nerves hummed and he bounced as he walked, pent-up energy for the upcoming fight rocketing around inside him. He might see her again today. She would likely be there.

The thought had barely registered before he scolded

himself. He shouldn't be thinking about that blue-haired witch. She had made a fool of him. Better she didn't have the chance to do it again.

Her face lingered in his mind, though. She had walked right up to him, sat and talked to him at the feast. Nobody had ever done that before. He knew now that her intentions were insincere, but gods did she have courage.

A flash of blue light through the fog snapped him out of his thoughts. He sped up, towards Antaeus.

'What was that?' he asked, quietly.

'I don't know.' They picked up their pace and in moments had cleared the canyon, the fog lifting and a great swamp visible before them.

HERCULES WAS HOLDING A HUGE SWORD, a weapon that looked like it was built for a giant rather than a human, which was glowing red as he slashed and twirled and leaped out of the way of at least a dozen terrifyingly massive serpent heads. The long necks looked as though they were tangling with each other and Eryx thought of Antaeus's writhing snake tattoo. There was another blue flash and he watched, amazed, as a severed snake head dropped into the black swamp with a huge splash. The severed stump was the source of the blue glow and what looked like liquid metal began to flow, forming a new head. Two new heads, he realised with a start. An orange light caught his eye on his right. Theseus was near the canyon entrance, along with the two women from his crew. He had an arrow nocked in a bow, orange flames flickering at its tip. The beautiful dark-haired woman, Hedone, tugged at his arm, shaking her head. Theseus ignored her and let the arrow fly.

'Hercules!' screamed Hedone. Eryx looked towards the

massive man as the arrow struck. It bounced harmlessly off him as he rolled under a writhing mass of necks. The beasts' heads were starting to snap at each other.

'Stop cutting off heads, you fool,' shouted Theseus, shaking his head. 'He's going to get us all killed,' he said and grabbed the now sobbing Hedone. 'Pull yourself together! We need a plan, come on!'

He began pulling her towards the canyon mouth but halted mid-stride when he saw Eryx and Antaeus, then carried on, dragging the gorgeous girl with him. The older woman scowled at the swamp and then set off after them. Antaeus nodded as he passed them.

'Leaving so soon, clever Theseus?' he said. Theseus did not reply, just started running back down the canyon path.

19

HERCULES

He couldn't keep this up. Even with unfailing strength, an impervious coat and a magic sword, Hercules knew he wasn't going to win like this. He rolled yet again, barely stopping himself from burying the sword in yet another metallic shiny neck. It was so instinctual. He gritted his teeth as huge jaws snapped at him, desperately trying to think of a way to kill the monster.

'Hercules!' someone in the distance yelled. He didn't dare look away from the snapping teeth in front of him but he heard the arrow as it sailed towards him. It bounced off his lion skin and fell to the wet ground.

He growled. So his rivals were worried about his progress? The teeth got closer, forcing him to back up further towards the creature's body. He knew he had to be careful of the swamp, though; there was a reason it smelled of sulphur. His boot tip had sizzled and melted when he had last got too close. As he backed up slowly his eyes fell on the arrow, flames still flickering gently at its end.

Fire. Fire killed almost everything.

Hercules lunged forward, making sure he got under the

head that was looming over him. He was fast, but so was the Hydra. As his fingers closed around the arrow, a black tongue as thick as his arm shot out at him. The force of it knocked him sideways and the massive sword caught in the ground.

He let go of it as he spun across the soil towards another open set of lethal jaws. Superhuman strength surged through him and he pushed hard against the ground mid-roll. His strength launched him to his feet and he threw the arrow towards the swamp. It whistled as it flew past the now seemingly countless heads and disappeared into the darkness below. A few heads had followed its motion but most stayed focused on him. He crouched, ready to lunge for his sword, when there was a ground-shaking bang. Huge orange flames shot up from the swamp, leaping up between the columns of scaly necks. They grew as he watched, all of the Hydra heads shrieking and hissing. It stamped its massive feet but did not move from the fiery pit. Maybe it was unable to leave the swamp? The flames flickered higher, burning red. Triumph seeped into Hercules as he scooped up *Keravnos*. Let the monster burn.

A SCUTTLING noise was breaking through the sound of the monster wailing. Hercules raised his sword, wary. He could hear hundreds of tapping sounds, like an army of huge ants. He looked around, confused. Spinning, checking the canyon path, he was vaguely surprised to see the giant crew stood staring at him. They hadn't even got the courage to try to take on the monster. He laughed. The second Trial was his and once again, nobody else had got a look-in. Immortality was going to be easier to win than he'd thought.

Pain seared through his foot. He cried out and looked

down. A crab, as metal as the Hydra and the size of a small dog, had a sharp pincer clamped onto his melted leather boot. He lifted his leg and tried to shake it off but it wouldn't let go.

He brought *Keravnos* down, easily severing the pincer from the crab's body, but his triumph was short-lived. Crabs were pouring from the inky-black swamp, moving through the flames like they were nothing. He looked up at the Hydra heads, now lined up and quiet. As one, they bellowed, a mechanical screeching sound that made him drop *Keravnos* and fling his hands over his ears. He heard a giant behind him yell. Then the crabs swarmed over him and he could hear nothing but the clacking of metal pincers.

20

LYSSA

Lyssa gave an involuntary fist-pump as Hercules disappeared under the wave of crabs. Phyleus frowned at her.

'You know we have to get past the crabs as well?' he said.

'I couldn't care less about killing the Hydra if Hercules is dead,' she snarled.

'Even though it nearly killed you just now?'

'It didn't nearly kill me. I outran it easily,' she lied. She had outrun it but it certainly hadn't been easy. Sometimes being the girl who ran could have its uses. In truth, not only had the Hydra nearly killed her, she had no idea how they could kill it, crabs or not. They'd stayed out of reach of the beast since her close call and she had been unable to think of anything, watching in horror as Hercules slashed off heads with his ridiculous divine sword. The man was a maniac. The thing now had more heads than she could count.

'Captain, I think I have an idea,' said Len. He was pale, his bravery on invisible bridges not apparent when it came to enormous flesh-eating monsters.

'Thank the gods for that,' she said.

'I think one of the heads has different-coloured eyes. That one might control the rest of the being.'

Lyssa frowned at him.

'How in Olympus can you tell that? I can't even count the heads, let alone see differences in them. Is this another time where you can see different things to humans?'

'Maybe. I don't know. There are fourteen heads. I'll point it out to you,' Len said, his voice hitching at the last bit. They all turned from Len to the Hydra. It was ignoring the pile of crabs trying to tear Hercules apart, and all its heads were now snapping at each other or the huge flames that surrounded it. The firelight flickering off its metal scales made it look like it was made from gold. It was breath-taking, really, and she started to understand why Athena would create such a thing. It was both an engineering and strategic masterpiece.

'THAT ONE, there, at the back, fighting with the other two. It's got a lighter ring in the middle of its eyes, almost yellow.'

They all squinted.

'I can't see it,' said Phyleus.

'Me either,' said Epizon.

Lyssa looked hard. The eyes all seemed red.

'I'm sorry, Len, you're the only one who can see it.'

He paled further. 'I'm going to have to go out there, aren't I?'

'I'm afraid so.'

'So do we need to cut off that head? How we going to get to it? We can't just bait one of fourteen heads,' said Phyleus.

'We're going to go straight to it,' said Lyssa, staring at the snapping heads high above them.

'How?'

'We need a little help. I'll be faster on my own. Stay here,' she said, and sprinted towards the canyon mouth.

21

LYSSA

The fog had enveloped her before she made it a few feet into the canyon and she slowed, wary of the heavy silence and limited visibility. She trusted she couldn't go off course with the rock faces penning her in, but nevertheless she walked slowly, aware that the edge of the island was just ahead of her. Her eyes were fixed on the ground and she tested the soil with her toes before she committed any weight to her hesitant steps. She was so tense and careful that she nearly knocked Phyleus out when he said her name.

'Gods, it's only me!' he exclaimed as he ducked only just in time for her punch to sail over him.

'What the hell are you doing here!' she yelled, her temper soaring with the shot of adrenaline. 'I told you to wait, and I'm your CAPTAIN.' She grabbed his shirt front and shouted the last word into his face. 'If you can't follow orders, then you are off the crew!'

Phyleus had both hands raised above his head in submission.

'It was Epizon's idea, not mine! He said you might need

help. I told him I doubted it.' She glared at him. He stared back, defiance dancing in his deep brown eyes. She knew he wasn't scared of her. He had seen her fight. He had seen her fuel the ship, he had seen her sling dead bodies overboard. He had seen her escape from harpies and shoot at enemies. But he had never seen her truly lose her temper. He had yet to see the Rage when she couldn't contain it.

'Is this a game to you?' she demanded, letting go of his shirt. He brushed it down so it hung straight, and the sight of his vanity set her temper flaring inside her again. 'Leave your bloody shirt alone!'

'You may be my captain now but I can still dress myself, and take pride in how I look,' he said, standing up tall. 'And yes, it is a game to me. And to you, and to all the other heroes in this. A game devised by the gods. You are willingly participating.' His eyes held hers, challenging her.

'Willingly? You think I'm doing this willingly?' Her nails were biting into her palms.

'Who doesn't want immortality? Don't start your martyr bit about stopping Hercules, you wouldn't still be trying to kill the Hydra if you only cared about that.'

As he shot the words at her, Lyssa realised that they may be true. Why was she still trying? If Hercules wasn't dead under all those crabs, then winning Trials was the best way to stop him, she reasoned. She opened her mouth to tell him this, but was cut off by a scream, long and high. They both turned towards the sound, which had come from the opposite direction to the swamp. Lyssa started towards it, dropping to her hands and knees as she reached the island edge, feeling for the invisible bridge. Phyleus moved further along and began to do the same. It only took a moment to find the cool glass. As she was already kneeling she crawled out onto it, using her hands to check for the solid surface before shuffling forwards.. She moved along on her hands and knees as quickly as she could, with no choice but to look down. There was nothing below her but endless blackness and she sped up as much as she dared, desperate to be back on opaque ground.

When she thought she was about halfway across she realised there were others on the bridge ahead of her, not moving. She scowled. She had passed the giants, standing seemingly awestruck at the canyon mouth, so it must be Theseus.

'Are you all right?' she called. Two heads turned to her. She shuffled faster. It was Theseus, and his first mate, Psyche, standing on the bridge. They were bent over Hedone, who was crying gently, half lying down. 'What happened?' she said as she reached them.

Hedone was truly stunning, even with tears streaking down her face. Psyche looked down at her, annoyance plain on her dark face.

'Hedone fell,' Theseus answered. Lyssa's muscles constricted. She'd be a crying mess too if she'd fallen on this bridge. 'She'll be OK, but we need to get her back to the islands.'

'Why were you coming back over the bridge?' asked Lyssa, carefully standing up. Theseus looked at her but said nothing. Maybe he had the same plan she did. Lyssa could play this game, she decided.

'Can I help you?' asked Phyleus's voice behind her. He was talking to Hedone, she realised. Hedone gave him a wobbly smile.

'I just need a moment, then I'll be OK. I slipped and...' She faltered. Lyssa felt a wave of sympathy and found herself wanting to hear more of Hedone's husky, sensual voice. She wondered fleetingly what it would be like if her own power was to be ridiculously sexy instead of bad tempered.

'It's OK, take all the time you need,' Phyleus told Hedone, his warm brown eyes earnest. Lyssa grunted.

'We don't have *all the time you need*,' she parroted. 'We need to get back to our crew and kill that thing, remember?'

'Right. Sure.' Phyleus nodded, not taking his eyes off the beautiful woman. Theseus reached down and gently pulled her to her feet. She didn't struggle but fear filled her eyes. Lyssa felt another pang of sympathy but squashed it. She needed to focus.

22

LYSSA

As soon as they got to the island Hedone dropped to her knees, stroking the earth beneath her. Lyssa would happily have done the same, but she had a plan to see through.

'Is there anything—' Phyleus started to say but Lyssa grabbed his arm and yanked him towards the other side of the island and the bridge.

'She's not our problem, Phyleus. If you're here to help me, then you're helping me.'

'I'd be more help to her. You just yell at me all the time,' he protested.

'That's because you're deluded, self-obsessed and bought your way onto my ship instead of earning it.' She jogged towards the bridge, ending the conversation. It was a relief to use the glass handrail, and to be able to see the next island clearly and close. They sped back the way they had come, moving too fast to speak.

'Are we going back to the *Alastor*?' Phyleus was panting slightly as they entered a hauler and were forced to stand still for a moment.

'No,' she said.

He frowned. 'Where are we going, then?'

'Back to that island with the huge houses.'

'Right.' The doors slid open. They weren't far away now. They stepped out and jogged past neat rows of single-storey homes, flimsy railings defining outside gardens belonging to each. This was the suburbs.

'Do you think Theseus is running away?'

'No. I think he's got the same idea I have,' she said.

'Which is...?'

'You'll see.'

She heard him sigh, and smiled. If he was going to be here, at least she could remind him who was in charge.

SHE SLOWED as she reached the house she was aiming for, the one with the long balconies around it. She peered up at them, looking for signs of activity in the windows. Everything was still.

Lyssa headed slowly towards the garden, her boots making no sound as she stepped onto the lush green grass. And, as she had remembered, a brand new, fully equipped longboat was tied loosely to a wooden stump at the island edge. She held her hand out towards it.

'My plan,' she said, unable to stop feeling pleased with herself. Phyleus's eyes widened.

'We're going to steal it?' he hissed.

'Yep,' she said, making her way to the boat.

'No, we can't do that,' said Phyleus.

She glared at him over her shoulder. He looked more scared than he had of anything else they had encountered so far.

'Then you can stay here. Bye.' She skirted around a children's swing and prayed that the owners of the house weren't at home.

When she reached the boat, she pulled gently on the tether. It floated right up to the island edge and she stepped easily on board before sitting down on the wooden bench and starting to undo the knots keeping it tied to the post. Phyleus stood in the garden and looked at her beseechingly. She raised her eyebrows at him and carried on working the rope with both hands. A moment later, he hurried towards her, passed the swing and clambered into the boat.

'I can't believe you've made me do this,' he hissed as he sat on the other bench, folding his arms. 'You've turned me into a common criminal.'

'What do you think we do on the *Alastor* when we're not trying to stop an evil bastard from becoming immortal?' she shot at him dryly. Phyleus didn't answer.

'Aha,' she said as the rope swung loose. She climbed over the bench seats to the front of the boat and grabbed the small wooden wheel, projecting herself at the little boat, trying to make a connection. 'No more invisible bridges.'

Lyssa smiled as the longboat responded to her touch, rising and turning straight towards the centre of Libra.

23

ERYX

E ryx stared in dismay as Bergion flew through the air above him. There was a sickening thud as the giant crashed to the earth. A long groan escaped him.

'He's alive,' Eryx breathed, relieved. Albion, on his left, roared and charged towards the closest reptilian head as it swooped and swerved, looking for its next victim. 'Wait!' Eryx yelled.

Albion ignored him and kept running. Eryx turned desperately to Antaeus, who was breathing heavily beside him. 'We can't win like this, Captain.' Antaeus grunted.

'For once, I agree,' Busiris said behind him. Eryx huffed at the cowards voice. Busiris hadn't even attempted to get near the beast. 'One of the heads is different to the others,' Busiris said, eyes fixed on the weaving mass of slick serpent heads.

'Really?'

'Yes. The horns are longer and there's something different about the eyes. You need to get to that head.' As he spoke there was a flash of light behind them. They all looked up as a longboat, sails shimmering in the fog, flew over them, towards the beast. Eryx saw a flash of red hair. It was Captain Lyssa.

The boat flew over a snapping Hydra head and Eryx yelled as his attention refocused on the creature. Albion was halfway up one of its long, scaled necks. Other heads were snapping at him but he had his legs clamped firmly around the things' neck and was batting the heads away with his barbed club. Admiration pulsed through Eryx. 'We need to help him,' he shouted and started forward.

'Wait! I have a better idea.' A shadow moved over them and they looked up in unison as another longboat, this one narrower with sails like those on a Typhoon, soared over their heads.

'Theseus,' growled Antaeus.

'Get on one of those longboats and get to that head. The one that's different. That one will be controlling the monster.' Busiris said, urgency in his voice. Antaeus looked down at the gold-skinned man.

'I'm too big for one of those boats,' he said. 'You two go.'

'Me?' Busiris spluttered. Eryx narrowed his eyes.

'You know which head it is. Come on,' and he grabbed Busiris's arm before he could protest any further.

ERYX SPRINTED TOWARDS THE SWAMP, every nerve alert as he got within range of the lethal snake heads. Most of them were distracted, snapping at Albion, who was still resolutely hanging onto the scaly neck and swinging his club mania-cally. Eryx glanced up and saw that Theseus's longboat was high above the Hydra. Three heads were shooting up out of the writhing mass, snapping at the quick little vessel as it darted about.

'Which head?' Eryx yelled as they got closer.

'I can't tell from here,' shouted back Busiris. His voice was strained. Cowardly idiot.

There was a screech and Eryx's head snapped up. They had caught the beast's attention.

24

LYSSA

P hyleus wasted no time getting off the longboat when Lyssa sailed to a stop next to Epizon and Len.

'Come on, Len, get in,' she shouted impatiently. The satyr reluctantly hauled himself into the small boat.

'Stupid human eyes,' he muttered as he righted himself on one of the benches. The boat rose back into the air quickly and Len yelped, grabbing at his seat as they soared over the top of the Hydra.

'Which head is it?' Lyssa asked, keeping the boat higher than the snapping jaws below. Len peered cautiously over the edge.

'Erm...' he said. Lyssa groaned.

'Come on, Len!' She could see that Theseus had indeed had the same idea as she had, and his boat was zipping between heads below them. She could see Psyche in her gleaming gold armour, firing perfectly aimed arrows at the beast's heads any time they got too close. 'It looks like Theseus is looking for something in particular too.'

'Captain, look,' said Len, sounding surprised. She leaned over the edge of the boat, following his pointing hand. Eryx, the half-giant, was climbing one of the great necks of the creature, pulling himself up each metal plate with his strong arms and legs. Lyssa frowned.

'What's he...' She trailed off as, with a roar, Eryx launched himself at Theseus's boat, just as it whizzed past him. He caught the back of it and his weight pulling the vessel down propelled Theseus and Psyche backwards, over his head. Lyssa heard Psyche scream as she started to fall.

Lyssa thrust her hand onto the mast and willed her control into the boat. It didn't respond like the *Alastor* but it did shoot forward. She aimed the boat down, through the entwined necks of the Hydra, its teeth flashing on either side of them. Len began to yell unintelligibly but she ignored him, focusing on the falling figures framed against the burning swamp below. The flames grew hotter as they raced downwards but she held her nerve, willing the little boat to move faster. Just a few feet from the flames she passed their falling bodies and spun the boat sharply. There was a thud as they landed hard against the wood in the bottom of the boat, and Len squealed as he was bounced off his bench and into the hull with them.

'Hold on,' she yelled as a Hydra head swooped after her and she sped in the opposite direction with a lurch.

'Thank you,' Theseus gasped behind her, and a sickening crunch accompanied another lurch. She spun around and came face to face with yellowing teeth as tall as she was. A huge jaw had bitten through the back of the boat. Theseus and Psyche were scrambling towards her and Len, away from the teeth. She refocused her concentration and the boat rocketed forward. She watched as the head reared back, eyes flashing, and then darted towards them again. They were only just out of reach when its jaws clamped shut, closing on thin air.

'Ha!' she yelled before she could stop herself. Rage-fuelled confidence powered through her.

'Captain! Captain, that's the head!' She realised Len was shouting at her. 'The one that just tried to eat us, that's the head!'

She slowed the broken boat and willed it towards the ground, well out of reach of the Hydra.

'Everyone out!' she yelled, and turned to the dishevelled Theseus and Psyche. They were both still on the bottom of the boat, gripping the wooden bench that was left and looking dazed. 'Out!' she yelled again. The boat hadn't stopped but it had slowed and they were not far off the ground. Len saluted, grabbed the side of the boat and vaulted over the edge. Theseus got to his feet quickly, pulling Psyche up with him.

'Consider your debt paid, Captain Lyssa,' he said, and followed Len out of the boat. Psyche nodded at her as she went after him. As soon as the boat was empty Lyssa steered it back round to face the Hydra head. It snapped at her as she hovered just out of reach, its fat tentacles writhing a few feet above the fiery swamp, the flickering light reflecting off its dark metal scales.

'Gods, I hope that satyr is right,' she muttered, and flew the longboat straight at the monster.

25

LYSSA

L yssa veered sharply upwards as the creature's black tongue darted out towards her. She tried not to hold her breath as her boat shot over the top of the horned head, missing the slimy tongue by inches. *She was not the girl who ran.* Rage poured through her and her muscles ached with tension. She gripped the wood hard and concentrated, almost completely reversing her direction and dropping sharply. The boat plummeted and her red hair flew up around her face. She counted to three and halted the boat in its tracks. The Hydra had tried to spin around to get her but her manoeuvre had been too tight.

SHE WAS right behind it and it couldn't see her. The head moved around slowly, tentacles probing the air, looking for Lyssa and her little boat. She crept along behind, anticipation building almost unbearably. She was only a few feet behind the huge horns framing its long head. Just a little closer and she would be able to jump onto its neck. She climbed onto the bench and started to count backwards, crouching down on the balls of her feet. Three... Two...

There was a roar above her and the Hydra's head snapped back suddenly as it looked towards the sky. Lyssa barely had time to register the largest horn as it impaled the side of her longboat. There was a sickly hiss and the Hydra spun its head, aware now that something was caught in its horns. The boat was thrown from side to side, the shining horn protruding though the splintered wood, and Lyssa threw her arms around the bench as she slipped, scrabbling to keep hold of something.

Her mind whirled as she was thrashed about, desperately clinging on as the creature tried to displace the boat. If she let go for a second she would be thrown to the fiery swamp below, and no amount of inhuman strength would save her from that. The roar sounded again, then there was a loud clang and the beast stopped moving. The boat creaked and swung sharply, now dangling vertically from the righted horn. Lyssa scrabbled up the bench seat as fast as she could and launched herself up towards the horn. As she grabbed at it with one hand, another, much bigger than her own, appeared around it. Eryx, the half-giant, hauled himself up into her view. He had both legs wrapped around the creature's neck and was pulling himself up to get to the snakelike head.

The beast began to thrash again and she reached for the horn with her free hand. She pulled herself up using her arms, feeling the Rage pulsing though her and drawing confidence from using her strength. She tried to imitate Eryx, wrapping her legs around the back of the Hydra's neck, but she was much shorter than him and couldn't get any purchase on the gleaming metal. Suddenly something grabbed at her leg. She kicked out hard but she had reacted too late. In a heartbeat she was torn away from the horn she'd been gripping, her desperate hands sliding against smooth metal. She yelled in fury but couldn't get a grip on anything and then she was swinging by her ankle, upside down over the flames. She used her strong stomach muscles to curl up, trying to right herself. Eryx was looking down at her, hanging from the Hydra's neck by his massive legs as it snapped its jaws uselessly. His dark eyes were alive with excitement and in that moment she knew she was not the only one who revelled in a flood of adrenaline.

'Sorry, Captain Lyssa,' he called, and let go.

26

ERYX

E ryx tightened his legs around the Hydra's neck and hung on a moment more, conscious he was wasting precious moments but unable to stop himself. He needed to make sure the red-haired girl landed in Theseus's longboat, where he'd tried to throw her. He wanted to win, but he didn't have a taste for killing innocent folk.

Relief washed through him as he saw her hit the wood with a thud and she began to roar curses at him. He smiled. He hadn't meant to fling Theseus and Psyche from their boat so he owed Captain Lyssa for keeping their lives off his conscience.

He pulled himself back up around the serpent's neck and got his arms wrapped around two horns just as the Hydra head lurched forward, moving down dangerously close to the flames, then veered sharply back upwards. Eryx clamped his mouth shut and gripped the metal beast harder. He narrowed his eyes as they ducked down towards the fire again, adrenaline coursing through his tense body.

The beast wouldn't get rid of him that easily. He pulled hard on the horns, turning his massive body slowly as the thing weaved back and forth and up and down, trying to dislodge him. After a few painstaking minutes he had rotated himself far enough that he was on the back of the thing's neck instead of hanging under its jaw.

Lyssa's wrecked longboat hung beside him, smashing against the gleaming metal scales every time they swerved. He reached forward and grabbed the huge central horn. Just as he wrapped his other hand firmly around it there was an almighty crash and he was catapulted sideways as another gleaming serpent head smashed into the one he was riding. He was barely able to hang on as they flew sideways, both beast heads snarling and hissing. The bottom half of Eryx's body skidded across the scales as the creature recovered, then darted back towards the gaping maw of the new head.

He needed to finish this, now.

Eryx bared his teeth and summoned all of his strength, struggling to get his feet on the writhing neck. He got one huge boot flat against the metal and used the purchase to heave himself forward, reaching his right arm over the fierce horns. Pain lanced through his ribs and he jerked his body backwards. One of the horns had pierced his skin, under his arm. He ignored the stinging pain and scrabbled around with his hand, trying to feel for the Hydra's eye. It thrashed harder as his fingers brushed across something angular and jagged, different to the smooth metal scales. He planted his other boot against the thing's neck and stretched, trying to see over the horns without them impaling him. Another burning surge of pain shot through his torso and he hissed. He clenched his hand into a fist and punched blindly at what he hoped was the Hydra's eye.

A shadow moved over him and he glanced up. The other head was above him, and it was looking straight at him. It opened its mouth slowly, showing lethal teeth, and flicked its tongue out.

Eryx smashed at the eye again with his fist, as hard as he could. With a crack it shattered beneath his hand and the monster roared, whipping its head back. Instinctively he gripped the hole he had just made, surprised to feel nothing inside the thing's head. He pushed his hand further in, feeling around for anything that might control the creature. A loud hiss above him accompanied liquid dripping on his back. Saliva. He was out of time. His hand closed around something cold and spherical and he yanked his arm out of the eyehole, pulling the sphere with him. The effect was instant.

Everything froze. Both the head above him and the one he clung to simply stopped moving. The fierce red eyes glaring down at him dimmed to nothing. The only movement he could see was the flames dancing and flickering below him.

He let out a long breath he hadn't realised he had been holding and looked at the sphere in his hand. It was made of the same dark shining metal as the Hydra and had an intricate pattern carved into it, covering the whole surface. The pattern was glowing faintly blue.

'Well done, Eryx,' said a deep female voice in his head. He was so startled he nearly dropped the sphere, and as he looked around for the source of the voice everything went black.

IT WAS ONLY dark for a split second and then Eryx was standing on the banks of the swamp, alongside his captain.

Antaeus beamed at him, and clapped him hard on the back.

'Congratulations to our victors, the *Orion*.'

Athena was standing before them. She was as beautiful as ever, and pride swelled in Eryx. He had won. He had destroyed the Hydra, won the Trial and was now being addressed by a goddess.

'You will want to attend to that wound,' she said, and gestured at his chest.

He looked down, surprised. Blood was streaming from the tears in his shirt. He couldn't feel it, though. He tentatively touched his chest near the rips. Nothing. 'Your next Trial will be announced in one hour,' Athena said, and vanished.

'WE HAVE something that can help with that.'

Eryx spun around to see Captain Lyssa, with her crew fanned out behind her. She pointed at his chest. 'My medic, Len, tells me that will kill you before the next Trial starts if you don't treat it now.'

'Is it numb yet?' the satyr asked. Eryx nodded.

'Why would you help him?' demanded Antaeus. 'He stopped you winning.'

The red-haired girl shrugged. 'Rather you than Hercules,' she said. 'Has anyone seen him?'

'No. Last I saw he was buried under the metal crabs.'

Eryx blinked at his captain. There were two of him. He knew that wasn't right.

'Er...' he managed to say before he crashed to the ground.

'Get me my bag!' demanded the satyr, rushing over. 'I'm sorry, Captain, but we may already be too late.'

'We can't be. Athena told me to help him. She said he was important,' Lyssa protested.

'Hold on,' was the last thing Eryx heard Antaeus say before everything went black again.

ARTEMIS

SKIES OF OLYMPUS

TRIAL THREE

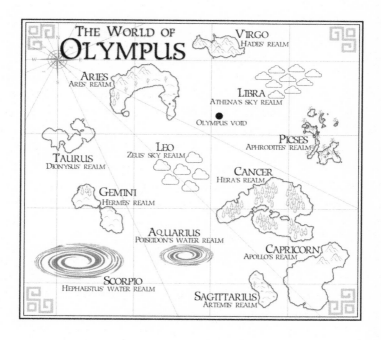

THE WORLD OF
OLYMPUS

VIRGO
HADES' REALM

ARIES
ARES' REALM

LIBRA
ATHENA'S SKY REALM

Olympus void

PICSES
APHRODITES' REALM

LEO
ZEUS' SKY REALM

TAURUS
DIONYSUS' REALM

CANCER
HERA'S REALM

GEMINI
HERMES' REALM

AQUARIUS
POSEIDON'S WATER REALM

CAPRICORN
APOLLO'S REALM

SCORPIO
HEPHAESTUS' WATER REALM

SAGITTARIUS
ARTEMIS' REALM

1

HERCULES

'I thought you weren't supposed to interfere,' said Hercules through gritted teeth.

He immediately regretted speaking. Pain surged through him from head to toe. He couldn't bite back his scream.

'For that, I'll leave some of these wounds unhealed,' Zeus replied, his voice deep and angry. 'I admire your courage, but deplore your stupidity. Next time, you take the girl with you. She can help.'

'Yes, Father,' Hercules mumbled, trying hard to sound contrite.

'If any of the other gods had seen me pluck you from Athena's metal abominations you would have been thrown out of the competition. Without the lion skin the crabs would have killed you. Fool.'

Hercules closed his eyes. There was no good to be had from losing his temper with the lord of the gods. Especially when Zeus was saving his life.

He was back on the *Hybris*, on the cold white marble floor of his washroom, where his father had transported

him. He hadn't felt close to death when he had been in the
middle of the heaving mass of metal crabs and he was sure
he would have fought his way out eventually. But these
wounds would have slowed him down for the next Trial,
that much was true.

'I have enough to worry about, without having to nurse
you,' Zeus snapped as Hercules straightened up. 'That's as
much as I can do without making it obvious I have been
involved. For the next Trial, use your head, and use the girl!'
He vanished in a flash of bright white light.

Hercules let out a groan and used the copper bath-tub to
pull himself to a sitting position. His head swam. He looked
down at his torso and fingered his shredded shirt. Maybe
the crabs would have killed him. The few that had gotten
under the lion skin appeared to have done more damage
than he had realised. He tenderly touched the already
fading scars on his chest. If Zeus said he should use Evadne,
he would. It didn't make him weak to follow a god's orders,
he decided. He concentrated on a mental image of her face.

'Evadne, come to my quarters,' he said.

'Yes, Captain,' she replied immediately, surprise clear in
her voice. He stood up, tentatively, and began to peel off his
shredded clothes.

EVADNE ARRIVED at his rooms in moments and he ordered
her to bathe him. Willingly and carefully, she wiped away
the blood and grime as he let the hot water soothe his
muscles. He didn't ache, exactly, but he was sore where the
pincers had repeatedly bitten into his skin and muscle.

'How...' Evadne started, but she trailed off. He looked
at her.

'Who won the Trial?'

Her eyes dropped from his.

'The *Orion*. Which is good, really. Theseus is your biggest rival, and obviously...' She paused and looked nervously at him. 'Obviously you wouldn't want the *Alastor* to win.'

She was right. If it wasn't him, the giants winning probably was the best outcome of a bad situation. He closed his eyes.

'When is the next Trial being announced?'

'Soon.'

He sat up, water sloshing over the side of the bath. Evadne jumped back, startled.

'How soon?'

'I'm not sure. Asterion is watching the flame dish,' she answered. He stood up, barely able to suppress the shiver caused by the water rolling down his body.

'Get me a towel. Olympus needs to know that their hero lives.'

'Yes, Captain.'

2

ERYX

E ryx coughed as light filtered painfully through his half-closed eyes.

'Welcome back,' rumbled Antaeus.

'Captain?' Eryx croaked, unsure where he was. He raised his head gently, pain throbbing in his skull as he looked around. He was in a bed that wasn't his, but the wood-panelled walls looked like those of the *Orion*. Antaeus was sitting in a big chair beside him, smiling. 'What...'

His voice tailed off as memories started to slam into him. He had been on the Hydra head over the burning swamp, he had smashed its eye and got that weird metal ball, he had... 'Did we win? I thought I saw Athena...' Antaeus cut him off with a deep belly laugh.

'Yes, Brother. We won. You won.' Pride swelled in him and he tried to sit up but his chest constricted painfully.

'Where are we?' he asked, wincing.

'My chambers. Don't get used to it, it's just until you feel better,' he said as Eryx's eyebrows shot up. 'You had us worried. It was close for a while but Captain Lyssa's medic knew about the poison in the Hydra's horns and was able to treat it. He just left.' Antaeus tapped his shoulder, more gently than Eryx would have thought he could manage. 'You've been blue for the best part of the last hour. I didn't know if you would make it.'

'Why would they help us?' Eryx asked slowly, looking down at his bandaged chest. His skin was so pale it was almost white. Antaeus shrugged.

'She said that they were more interested in stopping Hercules than winning themselves, and it was the decent thing to do. But I heard her say something to her medic about Athena believing you were important.' Antaeus leaned forward. 'You know anything about that?'

Eryx screwed his face up.

'I've never spoken to a god in my life,' he said. 'Even Poseidon. You know that.' Antaeus nodded and stood up, his massive frame filling Eryx's vision. 'And I'd have told you if something like that happened.'

'That's what I thought. Get some rest. You need to drink all of that.' He gestured at some sludgy blue liquid in a glass on the stand next to the bed. 'The next Trial will be announced soon.' He strode to the door, paused and turned back. 'Eryx, you did good. Really good.'

Eryx beamed.

WHEN ANTAEUS HAD GONE he laid his head back on the pillow, enjoying how much nicer it was than his own. He'd done it. He'd redeemed himself in his captain's eyes and shown himself a hero to all of Olympus.

A slow cramping pain rolled through his chest and he took a sharp breath in. He reached for the sludge and sniffed it warily. Saliva filled his mouth at the sour smell and he grimaced. If what Antaeus said was true, he'd been saved

for a reason. Why would Athena think he was important?
Was he important?

His fingers were weakening around the glass as he held
it. He tipped some of the blue sludge cautiously into his
mouth and spluttered as he tried to swallow. It was disgusting. But barely moments after he had forced half of the foul
stuff down his throat, the pain in his chest receded to
nothing and a warm drowsiness engulfed him.

3

LYSSA

L yssa scrubbed hard at her smudged, dirty head-
scarf. She'd become quite attached to it, after her
initial protestations. It was more comfortable than
tying her hair back, and though she wouldn't admit it to any
of her crew, she did think it looked good. She held it up to
the porthole in her washroom, inspecting it for lingering
dirt, then, satisfied it was as clean as she was going to get it,
wrung it out over the basin. Hope was skittering around in
her belly, making it impossible for her to settle. Hercules
had been buried under the metal crabs. He had the impervious lion skin and Zeus's sword, but... There had been a lot
of pincers, and nobody had seen him since.

'On board, Captain.' Len's voice sounded in her head.

'Good. Eryx?'

'He'll make it.'

Lyssa didn't reply. She wasn't sure how she felt towards
the giant who had dangled her by the ankle and dropped
her over a pit of flames, and she didn't know why Athena
had told her to save him, or told Len how to. Why had
Athena proclaimed her a hero, forced her into the Trials,

then insisted they save their rivals? She had transported everyone to their own ships when Eryx collapsed; all except Len, who she sent straight to the *Orion* to help Eryx. Were the giants going to win? If so, why did she have to be involved at all? She scowled at her reflection as she wrapped the damp head-scarf across her wild curls.

'Stop being stupid,' she muttered aloud. Of course an omnipotent goddess kept things from her. She'd been chosen for a reason. She was going to help stop Hercules. It didn't matter if the *Orion* won.

Immortality. The word popped into her head, with surprising clarity. She stared at her own green eyes in the mirror. Was Phyleus right? Did she want to be immortal? What would living forever mean? It wouldn't just be her. She would have Epizon, and Abderos, Len and... And Phyleus. Maybe she should make more of an effort with him, if she might have to put up with him for a long time.

She snorted aloud at the direction of her thoughts. They hadn't won a Trial. Worrying about who she would be spending her immortal life with was laughably pointless. 'One step at a time, Lyssa,' she said, stepping back from the mirror. Hercules hadn't won. He might even be dead. And that was something to celebrate.

LYSSA HAD no idea where her first mate was, but she wanted to talk to him. 'Epizon?' she asked mentally.

'Cargo deck,' came his quiet response. She sat down on the end of her bunk and laced up her boots, then headed out of her rooms to the hauler at the back of the ship. When she reached the cargo deck Epizon was sat on the crate again, watching Tenebrae. She was staring back at him, her purple scales shimmering in the light from the portholes and her eyes bright and unblinking.

'You sure it's a good idea for you to be alone with her down here?'

Epizon looked at Lyssa, his eyes slightly unfocused. She thought of when she'd been alone with the creature. How happy and detached she had felt, for no reason. Her eyebrows creased in concern. 'Ep?'

He blinked.

'Yeah, it's fine,' he mumbled. 'Len said there's not enough light down here for her to do anything serious.'

'Len is guessing,' replied Lyssa, pulling herself up onto the crate next to him. He handed her a hip-flask and she took it gratefully.

'Long few days, huh?' he said. She nodded as she tipped the flask back, relishing the burn of the ouzo. 'How are you doing?'

'Good. I'm good. I don't know why Athena wanted us to save the half-giant.' Epizon scowled.

'Because it's the right thing to do? And he could have dropped you into the flames but he dropped you safely into a longboat?'

'Not everybody is as virtuous as you, Ep. There'll be more motive than that. We should keep an eye on the giants. I wonder if they're supposed to win.' She tipped the flask to her lips again.

'Nobody is *supposed* to win, Lyssa. It's a competition between mortals; the gods can't decide who'll win, it's up to us. The heroes.'

She snorted, handing him back his flask. 'So you're saying the gods aren't getting involved? Why was Len transported back to the *Orion* to help, then? If Athena is breaking the rules, you can bet Zeus, Poseidon and Aphrodite are too.'

'Hmmm. Hercules did pull that sword out of nowhere,' Epizon conceded. He took a long drag from the flask and they sat in silence. Tenebrae stared, eyes flicking between them.

'Do you think he's dead?'

'I hope so. But until we know for sure...' She nodded at him.

'I know. We assume the worst.' They lapsed into silence again.

'Do you want to win?' Lyssa said eventually. Epizon turned to her, surprised.

'Well, yeah. Don't you?'

'Honestly, I hadn't got past the thought of facing Hercules. Now we're here, doing this, risking our lives... It's hard not to think about it.'

'Imagine what you could achieve with eternity,' said Epizon.

'What? What would you achieve? It would just be us and the gods. Forever. Might be kind of lonely.' Epizon put his hand on hers, for the briefest moment, then pulled it away.

'You'll never be alone again, Lyssa. We win this together, or not at all.'

A small laugh escaped her. 'We should probably start winning before we see this conversation through.'

He smiled at her. 'The next one. The next one will be ours.'

'What do we do about her?' she inclined her head at Tenebrae.

'I don't know. Should we take her up top again, try to communicate?' He sounded wary.

'Let's see what the next Trial is, how much time we have.

And we should ask Len.' Lyssa looked down, fiddling with her hands in her lap, uncomfortable with what she was about to ask. 'Do you... Do you want to talk about what happened? What you saw when you collapsed?'

'Not today,' he answered, softly. She was relieved. She would do anything, anything at all for Epizon, and she couldn't stand to see him in pain. She had avoided asking him how he'd ended up on Libra for years, because she didn't want to shatter the image she had of the strong, kind man before her. She knew it was selfish. That he may want somebody to tell. That maybe he had no story at all, and she was unnecessarily creating one. Either way, she sagged in relief at knowing she wasn't going to have to find out today.

'Hercules is alive,' Phyleus's voice rang across the quiet cargo deck. Lyssa's head snapped up as he strode over to them.

'How do you—'

He cut her off before she finished. 'He just sent a flame message out to all the ships. He said that he wanted everyone to know that he was saved by his almighty lion skin and that he was fighting fit for the next Trial.'

Anger and disappointment coursed through Lyssa. She had been stupid to hope.

'No gods involved, my eye,' she growled. 'There's no way he survived all those metal pincers on his own.'

'Didn't Athena just save the half-giant?' Phyleus shrugged. 'He's not he only one getting help.'

'Athena is supposed to be backing us! Poseidon should be helping the giants, Athena should be helping us!' She realised as she shouted the words that they sounded petty. But it was true. Athena was using her, not backing her. Even the god who chose her didn't think she could win.

· · ·

SHE JUMPED OFF THE CRATE, skin tingling as her temper soared. Phyleus took a step back.

'You really wanted him dead, huh?' he said.

'Of course I did,' she hissed. 'I was wrong to hope it would be this easy.'

'Easy?' Phyleus said incredulously. 'Easy isn't a word I would use to describe the last few days.'

'Nobody has died yet,' she snapped. He gaped at her.

'And that's your definition of easy?'

'Grow up, Phyleus. Join the real word. The real Olympus. The one outside your aristocratic courts and mansions, the one where people die.'

Anger flashed across his face, the first time she had seen something stronger than defiance or annoyance since the loathing glare he had given Lady Lamia.

'I've seen more than you give me credit for, *Captain*. You know as little about me as I do you. You should take your own advice, and stop acting like a jealous child.'

'Jealous!' She stared at him. He was more deluded than she thought. 'You think I'm jealous of you? Do you have any idea—'

'Captain, we should all go up to the quarterdeck for the Trial announcement.' Epizon's voice sliced through her own, deep and calm, and she closed her mouth. She and Phyleus glowered at each other, tight-lipped and tense. 'We wouldn't want to miss it.'

Epizon eased himself off the crate and walked slowly between them to the hauler. Lyssa bared her teeth and followed him.

4

LYSSA

Abderos was by the navigation wheel as usual, flicking through a book filled with drawings of ships. Len was sat on the bench along the back of the deck, reading a book with 'Herbs native to Gemini' written on the cover.

'Captain, I hope we're going to Gemini next,' he said as she stepped out of the hauler, waving the book at her. 'They've got some stuff I'd really like to pick up. Very interesting properties, some of these have.'

'Nothing to do with the large number of nymphs and sirens in Gemini, then,' teased Abderos. Len sniffed, but said nothing, pointedly opening the book again.

'How did it go on the *Orion*?' Lyssa asked the satyr. He looked up from his book, face serious.

'I really thought I'd lost him for a while. He was completely blue. But the concoction Athena told me to make worked. As long as he drinks it all, I think he'll be all right.'

'Did you learn anything useful about the *Orion* while you were there?' She asked hopefully. He shook his head.

'I only really saw the captain's chambers, then he took me up to the top deck in a hauler and rowed me back in their longboat. It's massive. Reinforced handrails and haulers, and the sails were in really good condition, but I can't tell you anything we couldn't see from getting up close.'

'They put him in the captain's chambers?' Lyssa didn't know why she was surprised. She would do the same for any of her own crew.

Len nodded enthusiastically.

'Captain Antaeus was very worried. It was quite touching, really.'

'Huh,' she said softly. At least it sounded like Athena was helping the good guys.

'CAP,' Abderos said urgently. She spun around as the gentle orange flames roared white in the dish. The blond man materialised as they died down, smiling his fake-looking smile.

'Good evening, Olympus! Well, that last one was exciting, wasn't it? Are you ready to find out what's coming next?' He beamed and spread his arms out. 'Trial three, everybody!' He faded from sight and was replaced by a slight, tanned figure with blond hair in long braids and a bow as tall as she was slung over one shoulder.

'Artemis,' breathed Epizon.

'Good evening, heroes. As the goddess of the hunt, I want to pose a different kind of challenge than your last two.' Her voice sounded young and innocent, compounding her childlike looks. 'Make your way to Sagittarius. Your Trial will be revealed there at sunrise tomorrow.' She faded from the dish and the flames flickered gently again, their orange colour seeping back.

'Sagittarius!' Len squeaked.

'Captain, do you know how few people see Sagittarius?' The excitement in Epizon's voice was infectious and she couldn't help smiling. He had long spoken of wanting to see how the centaurs lived. Now he may get a chance.

'I didn't think we would go somewhere forbidden so soon!' Len said.

'Do you think we'll be hunting something?' asked Phyleus.

'I suppose you're good at hunting?' she said, sitting down in the captain's chair. He shrugged. 'Have you been to Sagittarius before?' She knew the answer was almost certainly 'no'. Phyleus shook his head.

'No. I've only been to one forbidden realm.' Everyone looked at him, interest piqued.

'Which one?' asked Abderos. Phyleus grinned at him.

'That would be telling.'

'Ahh, come on! You're on the crew now! You have to share secrets!' Abderos cajoled.

Lyssa wrinkled her nose. 'It's obviously Pisces,' she said. 'Invited to exclusive parties, I imagine.'

Phyleus turned to her, his playful grin nowhere to be seen.

'I have never been to Pisces,' he said and strode off into the hauler.

'Cap, he's not so bad, you know,' said Abderos, once the hauler had dipped out of view. 'I like him. Give him a chance.'

'He didn't earn his place here,' she grumbled, trying not to feel guilty at the look on her navigator's face.

'Let him try and earn it now, then,' Epizon said quietly behind her.

5

HEDONE

Hedone held her breath outside her captain's chambers, sure that the goddess of love must know she was hiding and listening. Hedone had been walking down the wide corridor that led to her quarters when she had seen the blinding white flash that signalled the arrival of a god around the edges of Theseus's door. On impulse, she stopped. The gods weren't supposed to get involved in the Trials. Were they here to help or hinder? Creeping to the door, she had not been very surprised to hear Aphrodite's voice through the wood.

'It is hard for me to visit, or to help you, good Theseus,' she was saying. 'Zeus is particularly vigilant just now.' There was the sound of liquid pouring. 'Thank you,' the goddess sang. Her voice made Hedone's skin tingle.

'But Zeus gave Hercules *Keravnos*, as you said he would,' Theseus said.

'He is the lord of the gods. He has a certain amount of... flexibility we don't all share. But I have recently made a discovery that should keep him busy for a while.' Hedone could hear the smile in the goddess's voice. 'There's nothing like one of his brothers misbehaving to distract our lord, and Hades has been a very naughty boy indeed.'

'Do you know when we will visit Hades' realm? I've always wanted to see Virgo,' asked Theseus. The goddess laughed a tinkling laugh and Hedone found herself smiling involuntarily.

'It was an almighty row, getting Hades to allow any Trial to occur in his beloved realm after he has spent so long trying to keep everyone out. No, we choose the Trials at random just before they are announced, so as to avoid any cheating.'

'What has he done that will upset Zeus?'

'Ah, Theseus, I can't tell you that. Knowledge is power, and you must earn it.' Hedone heard movement, then a long sigh from Aphrodite that sent pleasant shivers through her own body.

'There's more to Olympus than meets the mortal eye,' she breathed. 'No map will show you what a god can.'

HEDONE WAITED STILL and silent by the door for another five minutes but she heard no more talking, just soft moans and long breaths. She carried on down the corridor to her own rooms, her mind whirring. She didn't think Hercules needed Zeus's help, but he should know that his father would soon be distracted. What had Hades been up to? The goddess' words rang in her mind. *Knowledge is power.*

The men and women she met fell over themselves to tell her anything she wanted to know, but she had tempered her desire to control them long ago, knowing how much better true love would feel. Theseus's dark, smiling eyes swam before her, blurring abruptly into Hercules's sharp grey ones. She had found the man she was meant to love. She paused, with her hand on the door of her quarters. She didn't have enough knowledge to be powerful yet. Not about the gods, or the Trials or Olympus. But that didn't mean she had to be weak. If she wanted to help Hercules she needed control over her own crew. And she knew just where to start.

SHE KNOCKED LIGHTLY on Psyche's door.

'Come in,' she called.

Hedone pushed the door open. Psyche's rooms looked nothing like her own. Typhoons were long ships and the living quarters stretched the full width of the ship, only leaving room for a long corridor all the way down the port side. Every Typhoon had a living room, with a bedroom and washroom on either side, but that was where the similarities ended. Where Hedone's rooms were draped in soft, light silks and the furniture made of rich-coloured mahogany, Psyche's were bold and bright. Throws hung on the wooden walls, patterns made of a hundred colours springing to life in the fabric. Her furniture was rough wood, the book-shelves and tables looking like she may have made them herself. Weapons from all over Olympus adorned the rustic surfaces, spears made of bone and bows made of wood.

Psyche herself was sat on a bright purple armchair, braiding her thick black hair. She looked surprised to see Hedone.

'Can I help you?' Her tone wasn't cold, but there was no warmth either.

Hedone swallowed.

'I've been thinking about what you said. On Libra.'

Psyche raised her eyebrows, fingers still working on the tight braids. 'You're right. I want to be more useful to the crew.'

'OK,' Psyche said slowly. Hedone took a slow breath in, lifting her chest, wetting her lips. She poured her power into her voice.

'Teach me to fight,' she said.

Psyche's hands dropped from her hair and she stared at Hedone.

'Really?'

'Yes. I need to be able to defend myself, to stop getting in your way.'

Psyche stood up, appraising her.

'It's a bit late, to be asking now.'

'Not at all,' said Hedone. 'We're leagues and leagues from Sagittarius. Theseus said it would take all night to get there.'

'And you want to train all night?' said Psyche, picking up a spear as she walked slowly towards her.

'No, but we could start. It's just...' She looked down, channelling innocence. 'It's just, you were so impressive with those arrows, against the Hydra. I wish I could help Theseus like that.' She looked up again, hunting for signs the flattery was working.

'I seem to remember you shouting Hercules's name,' said Psyche, coming to a stop in front of her and setting the spear butt on the floor.

'I... I hate to see anyone hurt. I can't help it.'

'Then you are ill-suited to fight.'

'I can learn. The more I see it, the more I'll cope,' she protested.

Psyche held her gaze, saying nothing. There was no sign she found Hedone compelling. Maybe Hedone's powers had waned; she hadn't used them for so long. Psyche stepped towards her, tilting her own chin down so her hair fell forward, brushing her cheek.

'How much has Theseus told you about me?' Psyche said.

Hedone frowned. 'Not a lot. That he trusts you with his life.' 'There's a lot you don't know about me, Hedone. About my family. My husband.'

Hedone raised her eyebrows, jealousy surging through her. 'You're married?'

Psyche nodded. 'I am. Your powers won't work on me.'

'What? I'm not, why would I...'

Psyche cut off Hedone's spluttering.

'If you truly want to learn to fight, then I will teach you. You do not need to seduce me into agreeing.'

Hedone's face heated and she said nothing.

'Do you want to learn?' Psyche continued.

She nodded. Psyche tipped the spear towards her. 'Top deck, now,' she said.

EVADNE

E vadne slid, as quietly as she could, out of the soft sheets. Hercules didn't stir. The cold air made her shiver as she crossed the room on silent feet. Although the sky did dim at night, it was never properly dark in Olympus, so the room was lit well enough for her to see where she was stepping. She picked up Hercules's shirt, which lay discarded on the floor, and pulled it on before creeping to the bedroom door, closing it quietly behind her and making her way to the bar. She lit a lantern and pulled *Realms of Olympus* by Apollodoros from the one of the huge bookcases. Easing herself into the soft armchair and placing the lantern on the stand, she crossed her legs beneath her and began to read.

IT WAS AGREED, by all of the gods unanimously, that they would divide Olympus into equal realms. They could govern these realms as they pleased, choosing which races made their home within their boundaries and which races were welcome as guests. Realms could exist within earth, sea or sky and anything between could be used freely by mortals. Zeus claimed a realm first in the centre of Olympus and, not willing to risk further warring between themselves (or indeed his mighty wrath), the other gods accepted this and claimed their own around his. Two created two sky realms; Zeus and Athena, two created ocean realms; Poseidon and Hephaestus, and the rest created islands floating in unclaimed water. All realms have climates controlled by the gods, Apollo's Capricorn typically experiencing the most extreme seasons. Four gods chose to forbid all but a few races from entering; Artemis, Hades, Aphrodite and Hephaestus. Dionysus's realm and Ares' eponymous realm are forbidden to no creature but are generally considered too dangerous for most to visit.

EVADNE SCANNED THE WORDS, stopping whenever she saw 'Artemis' or 'Sagittarius' in the text. The best way she could prove her worth outside of Hercules's bedroom was to know as much as possible about what they were getting into; preferably more than anybody else did.

'WE'RE HALF AN HOUR AWAY.' Asterion's voice in her head jolted her out of a riveting account of the last mortal attempt to breach the border mountain-range on Virgo. She heard Hercules stirring in the bedroom and stood up, stretching her arms above her head. It was still dark. Artemis had said the Trial would be explained at sunrise. Apollo, Artemis's twin brother, controlled sunrise and sunset, though Olympus had gone through many suns in its long life. Another nugget of information gleaned from good old Apollodoros. She reached down, patted the book on the chair fondly and made her way back to her own quarters to dress.

. . .

WHEN SHE ARRIVED on the quarterdeck, Asterion and Hercules were already there, waiting expectantly for the flame dish to leap into life. She looked out over the railings, past the ballista turrets and tall triangular sails, at Sagittarius. They were hovering, maybe twenty feet from the ground, over bare pale plains. Dusty, yellowing grass covered the flat expanse and low green hills rose up on all sides. Clouds glittering with orange and green swirled through the sky above her and she could smell the rich odour of soil. The *Alastor*, the *Virtus* and the *Orion* were all moored over the same field, looming quietly in the morning dusk.

Hercules didn't look at all like he had nearly died the previous day. He stood tall, his muscular frame filling the black shirt he wore, his grey eyes reflecting the dancing orange flames. She had felt every inch of his body last night, and barely a scar remained from Athena's metal beasts. She knew Zeus must have helped him. A thrill ran through her at the thought. The lord of the gods himself. Quite an ally. The flames flashed white and Artemis appeared in the dish. She didn't look older than fourteen, with no curves to her lithe body or lines on her honest face.

'Good day, heroes. I want you to catch my prize stag, Cerynea, on his way across Sagittarius. He is very fast and you will need to use a longboat to keep up and navigate the route he takes across my realm. If you can't catch him then the first to make it across my realm after him will win. You must take the route he does, or you will be incapacitated. And incapacitated means your longboat will disappear from under you, instantaneously, regardless of where you are when you break the rules. You have until sunrise tomorrow to prepare your vessels, though you may not leave the plains you are currently moored in. If this rule is broken, you will be executed, immediately.'

Evadne swallowed. It was unnerving seeing the young girl talk so simply about death.

'Good luck, hunters,' concluded Artemis. 'And I beg you, do not break my rules.' She vanished from the flames.

'It's a race. In longboats,' said Evadne. Hercules nodded, a smile spreading across his face.

'We have the best longboat silver can buy.'

7

LYSSA

'Why didn't I get the bloody longboat fixed?' It was the third time she'd yelled that and it still wasn't making Lyssa feel any better.

'Captain, we have twenty-four hours to fix it. We'll be fine,' Epizon told her calmly.

'Fix it with what?' She kicked moodily at the base of the flame dish and it wobbled precariously.

'Whatever we have in the cargo deck, Cap.' Abderos had a stack of paper on his lap and was drawing frantically. 'In fact, a broken longboat isn't much of a hindrance, if we build what I'm designing. We'd pretty much have to destroy it to rebuild it anyway.'

'Ab, we have a day. How much can we do in a day?'

He looked up from his drawing, eyes shining.

'Plenty. This is going to be the best longboat you've ever flown.' He held the drawing up. Len hustled forward to look and Phyleus pushed himself off the quarterdeck railings, eyebrows raised.

'Are those red sails?' he asked.

'Yep.' Abderos beamed.

'Rage-fuelled sails?' Lyssa said slowly, bending to look at the drawing more closely.

'Yep.'

'I couldn't fuel a longboat with my Rage, unless I sailed it every day for a year to bond with it.'

'You can if it's made from a ship you're already bonded with.'

'What? I'm not damaging the *Alastor*!' she exclaimed, alarmed.

'Relax, we'd just take a small amount of wood out of the back mast.'

Lyssa shook her head vehemently, the thought unbearable.

'No. No way. You can't just pull bits off her.'

'We wouldn't be *pulling bits off her*. We would be giving her an additional lease of life. On a smaller, more manoeuvrable vessel, still controlled by you – her captain. She'll love it!' Abderos waved the paper at her. 'This is our Trial, Captain. We're fast. Your Rage makes the *Alastor* the fastest ship in Olympus. We can win this.'

Pride in her ship tempered Lyssa's outrage slightly. 'How can you cut out part of the mast without causing damage? Will the mast still be stable?' She asked, warily.

'We'd cut small sections in a spiral up and around it. It won't affect the integrity at all. And it might even look quite good.' He scribbled a sketch of the mast on the edge of the paper, marking where he wanted to cut.

'I don't know...' Lyssa frowned down at the drawing.

Epizon coughed.

'Captain, why don't you think about it while we repair the sails? Having *Alastor* wood on board makes no difference if we have no sails,' he said.

'That's true enough,' Abderos agreed. 'Phyleus, you bought everything on that supply list, right?'

'Course. Including enough canvas to replace a full sail on the *Alastor*.'

'Perfect,' Abderos said, and wheeled himself off the quarterdeck, down the gentle slope towards the cargo deck hauler. Epizon and Len followed after him and Lyssa scowled.

'What do we do if anything happens to the *Alastor*'s sails, and we've used all the material up on this?'

'Hopefully we won't find out.' Phyleus shrugged.

8

LYSSA

L yssa's gut wrenched as the axe bit into the *Alastor*'s mast with a thunk. Epizon looked guiltily at her as he pulled the steel from the wood. She wanted to give him a reassuring look back but she couldn't. He swung the axe again and she looked away, glaring at the deck. Abderos had said it wouldn't harm the ship. And when they were finished they would have an unbelievably powerful longboat, faster than any of their rivals but still firmly a part of her ship. She clung to the words, praying he was right. A Rage-fuelled longboat wouldn't just help them in this race. It could be the edge they needed in the whole Trials. But if it didn't work and it damaged her bond with the *Alastor* then she would never forgive him. Or herself.

'Cap, we need your help with the sail.' Len's voice came from behind her.

'Sure,' she said, relieved not to have to oversee Epizon hacking at her ship. She followed the satyr across the deck to the front of the ship, where they had set the broken longboat up on some of the wheeled bases from the cargo deck. It was raised so that it was higher than her shoulders, so she didn't see Phyleus inside the boat until he straightened and stood up.

'It's warmer here than Libra,' he said, wiping sweat from his brow with the back of his hand before throwing a broken bit of wood out of the boat and onto the deck.

Lyssa's steps faltered involuntarily. Phyleus had taken off his shirt and tucked it into the low waistband of his trousers while he worked. He was nowhere near as muscled as Epizon or Theseus, or in fact most of the other men in the Trials, but her eyes fixed on the lines of his chest, and his bare, tanned skin filled her vision. He was right. It was warmer. Sweat glistened on his body and she swallowed, reminded of the last bare chest she'd seen shining with sweat. Other than her own, it had been the only bare chest she had ever touched, and the sweat had been hers. Heat flooded her face and she closed her eyes a moment, squashing the pleasant memories of her last trip to Pisces.

'So, we've pulled out all of the benches. We didn't know if we should put new ones in or just create one big seat for you and leave space in the back for stuff.' Len began talking at a hundred miles an hour beside her, and she tried to concentrate.

'One bench across this middle,' she said as they reached the boat. She hopped up onto the crate they were using as a step, then climbed over, trying not to make eye contact with Phyleus. If he'd noticed her reaction to him he was keeping it quiet. 'I think just one bench here, near the mast,' she clarified. She looked around, leaning on the bare mast. They had done a good job repairing the damage to the hull.

'How'd it get so beat up in the first place?' Phyleus put both hands on his hips. 'A torn-up sail and a huge hole in the side isn't your standard wear and tear.'

'Delivery job gone wrong,' she shrugged, trying to ignore the sounds of the axe in the background.

'What were you delivering?'

'Don't know. We don't ask.'

'Doesn't that bother you?' he said, his eyebrows drawing together.

'If everyone sticks to the code then we shouldn't need to ask,' she snapped, guilt lacing her defensiveness. 'Len, where's the sail?'

'Down here, Cap,' he called. 'I've cut it to size and sealed the edges.'

She climbed back out of the boat and retrieved the sail from Len. It was heavy but she didn't need to rile herself up to get the strength to lift it. Phyleus had done that for her. She threw it up over the edge of the boat, a satisfied smile spreading over her face when Phyleus yelped as it landed with a loud thud in the boat. She hoped it had hit him, rather than just startled him.

'Sorry,' she lied as she climbed back in. He glowered.

'Honestly, you're so immature. It's like a child running a ship,' he said, crouching down and lifting a long plank of unbroken wood.

'Right, and you're so grown up. How old are you, anyway?'

'You first,' he answered, not looking up from balancing the wood across the boat, marking where the bench would sit with a thick lead pencil.

'I'm eighteen. You hardly needed to ask. The whole of Olympus knows Hercules was put on trial for killing his family four years ago and that his fourteen-year-old daughter survived his attack,' she said.

'I'm twenty,' he replied. 'I just wanted to see if you would tell me. Are you the youngest on board?'

'No. Abderos is sixteen.' He looked up at her in surprise. 'I thought you two were pals. Did he not tell you?' Phyleus shook his head.

'No. I mean, I know he looks young but... What's he doing away from his family, on a smugglers' ship with...' He trailed off.

'With a bunch of hard-up misfits?' she finished for him.

He shrugged.

'Not my story to tell,' she said, and started to shake out the huge piece of white material. It glittered as the light moved over it and a peaceful feeling pulsed through her. 'Len is over a hundred,' she said, smoothing out the creases.

'You're joking,' Phyleus said. 'I thought satyrs only lived to a hundred?'

'Most satyrs, yeah, but not his species. Blessed by Pan himself, Len says. In fact he's relatively young.'

'What about Epizon?'

'I don't know,' she admitted. 'Epizon doesn't talk about his past. At all.'

'Huh. So you don't know where he's from?' She shook her head and grabbed the mast, preparing to climb up with the sail over her shoulder.

'Captain!' Len's voice sounded urgently in her head as well as out loud, below the boat.

'What's wrong?' she said, dropping the sail and vaulting over the edge of the boat. Her breath caught as she landed.

'We... We have a visitor,' he said, pointing to the centaur standing on the deck of the *Alastor*.

Lots of female centaurs wanted Cyllarus's affections but he was only interested in Hylonome.
She was the prettiest of all the half-beasts in the forests. She won him by loving him and
telling him so. They did everything together, roaming lands, exploring caves and fighting,
side by side.

In one fight Cyllarus was wounded, in the heart. Hylonome put her hand on the wound and
kissed him, trying to stop his last breath from leaving him. When she realised he was dead,
she took the weapon that had killed him and used it upon herself, falling on her husband's
body.

EXCERPT FROM

METAMORPHOSES BY OVID
Written 8 A.D.
Paraphrased by Eliza Raine

9

LYSSA

T he centaur bowed her head and Lyssa took a hesitant step forward. She was breath-taking. She had a sleek mahogany mare's body, smaller but more agile-looking than the warriors they had seen at the feast. Her pale white chest was clad in shining steel armour with massive shoulder plates laid over leather gauntlets that wrapped around her arms. More shining plates were strapped across her human waist, hanging down to protect her flanks, and two long scabbards ran behind them. But most striking was the mane of white hair flowing from her steel headband down her back and spilling over her dark coat, matching her tail perfectly.

'How did you—' started Lyssa.

'Captain Lyssa. Allow me to introduce myself. I am Hylonome-nestor-cyllarus.' Her serious face barely moved as she spoke and Lyssa couldn't make out what colour her eyes were. She took another step forward.

'That's quite a mouthful,' she said.

'You may call me Nestor.'

Lyssa nodded. 'How did you get on my ship?'

'I have Artemis's blessing.'

Lyssa swallowed. If a goddess had sanctioned this visit, the centaur was going to get what she wanted.

'And how can I help you?'

Nestor's tail flicked. 'Actually, it is I who can help you. You were there when my love was slain.' A sick feeling swamped Lyssa's gut. The centaurs at the feast. 'Hercules killed Cyllarus, my husband, and you want Hercules dead. I am here to help you.'

'I'm sorry for your loss, Nestor, I truly am. I know how it feels to lose somebody you love.' She looked down a moment, forcing the sound of the centaur's legs snapping out of her mind. *Please let her husband have been one of the other two poor creatures*, she prayed silently. 'How can you help us?' she asked.

'I will join your crew and make sure Hercules dies during the Trials.'

Lyssa blinked.

'Join the crew?' Nestor said nothing. 'But...' Lyssa couldn't take on another crew member. She didn't even want Phyleus on board, and a centaur simply wouldn't fit on the *Alastor*.

'I can fight. I have knowledge passed down through many generations, some of which I can share with you. I have the favour of Artemis.'

Lyssa took a long breath. 'I need to talk with my crew first.'

Nestor nodded. 'I will return in one hour.' She vanished with a small flash of light.

Len let out a long whistle.

'Wow.'

'Wow,' echoed Phyleus, still in the longboat.

'Was that a centaur?' Epizon was jogging across the deck towards her, Abderos wheeling his chair along behind him. 'Captain, my eyes weren't playing tricks were they? Was a centaur just on the ship?'

'Yes.' She didn't know what else to say.

'What did she want?' Epizon's eyes were alive with excitement as he reached her. 'I would have come over but I didn't want to scare her.'

Len snorted. 'I don't think you could scare her. Or, in fact, make her laugh.' The satyr looked up at Epizon. 'Her husband was killed at the feast. She wants to join the crew to try and get revenge on Hercules. By killing him.'

Epizon's mouth fell open. 'A centaur on our crew! Captain, this is incredible!'

'Slow down, Epizon. The *Alastor* is at capacity. We don't have the space for a centaur on board. We don't have the supplies for another crew member. We don't know anything about her.' She shot a look at Phyleus. 'She hasn't earned a place on this crew.'

'Lyssa, if anyone has earned a place fighting at your side, it's somebody who has lost a loved one to Hercules.' Epizon never addressed her as Lyssa in front of the crew. She frowned at him.

'Her desire for revenge might make her do something stupid,' she said. Epizon raised his eyebrows and Phyleus coughed. Anger flashed though her. 'Since when did being Captain mean I can't make any of my own bloody decisions! This is not a democracy.' She stamped her foot as she said it, painfully aware of Phyleus's accusation of immaturity only moments earlier.

'Yes, Captain,' said Epizon, visibly trying to suppress his excitement, and failing. 'But centaurs are some of the best fighters in Olympus, and not prone to acting irrationally or—'

'Enough, Epizon. I'll think about it.' Lyssa held her hand up and he stopped talking immediately. 'Get on with ruining my ship.'

10

EVADNE

'Captain, there must be something useful we could be doing with our time.'

Evadne twirled her hair around her finger as she spoke, watching the colour change between black and blue as it moved in the warm daylight. She needed to handle this conversation perfectly. There was no way she was being left out of another Trial.

'Our longboat is in perfect condition, and we have the new slingshots. There is nothing we need to do.' Hercules was sitting in his captain's chair on the quarterdeck, his eyes closed and his face tilted up towards the sun.

'I wonder how the others are getting on, improving their boats,' she mused casually. 'Shame they were given time to make amendments. You could even say it's not really fair, when we took the time to make ours perfect before the Trials began.' She glanced at him. His eyes were still shut and he hadn't moved. She stood up slowly, stretching, and walked to the railings along the edge of the high quarter-deck, making sure her boots thudded on the planks as she went. The Whirlwind-class ship's high quarterdeck meant she had a great view of the decks of the much lower *Alastor* and *Virtus*, but the giant's huge Zephyr rose just above them, out of sight. 'Looks like Captain Lyssa's longboat is being patched together out of rags; I don't think we've much to worry about there. I can't see Theseus himself, but his longboat is up on deck. I wonder what's happening on the *Orion*. It's frustrating we can't see from here.' There was still no reaction from Hercules. 'How long would it take to reach one of the other ships? They're moored so close,' she muttered to herself. She heard movement behind her. 'It really isn't fair that they all get to make enhancements to their boats.' His chair creaked and boots thudded on the deck towards her.

'Evadne, I have an idea,' Hercules said. She felt a satisfied smile spread across her face, but replaced it with a neutral expression before she turned to him.

'Yes, Captain?'

'Artemis said we could use this whole area. And there are three other ships in this area. I think that sounds like an invitation.' Evadne raised her eyebrows innocently. 'Why don't we pay the others a little visit, and see first-hand how they're getting on?'

'I take it we will be undoing their hard work?' she asked.

'Of course. I'll go to the *Virtus*. You go to the *Alastor*,' he said.

Annoyance sliced through Evadne. That hadn't been her plan.

'We can see from here that the *Alastor* is no threat. Perhaps it might be better to find out what's happening on the *Orion*.' She worded her suggestion meekly, careful not to sound like she knew better than him. Hercules looked over her shoulder at the *Alastor*. She followed his gaze. It was easy to make out the little boat they had set up on the top deck, and a tiny figure fighting to attach a sail to the single mast.

'Fine,' he said. She stopped a smile from flashing across her face and nodded sedately. 'Go to the *Orion*.'

'I'll go now,' she said.

'Asterion, prepare the longboat,' Hercules instructed aloud, then looked at her. 'Yes. It'll take you a while on foot.'

She gaped at him.

'On foot? I'll never get up onto the *Orion* on foot. I'll wait and go when you return from the *Virtus*.'

'No, you'll go now. On foot.'

Evadne felt her eye twitch as she stared at him, trying to control her tongue.

'Yes, Captain,' she spat eventually, and wheeled away, towards the steps that led down from the quarterdeck. He was going to take his time on the *Virtus*. Her fists clenched as she remembered how he had looked at Hedone at the feast. *Two can play that game*, she thought, grabbing a coil of coarse rope off the deck and tying it to the metal railing. There was a reason she'd gotten him to send her to the *Orion*, and it wasn't just to sabotage their longboat.

EVADNE THREW the rope over the edge of the *Hybris* and climbed over the railing. Carefully coiling a length around her wrist she tested the rope with both hands. Satisfied it would hold her weight, she eased herself over the edge of the ship, planting the flats of her feet against the sheer metal plating of the hull. She began to walk down the metal, one hand moving over the other on the harsh rope. When she was a few feet from the bottom and the hull began to curve away beneath her she let go, landing softly with her knees bent. The smell of soil was stronger on the ground and she took a moment's pleasure in feeling it beneath her feet. Yellowing grass crunched as she began to walk towards the Zephyr. Not all of Sagittarius was this hot, she'd read. Some areas were shady forest and she was sure there was a mountain range somewhere on the island. Mountains were usually colder, she thought, though in Olympus you could never assume anything.

What had looked like a short distance from the high quarterdeck felt like miles to Evadne as she sweltered under the hot sun. She was regretting the black leather vest she'd worn as she trudged across the dry ground, the *Orion* looming larger as she approached. She studied the long wooden planks of the hull, lined with portholes and ballista windows, trying to figure out the best way to sneak on board. It didn't look like she would be able to climb all the way up onto the deck – the ship was too large and anyone on either of the two quarterdecks would spot her when she reached the top.

She decided she would climb to one of the ballista windows and pray that she could squeeze through the gap between the weapon and the frame. It wasn't until she was a lot closer that she realised most of the ballista windows were empty. That was interesting. The *Orion* hadn't equipped most of the ballistas, either meaning they couldn't afford to or that they had weapons elsewhere. She would need to tell Hercules.

The Zephyr was hovering eight feet off the dry grass and Evadne began cursing her captain under her breath when she jumped for the bottom of the ship and failed to get a grip for the third time. Panting, she crouched down on the balls of her feet and counted backwards from three, before launching herself up again. This time she got her fingers into the gaps between the lowest planks and she cried out in pain as her fingernail tore on the rough wood. She didn't let go, though, pulling her legs up after her, trying to get purchase on the hull.

She ignored the pain in her finger as she climbed, slowly and carefully, to the nearest ballista window. Peering cautiously round the edge of the frame, she checked the room beyond was empty and silently eased her way through the window and onto the wooden floor.

She was in the enormous cargo deck, she realised, looking around at dusty crates lining the hull. It was nothing like the cargo deck on the *Hybris*. For one, it barely had anything in it, despite it being three or four times the size. The ceiling was probably double the height of the *Hybris*, she estimated as she crept towards the hauler in the middle of the other wall. She was hoping that the crew would all be up on deck, leaving her free to find the one person who wouldn't be working on the longboat. She needed information, and she knew just the man to provide it.

11

ERYX

'ntaeus? How's it going with the—' Eryx was cut short as he realised the figure entering his room was too small to be Antaeus. It was too small to be anyone on the crew. 'You! What are you doing here?'

'Shhhhh,' hushed Evadne, quietly closing the wooden door behind her. 'You'll give me away.' Something like concern flitted across her face when she took in his bandaged chest. 'I saw what happened in the flame dish. I have to admit, you were pretty impressive.'

She walked towards the bed and he struggled to sit up. He was back in his own rooms and had been waiting desperately for news of his captain's progress. He certainly hadn't expected any other visitors.

'You shouldn't be here,' he said, pushing his long hair back from his face. He hated anyone seeing it out of its usual knot. She smiled.

'I thought you might be lonely, in your sickbed.' She sat on the edge of his bed and leaned over, picking up the glass of sludge. She tilted it from side to side before sniffing it. 'Gods, that smells vile,' she exclaimed.

'It is. Why are you here?'

'I just told you, I wanted to talk to you. And...' She trailed off, then looked him in the eye. 'And to make sure you were OK.'

Eryx crossed his arms as gently as he could over his tight chest. It made him angry that he wanted to believe her. He didn't, of course, but his traitorous mouth opened anyway.

'Talk to me about what?' he asked.

'About the Hydra. About how brave you were.' She smiled at him. 'It really was impressive.' Her long ponytail fell across her bare shoulder as she cocked her head at him. He swallowed as he unintentionally followed the movement down to the tight leather vest she was wearing. 'Eyes up, big boy,' Evadne said. His face flushed immediately and she laughed. 'Well, at least you're getting some colour back.'

'I'm not talking to you. You shouldn't be here.'

'You're always saying that to me,' she pouted.

'You're always in places you shouldn't be!' he snapped. 'Why are you really here?' Evadne looked at him a moment more, then sighed and stood up.

'Fine. I wanted to ask you about Poseidon.'

Eryx raised his eyebrows in surprise.

'Then you've picked the wrong giant to talk to. I don't know anything about him.' He looked down at his folded arms as he spoke.

'He's your father. You must know something,' she pushed.

'That's not how it works. Poseidon, Zeus, Hermes, all of them, they all have abandoned children all over Olympus. I've never met him. Never spoken to him.'

'Oh.'

'Yeah. Why did you want to know about him?' he grumbled.

'I read... I read something interesting about him. About his realm, Aquarius. Have you been there?' Eryx nodded.

'I grew up there. Moved to Ares when my mother died.' He tailed off and looked down again, guilt washing over him that it had been so long since he thought of her. It would be ten years since her death this year.

Evadne was silent for a moment.

'Ares, huh? Dangerous place, I've heard,' she said eventually.

He looked up at her, pushing his chin out.

'Not for a champion boxer.'

'Ahhhh, you had a taste for life as a gladiator, did you?'

'Gladiators fight because they have to; boxers fight because they're good at it,' Eryx said. He knew he should tell her to go. He knew he shouldn't be telling her about himself. But she seemed genuinely interested. And he wanted to talk to her. He couldn't help it.

'What's Aquarius like?' she asked.

'You'll see it during the Trials. Why do you want to know?'

Evadne shrugged.

'Just curious. I know it's underwater and that everyone lives in sealed domes. Does Poseidon live in one of the domes?'

'I don't know. I told you, I don't know anything about him.'

'But you must—'

'Stop asking me about him!' She wasn't interested in him. It was clear she only wanted to know about his father. 'You need to go,' he said, meaning it this time. He wasn't playing her games. He was smarter than that. She sighed again, then stepped close to his side and leaned down towards him. She smelled of citrus and his breath caught as his muscles tensed.

'You really were impressive,' she whispered, and kissed him gently on the check. He felt a red flush roar across his face and she laughed again as she sashayed to the door, winking as she silently let herself out.

It took him nearly an hour to relax again. He'd heard nothing from Antaeus, or any of the rest of the crew about an intruder. He didn't know why he wasn't telling his captain about her visit. Women had talked to him in the past, sure, but rarely human women. And the giants and warrioresses he had spent time with on Ares were nothing like Evadne, who was lithe, quick and completely fascinating. He knew for certain that he would need to be on his guard around her when he got his strength back and re-joined the Trials.

12

HERCULES

H ercules kept his longboat low to the ground as he approached the *Virtus*, trusting that the ship's long front sail would keep him from view. The thought of Hedone when he'd last seen her, the desire obvious in her intense dark eyes, made him will the boat on faster. As he came up alongside the ship he turned to the minotaur.

'Come back for me in one hour.'

'Yes, Captain.' Asterion nodded. Hercules reached out of the longboat, grabbed the edge of a ballista window and pulled himself easily up and through, onto the *Virtus*. The weapons room was empty of people, just housing the long row of massive wooden crossbows lining the edge and the barrels filled with lead shot beside them. Hercules had been on Typhoon-class ships before, and knew they had lots of space dedicated to living quarters. With only four crew members needing rooms most of them would be empty, but he needed to make sure he found Hedone without letting anyone else know he was here. He had told her to expect him and it was unlikely Theseus needed much help with his longboat. He would find her rooms and if she wasn't there, he would wait for her. He wasn't leaving the *Virtus* without knowing the feel of those beautiful lips on his.

HE CREPT out of the ballista room and turned down the wood-panelled corridor, towards the back of the ship. It smelled different to his ship – a citrus scent lingering in the air. Did it smell like her? He hurried past a series of open doors until he heard voices. He stopped and pressed himself against the wall, listening. There was the steady clinking of metal and the noise of water splashing. He'd found the galley.

'Here, I can wash that up for you. It's the least I can do.' The soft, husky voice belonged to Hedone. Hercules's muscles constricted slightly.

'It's fine. You're getting better, you know. Not with the knife, perhaps, but at least you can lift a spear and aim a slingshot now,' an older female voice replied.

'The slingshot is easiest. I don't have to be near my opponent.'

'If you're half-decent, then you don't need to be near them to use a spear either. We'll start again in three hours, when that meal's gone down. Go and get some rest.'

'OK.' There was the sound of wood scraping on wood and Hercules held his breath as a door a few feet ahead of him swung open. Hedone swept out, before turning in the opposite direction to him and making her way down the hallway. She was wearing a tight leather fighting-vest, much like Evadne's but filled out in all the right places, and dark leather trousers. Joining her vest to her trousers at the back were flowing ribbons of sheer turquoise silk, looking remarkably like wings. Even in fighting garb she looked like

a goddess. She held her arm out as she walked, runi
fingers along the dark wood, humming softly. He le
breath slowly and crept after her.

THEY WALKED past another four doors and then she pushed
one open and went inside. Hercules gave her as long as he
dared and then went in after her. He found himself in a
lounge that looked a little like his own, save for the white
silk draped over the mahogany walls, softening everything.
There was a large white day-bed by a low table in the centre
of the room and a well-stocked bar and bookcases against
one wall. He couldn't see Hedone but he could hear her
humming through the open door at the back of the living
room. He stepped quietly across the room. She was leaning
over a huge bed, almost as large as his own, pulling back
sheets and arranging cushions. Lust pulsed through him.
He took one long stride through the open door and as he
came up behind her he covered her mouth and spun her
around to face him. Her wide-eyed panic subsided as soon
as she saw him and he moved his hand from her mouth to
her cheek.

'Hedone,' he breathed.

'Hercules,' she whispered back. 'How did you...?'

'I have one hour.' She let out a breath as he pushed his
hand into her soft hair, his thumb stroking her jaw. 'You are
so incredibly beautiful,' he told her.

Her face broke into a smile. 'Wait, I have to tell you
something,' she said.

Hercules softly tilted her head to one side, exposing her
long white neck. He leaned forward and kissed the bare
skin. Goosebumps rose across her neck instantly and she
gasped. 'I heard Aphrodite and Theseus talking. They said

Zeus had to deal with something to do with Hades and that he wouldn't be able to help you,' she said in a rush.

He straightened up, meeting her eyes.

'I don't need any help.'

'I can help you,' she said, staring up at him. 'Let me help you.' He could spend forever lost in those deep, intoxicating eyes. 'I can make you feel better than you ever dreamed possible.' Her voice was breathy and deep and she had that dark, hungry look again. 'One hour with the goddess of pleasure.'

Every part of his body responded to her as she pushed him gently onto the bed and brought her soft lips to his.

13

LYSSA

There was no way around it. She would have to accept the centaur onto the *Alastor*. For an hour Lyssa had been trying to work out a solution to Nestor's proposition but she couldn't shift the memory of the feast, the sound of the centaur's legs breaking, the maniacal look on Hercules's face. Epizon was right. There was nobody in Olympus who shared Nestor's pain or need for revenge more than she did. Any anyway, if Artemis wanted her on the ship, that was what would happen.

Lyssa was standing with her back to the rails, leaning on her elbows, waiting for the centaur to return and glaring at the back mast. It had shallow square patches of wood missing in a neat line that spiralled up the wood like steps. If she were being honest it was actually quite pretty. She pushed herself off the rail and hesitantly stepped towards the mast. She almost didn't want to touch it, just in case. In case her bond was damaged, or broken. In case her ship was angry with her. Her crew had convinced her it was a risk worth taking but they didn't know the *Alastor* like she did. She closed her eyes, took a deep breath and laid her hand on the mast, concentrating. The thriving hum of the ship filled her at once, the sense of the massive sails and the unending sky fierce and strong. Relief washed through her as she broke the connection, her hand dropping back to her side. They'd been right. She let out a long breath. If they were right about the transplanted bits of mast carrying the bond over to the longboat...

A SMALL FLASH of white light caught her attention. She turned to where Nestor was standing on the deck, exactly where she had been before. The centaur bowed her head.

'Captain Lyssa,' she said.

'Nestor.' Lyssa inclined her head in return. 'Please wait, while I summon my crew.' She'd barely finished the sentence before Epizon had bounded across the deck from where he'd been working on the longboat. He bowed low to the centaur.

'I'm Epizon. Welcome...'

Lyssa grabbed his shoulder, stopping him mid-sentence, and stepped past him towards Nestor. She stood in silence while Abderos wheeled his chair over, Len trotting on one side, Phyleus sauntering on the other.

'Nestor. I have decided to accept your help, with gratitude,' she said when they were all gathered. The centaur bowed her head again.

'You will not regret it. I will make sure your father does not see the end of the Trials.'

Lyssa's fists clenched at her sides.

'I appreciate your conviction, but if you ever refer to him as my father again you will lose your place on this crew.'

Nestor flicked her tail. 'I am sorry. It may take me a short while to understand some of the customs on this ship. We are a private race, and unfamiliar with the ways of modern humans.'

'Epizon and Len will fill you in, I'm sure. Phyleus,' she turned to him. 'You're going to have to share quarters with Abderos so Nestor has a room.'

His mouth fell open.

'Captain, I paid to furnish that room! You can't just give it away!'

'Yes, I can.'

'Len's the smallest, surely he should share!'

Len snorted, scraping his hooves on the deck.

'Trust me, nobody is ever sharing with Len,' said Abderos. 'Do you know what satyrs get up to in private?' He raised his eyebrows at Phyleus and shook his head. 'Don't ask. I wish I hadn't. Plus his room looks and smells like a forest.'

Phyleus looked back at Lyssa and she shrugged.

'It's true. Two human men sharing is the most sensible option. Deal with it.'

'I am sorry for causing upset,' said Nestor. They all looked at her.

'It's fine,' said Epizon quickly. 'Do you have belongings to move onto the ship? We have a large cargo deck to store them if so.'

'No. All of my belongings are tied too closely with Cyllarus. They are safe here on Sagittarius until I avenge him and can take pleasure in them once more.'

Lyssa shifted uncomfortably. She knew it was a selfish thing to think as soon as the thought entered her mind, but she couldn't help it: Nestor's solemn grief was definitely going to change the mood on board the *Alastor*.

. . .

'CAPTAIN, we're ready for you to try the longboat,' said Len.

'Good.' Lyssa was relieved to hand over the intense horse-woman to Epizon for a tour of the ship, and anxious to see if their plan had worked. She hopped up on the crate and into the longboat. The sail was up, the bench secured and the mast clad in the slightly dark patches of wood from the *Alastor*. She laid her hand on the mast and willed the boat up. It responded instantly, rising a foot above the deck of the *Alastor*. She let go of the mast and the ship hovered in place. So far, so good. She moved along the boat, checking the repairs Phyleus had made to the hull. She reluctantly acknowledged he'd done a good job. With his shirt off. She shook her head, clearing the image.

'Do you need any help testing your Rage?' Phyleus clambered into the boat beside her, struggling now it was a foot higher.

She scowled. 'You're certainly the best person to make me angry.'

He winked at her as he stood up straight. 'I know. That's why I volunteered.'

'It's not just anger.' She looked at him and sighed. 'Anger is the easiest way, but anything that produces adrenaline...' she paused. 'Excitement. Fear. They all trigger the Rage.'

Phyleus tilted his head at her.

'Huh. Must make for some... interesting experiences in your love life.'

She reached out, punching him in the arm. He yelped.

'Line crossed. Captain, remember?' she said, pointing at herself.

'I'm just helping you test the Rage,' he grimaced, rubbing his arm. She glared at him and reached out for the mast. She closed her eyes and concentrated. The truth was, she'd never tried to power the ship with anything like the

kind of fuel Phyleus had just suggested. She'd only rec
discovered that her power responded to ph
excitement.

As soon as she remembered that night on Pisces she
heard the sail snap taught. She allowed herself to remember
the details, the deep kisses and soft caresses. Energy
thrummed through her body, flowing fast and powerful. She
willed the ship up and heard Phyleus shout as they shot into
the sky. She felt a broad smile split her face as the wind
whipped through her hair, her imagination soaring with the
longboat.

'Lyssa!'

She opened her eyes. Phyleus was in front of her, sitting
in the bottom of the boat, clinging to the bench. She slowed
their pace, looking up at the blood-red sail. 'Gods, you
should warn me if you're going to do that!'

He was panting. Her eyes fixed on the rise and fall of his
chest, the beads of sweat glistening on his skin. Power
flowed through her like electricity, her own skin humming.
She wanted him. 'We're too high. Artemis told us not to
leave the plains, we need to go back down.'

His words filtered through her haze. Artemis. The Trials.
She took her hand from the mast and leaned over the edge
of the boat. They were high. The *Alastor* was far below them,
looking tiny so close to the other, larger ships.

'Huh,' she said.

'Yeah. So the Rage works on the longboat. Get us back
down.'

'Get us back down, *Captain*,' she said, looking at him. He
rolled his eyes. For a moment, she wanted to toy with him.
To drop the boat now, watch him scream as they plummeted
back towards the earth. She wanted him on his backside
before her, calling her captain. Epizon wasn't here to cut in,

to stop her, to remind her what was important. She could show this arrogant man that he should respect her. Even fear her.

'Please.' Phyleus said. She blinked. 'We don't want to risk upsetting Artemis and being expelled from the Trials. Especially as I reckon we can win this one.' He smiled a twinkling, excited smile that reached his eyes. She willed the boat down, gently, flexing her fists and forcing out the images of Phyleus kneeling before her.

The Cerynean stag was sacred to Artemis and had golden horns. Hercules did not want to kill or wound it so he chased it, for a full year. Eventually the stag took refuge on a mountain and Hercules shot and wounded it as it crossed a stream. He was now able to catch it and he threw it over his shoulders and started to head back but Artemis and her brother Apollo stopped him, angry that he had tried to kill the sacred animal.

EXCERPT FROM

THE LIBRARY BY APOLLODORUS

Written 300–100 B.C.

Paraphrased by Eliza Raine

14

LYSSA

'Are you ready for this?' Epizon asked quietly. They were standing together on the deck, watching the purple twilit sky slowly getting lighter.

Lyssa hadn't slept well. She put her unsettled feeling down to anxiety about the race, crushing the memory of how she had felt about Phyleus the previous day. She didn't want to work out if it was lust or something else she was feeling. Something dangerous.

'Of course I am,' Lyssa said.

'Who are you going to take with you?'

'Nobody. The lighter the boat, the better.'

Epizon shook his head.

'If you're channelling Rage and steering you need somebody with you. Somebody who is light, *and* a good shot. You can guarantee the others will have a navigator and a gunner.' She looked at him and sighed. She knew where this was going. Epizon shrugged. 'I'm too heavy, Abderos is a terrible shot and Len's too small. It's got to be Phyleus.'

'He irritates me,' she grumbled.

'Even better,' Epizon smiled. A horn sounded in the distance. 'Lyssa, be careful. Don't lose control.'

'It wouldn't slow us down if you were on board. My Rage can make up for it,' she said quickly.

'We need to win this. I'm too heavy.' He laid his hand on her shoulder and she straightened. 'Concentrate on the race, not your emotions. This one is ours, Captain.'

'So, sun's up. What happens now?'

Lyssa turned around at Abderos's voice. He was wheeling himself across the deck towards them. She opened her mouth to reply... and the world filled with white light.

SHE BLINKED, her vision clearing slowly. Sound filtered through to her. Cheering. She shook her head hard, and felt the scarf around her hair loosen. She was in the longboat. To her left and right were the other crews' boats, lined up and facing the same way. Banking them on either side, in tall stalls, were hundreds of creatures. Many centaurs lined the front rows, stamping their feet and beating their armoured chests, while dryads and nymphs called and cheered. Beings from races made up of animals Lyssa couldn't even name stared back at her, clapping their hands and shouting. Beyond them, the hills were gone. They were on a different plain, long yellowing grasses stretching in all directions.

'What in the name of Zeus...?' Phyleus made her jump. He was sitting behind her in the boat, looking around dazedly. His shirt was undone and she realised with a start that he had nothing on over his undergarments.

'Where are your trousers?' she hissed at him. He looked down at himself in shock.

'I was putting them on! I don't know how I got here!' He

scrabbled around the bottom of the little boat, looking for his trousers, crying out in triumph when his hands closed around them.

'Please tell me you have a slingshot,' Lyssa groaned. His face reddened as he pulled the trousers awkwardly along his legs without standing up and revealing himself to the crowds. She looked to the sky and blew out a long breath, then unstrapped hers from her belt. She handed it to him, along with the small bag of lead shot. 'You're my gunner. And... You'll need to tell me if I get... carried away.' She looked down as she said the last few words.

'Carried away?' He strapped the shot bag to his hip and tested the strap on the slingshot.

She scowled at him. 'Don't break that.'

He rolled his eyes and turned to his right. Lyssa followed the look. Hercules was waving to the crowds, his lion-skin cloak draped across his shoulders. Evadne, blue hair shining in the increasing light, was standing next to him with a small smile on her lips. Lyssa made a low growling noise and turned the other way.

Antaeus and the gold-skinned half-giant Busiris were in a longboat twice the size of hers, with two small masts. She wondered if that would make it move faster, or if their weight would still hinder them. Past them she could see the slender longboat from the *Virtus*, the same one she had landed in when Eryx had thrown her from the Hydra head. Theseus, Psyche and Hedone were all in the boat and, to her surprise, Hedone was armed with a long spear identical to Psyche's. She felt a stab of respect for the beautiful girl.

'Heroes of Olympus.' Artemis's young voice was amplified across the plain and the crowd fell silent immediately.

'Meet my prize stag, Cerynea.' The air ahead of them shimmered with glowing gold and slowly the light solidi-

fied, an animal taking form. He truly was a beautiful creature. Taller than Lyssa at his shoulder, and so pale he was
almost white, the stag had the most magnificent antlers she
had ever seen. They were shining gold, the light reflecting
from them every time he dipped his head. 'You must follow
him back to me, on the other side of Sagittarius. You must
not harm him, and you will not overtake him. You must take
the route he does. You will start when he does. If you believe
your life is in mortal danger, tell me you give up and I will
decide if you deserve to live.'

Lyssa looked at Phyleus and laid her hand on the mast of
her boat.

'You ready? I need you to keep the others away from us.'

He loaded the slingshot and nodded.

'I'm ready.'

15

LYSSA

The stag pawed at the ground, and Lyssa realised his hooves were shining too, gold glinting in the sun. He snorted loudly, and raised his magnificent head. Another horn sounded and in a flash of gold the stag was moving, not just forward but up. His golden hooves shone as he galloped through thin air, gaining speed and height simultaneously. There was a burst of noise from the crowd and Lyssa willed her boat forward, after the shining beacon ahead of her. They were barely off the ground when Hercules's boat smashed into the side of them. Evadne aimed her slingshot with a smile and Lyssa ducked as the lead flew towards her.

'Phyleus!' she yelled, turning to him. He was firing at Busiris who was on their other side, launching arrows from a bow in a high arc above them. One landed with a loud thud in the bottom of the boat. She looked down at the metal arrowhead embedded in the wood, and willed more of herself into the little boat. The thrum of power built in her veins, the wooden mast seeming to heat beneath her hands as they surged forward, out of reach of Hercules. She looked ahead to the flash of gold, now too small to make out as any specific form. The plains still rolled ahead of them, no mountains or hills in sight. The grass was changing colour, though, turning greener and longer as they sped over it. She looked back towards Hercules, not far behind her. Evadne was yanking at a series of arrows that were sticking out of the mast of his boat, the only part not covered in dull metal plating. She scanned the shimmering triangular sail for signs of damage but couldn't see any. White flashed past on her other side. It was Theseus, over-taking her. Hedone and Psyche were holding their long spears out on either side of the boat, ensuring nobody could get close enough to ram them. Smart move, Lyssa thought, but they had no ranged weapons. Theseus saluted as he made eye contact with her and she scowled.

'Can you hear buzzing?' called Phyleus.

'Buzzing?' She listened over the sound of the wind in her ears. There was something... She willed more of her power into the boat, wanting to keep up with Theseus but reluctant to build up her energy too early. She didn't know how long this race would last and it got harder to concentrate, the more power she was channelling. Something tiny and black flew past her, close to her face. She swatted at it. Phyleus was right, it was buzzing.

'It's some sort of bug,' he called. As he said it, the grasses below them began to move, rippling like an ocean. She watched as a black swarm rose from the ripples, engulfing Theseus's boat.

'Shit,' she cursed and poured power into the mast. They shot up, over Theseus's halting boat, the buzzing bordering on deafening. She fixed her eyes on the golden glint ahead and tried to ignore the writhing black in her peripheral vision. 'Are we above them?' she yelled to Phyleus.

'I can't hear you!' She barely caught his reply. A moment later she jumped as she felt a hand on her shoulder, causing the boat to swerve as she turned.

'Whoa! Only me.' Phyleus had climbed over the bench to the mast. He leaned over the side of the boat, gripping the edge hard enough that his knuckles were white. 'I can't see the others,' he said, scanning the sky.

'I can,' Lyssa pointed. Not far below them, but a long way in front, was a whirling red light, surrounded by the black swarm. Hercules was swinging his sword in wide circles, fast, keeping the throng of insects at bay. She swatted angrily at her hair again and pushed the boat faster.

'As long as we stay above the bulk of them, we'll be OK,' Phyleus said, still shouting over the roar of the wind and the drone of the bugs. Lyssa fixed her eyes ahead and nodded. She forced herself to ignore the urge to keep looking down at the red glow of Hercules's boat and concentrate on powering forwards, over the writhing, buzzing grasslands. She didn't know how long they'd been flying when Phyleus said, 'It's stopping.'

The fact that he hadn't needed to shout the words meant he had to be right. Lyssa blinked her stinging eyes and looked as far down as she could without letting go of the mast. The undulating black mass was thinning out. She could still see the red glow of Hercules's sword but he wasn't so far ahead any more.

'Where are the other two boats?'

Phyleus moved from her side, she presumed to the back of the boat. She didn't turn to look, not wanting to risk losing track of the stag. He may have kept a steady pace in a straight line so far, but she knew enough not to take anything for granted.

'They both made it. The giants are at the back,' Phyleus reported.

'The grass is changing,' she said. 'I think... I think there's water ahead.' She lowered the boat a little without slowing, ignoring the few lingering insects that buzzed around her. They were approaching a massive marsh.

16

ERYX

Of the three Trials so far, Eryx couldn't believe he had been forced to sit and watch two from the sidelines. The only one he had been involved in he had won, he thought ruefully.

Antaeus had moved him up to the rear quarterdeck so that he could see everything going on in the flame dish. Hercules was winning, emerging from the insect-infested field waving his sword triumphantly. The crews from the *Alastor* and the *Virtus* were level, the redhead from the *Alastor* keeping her boat high. Antaeus was at the back, his face a mask of concentration. Eryx scowled, wishing he was in Busiris's place. They were approaching marshland now, and if the insects were anything to go by, they should be on their guard. Busiris held his bow at his side, looking around nervously.

Eryx felt around for the jug of water beside him, reluctant to take his eyes off the race for even a second. He had downed pints of water now but he could still taste the remnants of the disgusting sludge. He took a long swig and poked at his bandaged chest. It was tender, but not painful. He supposed he was grateful he could feel at all.

The image in the flame dish changed, showing a closer view of Hercules, the lion skin bulking his muscular frame out further. Behind him, slingshot pulled back, blue hair in a high tail and eyes vigilant, was Evadne. Eryx's eyes flicked between the two. He could see why she would be attracted to Hercules, but the things the man had done? How could anyone be with a man who had murdered his own wife and had no love for his surviving daughter?

The image widened, showing Captain Lyssa speeding towards the marshland, gaining on Hercules. The sail on her small boat was rippling scarlet red, the same colour as Hercules's sword. A flash of movement below the tiny boats caught his eye and he leaned forward, grunting in discomfort. There was something in the swamp.

HE SQUINTED at the picture before him, watching the boggy ground the boats were flying over. Again he saw it, a splash and a fin of some sort, disappearing into the murky water. Antaeus and Theseus were flying close to the swamp, close enough to each other that Theseus's first mate was stabbing her spear at Busiris, her gold armour gleaming. Frustration welled in Eryx. They weren't watching the water. He pictured Antaeus in his mind and projected his voice.

'Captain, there's something in the water below you. Raise the boat,' he said, as calmly as he could. There was no answer. He watched the flame dish, desperate for any sign that Antaeus had heard him. His captain's face didn't change. There was another ripple of movement in the water, this one bigger than the last. Eryx watched in impotent dismay as more than just a fin rose from the murk. A dark green tail, lined with sharp triangular spikes, rolled up out of the reed-filled marsh then disappeared again. He'd seen a tail like that before on Aquarius. It belonged to a giant crocodile.

17

HEDONE

Hedone was feeling quite proud of herself, until the green lizard burst from the marsh below her, snapping its monstrous teeth and flicking a tail as large as their boat at them before diving back under the water. She was able to bite back her scream, but she dropped her spear as she stumbled backwards, the boat swerving as Theseus reacted.

'Shit,' barked Psyche. 'Captain, we need to get higher.' She held her spear out further as she spoke, swishing it from side to side. Hedone bent, fumbling to get her own back in her hands.

'I'm on it.' Theseus's voice was calm and clear.

'How high do you think it can jump?' Hedone stammered.

'They. There's more than one.' Psyche's eyes were fixed on the muddy water as the boat lifted.

'They must be fast, to be keeping up with us,' Theseus said. Hedone heard a small splash, then there was a loud thud and she was thrown from her feet. She flung her arms out to break her fall, her chest hitting a wooden bench and her chin banging down a second after. She tasted salt as blood filled her mouth – she'd bitten her tongue.

The boat swerved again and she lifted her head in time to see the slimy green skin of a lizard as it collided with the side of their longboat. They were thrown the other way and Psyche roared, 'Get us higher!'

'I'm trying!' Theseus shouted back.

Hedone gripped the side of the boat with both arms and pulled herself up to a crouch. Hesitantly she peered over the edge, looking towards the bog. Five or six lizards were leaping in huge arcs out of the water, narrowly missing their rising boat. The giants had not been able to get high enough. They were still moving, but close to the water, the huge Antaeus swiping and punching whenever the lizards leaped close to their boat, toying with their prey.

The gold-skinned smaller man behind Antaeus was aiming a bow but his movements were jerky and nervous and he wasn't releasing any arrows. Reeds from the bog were climbing, reaching for the boat and wrapping themselves around the wood, stopping it from escaping the lizards' game. Hedone's mouth fell open slightly as the shirtless Antaeus roared, his massive fist connecting with a lizard's head. The snake tattoo on his back writhed with his movements, clearly visible even from this distance. But more knobbly green lizard skin flashed in the water below them, the splashing increasing as the beasts surrounded the boat. He wouldn't be able to fight them all off. The smaller giant shouted something she couldn't make out and pointed ahead of them. She followed his gesture. The stag was changing course, veering hard to the right. Theseus saw it at the same time.

'Hold on,' he called, and banked hard to keep behind the creature. She gripped the edge of the boat and turned her gaze back to the giants. They hadn't been able to turn and follow the stag. The reeds had pulled them almost to a stop and it looked like they were shouting at each other. A small lizard erupted from the water beside them and Antaeus caught it by the throat, leaning back and then launching it into the distance.

She'd never watched giants before, as they didn't visit Pisces. They were truly impressive. But she couldn't see how they were going to get out of the marsh.

Antaeus clearly realised the same thing. With a bellow he stood up tall, holding both arms in the air. She just caught the few words he shouted.

'We give up!'

The air around his boat shimmered, and then the whole thing vanished.

18

ERYX

Eryx roared on the quarterdeck, his injured chest painful as he slammed his fist down on his leg in disappointment. There was a shimmering on the deck, and then Antaeus and Busiris were back on the *Orion*, still in the longboat, slimy reeds curled around the mast and bow. There was another shimmer and Albion and Bergion appeared beside the boat, transported from the watching crowd.

'Why weren't you watching the water?' shouted Eryx, looking directly at Busiris. He was supposed to be both lookout and gunner.

'I was dealing with that bloody woman on Theseus's boat,' he growled back.

'Both of you, stop.' Antaeus voice was laced with fury. He reached up to the sail and yanked on it.

'What...?' Eryx stared. The mast behind the sail was shredded. Long jagged gouges ran in rows across it from top to bottom, clearly the work of a serrated knife. There was murder in his captain's eyes as he spoke.

'The boat wouldn't respond properly. We couldn't get high enough. Somebody did this before we started.'

Cold clamped over Eryx's skin and there was a pounding in his ears. She'd said she wanted to know about Poseidon. He'd let himself believe that she was there to talk to him. That she was concerned about him. His stomach felt like it was tying itself in knots. He couldn't tell Antaeus. He would never be allowed to take part again; he'd be stuck watching the action from afar permanently. Antaeus was staring at him and he knew his red face was showing his anger.

'Do you know who did this?' Antaeus asked quietly.

Eryx shook his head, without hesitation. 'I never left your quarters, until you brought me up here. I can't believe anybody would stoop so low...'

Antaeus cut him off.

'You two were supposed to watch the boat. How the hell did this happen?' he shouted at Bergion and Albion. They both looked down, shuffling huge booted feet. Neither spoke. 'Get it fixed,' he hissed, and stormed over to the flame dish.

19

LYSSA

Lyssa hadn't dared look back as Phyleus told her about the giant green lizards attacking Antaeus. She felt a stab of satisfaction that the giants were out of the race and immediately felt guilty. The point was to stop Hercules, she reminded herself.

She was sure they were gaining on him. She had found a good rhythm, a trickle of her power flowing through her and into the boat, enough to keep them level at the front but not enough to drain her. She didn't know for sure that she *could* be drained of her power, but she wasn't taking any risks just yet. The Rage had burned within her for ten years, and it had only grown, but she'd never channelled her power gently for a long time. Short, explosive bursts were more her style.

'Are those flowers?' Phyleus asked.

She flicked her eyes down. 'It's a meadow.'

Long, low hills were appearing on either side of them, a bright inviting green. The boggy ground had given way to luscious grass, peppered with white flowers. As they sped along trees sprouted from the ground, thick with foliage. Red and yellow flowers sprang up to join the white ones.

'It's pretty,' Phyleus said.

She rolled her eyes. 'Then something ugly is about to happen.'

Her attention was caught by a large plant growing from the ground far ahead. It wound its way up and up, taller than any of the others. In fact, it wasn't stopping. It would be as high as they were by the time they passed it.

'Lyssa!' Phyleus shouted. A huge green shoot flicked in front of the boat. She swerved sharply, heading straight at another one. 'They're growing so fast! They're everywhere!' She narrowed her eyes, adrenaline pumping through her body as she banked again, avoiding another winding vine. She wouldn't be able to get higher than these. 'Hercules is cutting them down,' Phyleus shouted. Her eyes flicked to the flashing red on her right. He was whirling his sword again, slicing through the emerald vines as they flew between them, and Evadne's young face was screwed up in concentration. She didn't normally navigate, Lyssa realised.

She'd taken her eye off the vines too long. There was a thud as they bumped along the side of one and she stumbled sideways, her hand coming off the mast. The boat slowed immediately, the red draining from the sail. A loud crunch came from the back of the boat. A vine had curled around the peaked end of the boat and they lurched to a stop. She cursed and launched herself towards the vine.

'Shoot Evadne!' she yelled at Phyleus as she grabbed hold of the vine and tried to force it off the wood. It was as thick as an arm and strangely warm. It was also completely unyielding.

'They're out of range,' Phyleus called.

'Then help me.' He was at her side in a second, scrabbling around in the bottom of the boat. 'What are you doing?' she demanded.

'When I was looking for my trousers earlier I swear I saw... Yes!' He pulled a rusty knife up triumphantly and began hacking at the vine. Lyssa looked back towards the stag. It was only a small glow in the distance, barely visible through a maze of tall, undulating vines.

'Shit,' she muttered. A second vine appeared over the prow of the boat. 'Shit!' she repeated loudly. It was time for brute strength. She ran back to the middle of the boat, laid her hands on the mast and concentrated. She fixed Hercules in her sight, speeding ahead of her, and the sail snapped taught. The boat lurched beneath her as she willed it forward, pulling against the vines.

'Got it!' shouted Phyleus and she felt the release. The longboat rocketed forward, but spun, anchored to the vine around the front of the boat. 'I'm on it,' yelled Phyleus, scrambling past her.

Lyssa took a breath and opened her mind, letting ugly memories spill into her. There was a creak, then a tearing noise as they ripped free of the vine. Phyleus went flying backwards past her as they pivoted, and then they were shooting towards the golden stag, their sail shining red.

20

HEDONE

'Do either of you have knives?' Theseus spoke calmly but his eyes darted between his crew members and the vines curling around their suspended longboat.

Hedone shook her head.

'No, Captain,' said Psyche. 'I didn't think we'd be in close combat at any time...'

'Start pulling, then,' he said and grabbed at the plant closest to him. Hedone turned, trying to do the same. The creepers were thick and they were coiling themselves around everything they could reach. All around the boat more grew, blocking the light, causing a claustrophobic gloom to engulf them. She pulled uselessly at the warm vines as they stretched over more of the wood.

'Captain, what about your arrows?' Psyche said. He looked at her.

'The boat's made of wood. If we burn the vines we risk burning the boat.'

'I'd say the risk is worth taking,' she answered, scratching futilely at the plants.

'Hedone.' Theseus looked at her. 'If the boat burns, there's a chance we may need to jump. Can you do that?'

'Jump where?' She looked over the edge of the boat. The ground was thirty feet down.

'Onto a vine. Then climb down.' His deep, warm eyes burned into hers, his concern for her clear. Her stomach flipped, then annoyance pricked at her. She wasn't a child. What would Hercules think of her having to be coddled by his rivals? She pushed out her chin.

'Of course I can,' she said.

Theseus pulled his bow from his back and notched an arrow. He leaned out slightly and murmured, '*Pira*.' The arrow tip burst into flame. He aimed for a half a second then loosed the arrow, straight at the base of the vines.

All three of them leaned over the edge of the boat, watching expectantly. For a moment nothing happened, then Hedone saw an orange flicker. The flicker grew slowly, flames forming around the bottom of the plant as she watched. Theseus notched another arrow, aimed at the next vine, and fired. Hedone realised with a start that the creeping ends of the plant weren't spreading any further.

'Look!' she exclaimed.

Psyche pulled at the vine she was pointing to and it came away from the wood in her hands. Her face lighting up, Psyche pulled harder, ripping the whole shoot away from the boat and throwing it back over the edge. Hedone hurried to do the same, working her way along the edge of the boat. The plants were getting warmer, she noticed. Almost hot. She yelled as flames licked up the creeper she had just pulled from the wood, throwing it away from her just in time to save her hands.

'Theseus!' yelled Psyche. Hedone spun around, panic engulfing her. The flames had climbed the plants faster than they could rip them from the boat. Theseus was kicking at the flaming vines but the fire had already taken to the wood, crackling, growing.

Hedone needed to be fierce. Fierce like Hercules. His strong, powerful body, moving in time with hers, making her strong. She clung to the thought, baring her teeth as she tore at more creepers, trying to rip them from the boat before the flames took them. The more she ripped at the plants, the stronger she felt, her fear melting away. Hercules's face swam before hers, filling her with power. Then the image shimmered and world went black as she heard Theseus's voice.

'We give up!'

21

EVADNE

E vadne hated flying. Hercules had never allowed her to navigate on the *Hybris*, so she didn't have much practice, and she was the sort of person who thought things through rather than reacting fast or relying on her reflexes. She dared not try to do anything smart like zipping between the swaying plants; she just plowed forward as fast as she dared and trusted her captain to cleave his way through anything they might hit. So far Hercules had easily hacked his way through the meadow of giant vines with *Keravnos*.

They might very well win this one, she thought, clutching the mast with both hands and keeping her squinting eyes on the golden stag ahead. The swathe of green in front of her seemed to be lessening. The stag veered suddenly, and she panicked, swinging the longboat after it. Hercules stumbled at the front of the boat and threw her a furious look.

'Evadne!' he roared, but she returned her attention to the stag. It was still heading left in a wide curve. She willed the boat to follow, noticing with relief that the vines were definitely becoming sparser. She could see Hercules moving towards her in her peripheral vision.

'I'll take over,' he barked. She readily relinquished control of the boat and it juddered through the air for a split second. 'Idiot,' he spat, before the smooth movement resumed. 'Now we can pick up some speed,' he muttered.

A flash of red caught Evadne's eye and she looked up as a much smaller longboat with a red sail soared over them. Captain Lyssa.

'How did they get through the vines?' she asked aloud. Hercules growled.

'She has more of my strength than I estimated. Where's the new slingshot?'

Evadne crouched in the boat, scanning the bottom for the weapon. It wasn't really a slingshot at all; it was more like a hand-held ballista. They had called it a crossbow on Leo, the first of its kind. She found it, and pulled metal bolts from the pouch on her belt to load it. She knew they would be far more lethal than the lead shot everyone else was using. It didn't really feel fair, but all four crews had been chosen by the gods, they all had help, and most had means. This was a battle, and the prize was worth the cost. She slid a bolt in and pulled back the band.

THE LANDSCAPE around them was changing. The vivid greens were dulling, muddy browns and dusty oranges replacing them as dirt covered the grass. The rolling hills were growing in height, becoming thinner and jagged, and a canyon was forming before them. The stag began to weave between the spindly peaks jutting out of the ground.

'Are we supposed to follow its path exactly?' she asked, knowing the answer but wanting to make sure Hercules did too. He didn't answer but the boat moved to follow the path of the stag. They were close enough that they could see the gold flash of its hooves and make out the shining curves of its antlers. Lyssa was still above them, but not hugely ahead. She was following the creature precisely, rounding every spindle and rocky outcrop the stag did. Soon there was no grass left at all, the barren rock turning a deep terracotta. The valley they were flying through deepened and the jutting spires increased in number. Every now and again the valley would curve sharply, forcing them around bends so tight that they almost went back on themselves.

Evadne started to enjoy the feeling, now that she wasn't in control. Her ponytail whipped behind her as they picked up speed. There was no sign of the other two crews and Lyssa was not making up any more ground. Adrenaline pulsed through her as she thought about winning. How happy Hercules would be. How they would be that much closer to immortality.

'I'm going to take the boat up. Shoot when we get level,' Hercules called.

Her elation dipped.

'Shouldn't we just speed up? Win that way?' she said, before she could stop herself.

'Shoot when we get level,' he repeated.

She took a long breath and raised the crossbow.

'Yes, Captain.'

22

HERCULES

The indifference Hercules had felt towards his daughter when he began the Trials was gone. His grudging respect for her tenacity and spirit aside, he needed her out of his way, permanently. He'd never set out to kill her or her mother four years ago; those actions had been out of his control. But this time, he knew exactly what he was doing. Keeping the golden-horned stag in sight, he willed his boat higher. Lyssa was only feet ahead of him. He swerved around a rust-coloured rock spire, the boat still rising, but made no move to overtake. He held his arm high as they drew up behind the smaller boat. The useless boy she had as lookout was facing forward, in the same direction as her.

'Shoot!' he cried and dropped his arm. He heard the bolt loose from Evadne's weapon at the same time as Lyssa's boat plummeted towards the ground. 'What in Zeus's name is she doing?' he yelled, then realised he'd lost sight of the stag.

He launched his boat after hers, spotting the stag galloping headlong at the rocky ground. At the last minute it pulled up, heading fast towards a dark hole in the face of the canyon. A cave. Lyssa's shining red sail dimmed in front of him as both boats sped into the cave mouth, swerving immediately to follow the narrow channel winding through the rock. Dust flew up around them as they shot through the tunnel and Evadne began coughing.

It was pitch dark inside the rock, making the outline of the shining stag ahead crystal clear. The glow of both boats' sails shone off the rock walls as they zipped through the passage after the creature. Hercules glanced up at his already dimming sail, acutely aware that with no light at all it would start to lose power. He narrowed his eyes at the red rippling across Lyssa's sail in front of him. He had never channelled his own divine strength into a ship like that. Perhaps it was time he started. He assumed it would be the same as wielding *Keravnos*.

'The end of the tunnel,' said Evadne, around spluttering coughs. The tunnel was straightening and he could see bright light growing in the distance. There was a shout from ahead of him and he tensed.

'Get ready to aim again, as soon as there is enough light,' he told her.

'Yes, Captain.'

Something whistled over his head and there was a clank as it hit the rock wall.

'What was that?' Hercules demanded. He pulled his lion skin up over his head with his free hand and focused on the growing exit. There was more whistling and then a thunk, and the boat lurched, scraping against the narrow tunnel wall.

'It hit the boat!' Evadne called.

'What is it?' he growled, righting the longboat, the passage too tight to risk turning to look.

'Some sort of spear, it looks—' She was cut off by another whistling sound, then the clatter of metal on rock. 'They're coming out of the rock face,' she called, her voice muffled now. It didn't matter, as they would be out of the tunnel in seconds.

The next spear hit Hercules, ricocheting off the impervious lion skin. The power of the shot knocked him sideways, though, and the boat lurched with his movement, bouncing off the wall until they burst from the rock into the bright light. They were in a canyon, only a few feet wider than the tunnel they'd just emerged from, but filled with bright daylight. His sail tautened and shimmered as he looked to Lyssa's boat. Neither she nor her crew-mate had been injured by the spears, he noticed with disappointment.

Evadne was scrambling up the boat to get next to him.

'You're supposed to be shooting!' he barked.

She pointed ahead.

'It's the end of the race.'

He followed her arm. At the end of the long, straight gorge were the tiered stalls from the start, loaded with waving spectators. He couldn't hear them but it was obvious they were cheering. And next to them, standing on a floating platform, with her gleaming bow over her shoulder, was Artemis. He willed the boat towards her as fast as he could.

23

LYSSA

They were going to win. Lyssa knew it the second she saw Artemis at the end of the gorge. Her Rage had had kept her higher and faster than any other crew, and now there was nothing between her and victory. Excitement flooded her system and she felt the boat pull beneath her, reacting to her. A high-pitched ringing sounded in her ears, followed by a loud grating noise. Apprehension clamped over her.

'What was that?' Phyleus called over the rushing wind.

'I don't know, but it doesn't matter. We're almost there,' she shouted back. Something was glinting off the canyon walls ahead of them. There were spikes erupting from the rock as the stag galloped past it, growing in his wake and elongating as she watched.

'Captain...!' Hundreds of sharp metal points were growing horizontally, straining to reach the opposite side of gully. 'We can't go over, the stag has gone through the middle.' Phyleus was right. And once those lethal tips met in the middle, the finish line would be completely blocked.

'Then we'll have to speed up,' Lyssa replied, gritting her teeth and opening her mind.

SHE WAS NO LONGER the girl who ran. She could win. She *would* win. This was a fair fight, head to head, and she would win. Her hair whipped around her face as adrenaline poured through her body and she realised absently that her scarf was gone. She felt her hands heat against the wood, drawing the Rage from her body and filling the sail with power.

The rock walls on either side of her were a blur as they sped after the stag, her eyes watering in the wind. There was a thud and the boat shuddered hard, pitching her forward to land hard against the bottom of the boat on her knees. They slowed, momentum preventing them stopping completely, and she looked up in dazed shock. Hercules flew past, huge in his lion skin, Evadne holding a metal slingshot-type weapon and smiling. Time seemed to slow as Hercules fixed his eyes on her, a laugh big and obvious on his lips.

Fury pulsed through Lyssa so hard it hurt. She roared as she leaped to her feet, thrusting both hands onto the mast and hurling her fury into the boat. It moved so fast she barely kept her footing. Phyleus yelled as he was thrown backwards but she didn't care. She fixed her venomous glare on Hercules's boat and let the hatred flow through her like liquid fire. Her mother's broken body flashed through her mind and her muscles tensed so hard that for a second she thought she would break. But the pain morphed, cloaking her, lifting her. She was gaining on him.

'Lyssa, we're too close to the spikes!' Phyleus's voice barely registered. 'You need to stop, we're not going to make it!'

They were level with Hercules now. He turned to her, his smile gone, frenzied determination on his face. She knew the shining spikes were approaching on both sides but she didn't care. All she could see was him. All she had to do was stop him. *Kill him*.

'Lyssa, give up! Give up now!'

Deep red seeped into her peripheral vision, then flooded her whole field of view, and pounding blood crashed in her ears. Phyleus kept screaming but it meant nothing. There was nothing but power, enveloping her, elevating her, making her stronger than him. Stronger than *everyone*. The pounding in her ears was now a constant roar, her whole vision filled with dark, dark red and images of her standing over Hercules, her holding the bloody poker, her raising the weapon and bringing it down towards her cowering father—

Something hit her, hard. Something bigger than her. The boat jolted as she crashed to the wooden floor, and she kicked out hard. As her leg extended, crippling cramps racked her entire body. She screamed in pain as the energy that had been coursing into the boat paralyzed her, trapped with nowhere to go. She could hear Phyleus through the confused haze of pain and anger.

'I'm sorry, shit, I'm sorry,' he was babbling.

Lyssa curled up, her body shaking as her muscles constricted so hard she couldn't breathe. She tried to concentrate on anything except the pain. The boat had stopped moving. The spikes. Why weren't they dead? Another wave of convulsing cramps ripped through her. Was that cheering?

'Phyleus?' she stammered.

'I'm sorry, I didn't know what to do. We only just made it through the spikes; you nearly killed us! Then you wouldn't stop and the sails were turning black and I didn't know what to do.' He was talking so fast she could hardly understand him. The pain in her body was subsiding. She rolled onto her back. Phyleus was leaning over her.

'*You* knocked me over?'

'I had to get you away from the mast. We had to stop.'

'Did we...?'

A small smile appeared on his lips. 'Yes. We got here first.'

She sat up quickly, immediately bashing her head into his.

'Ow! What in Zeus's name is wrong with you?' he yelled, rubbing his forehead.

'We won?'

'We won. Hercules never made it through the spikes.'

Lyssa leaped to her feet, immediately regretting it when a wave of dizziness hit her hard. She gripped the side of the boat and leaned over, looking towards the wall of shining horizontal spikes.

'I can't see any bodies.'

'No. Guess he gave up at the last minute.'

Lyssa scowled. 'Hercules would never give up.'

Phyleus shrugged. 'Maybe Evadne did for the both of them.'

Lyssa looked at him. 'Why didn't you? Why did you let me carry on?'

He stared back at her.

'I knew you could do it,' he said eventually.

'WELL DONE, HERO LYSSA.' Artemis's commanding voice rang across the cheers. Lyssa spun around to face the goddess on the podium. The Rage was leaking away and only her hands were now shaking. 'As the only hero to finish this Trial, I will gift you these.' An enormous golden set of antlers appeared above the goddess, spinning slowly. 'Any ship with these horns afront its prow is welcome on Sagittarius.'

Lyssa dropped to one knee, her heart skipping. Access to a forbidden realm could change their lives. Epizon would be thrilled, if they survived long enough to use it.

'Your next Trial has already begun,' Artemis said with a small smile, then vanished.

Immediately Lyssa heard voices in her head.

'Captain? Captain!'

'It's no good, she can't hear you. Ship communication hasn't been working since the start of the race...'

'Hey!' she shouted across them. The voices stopped. 'I can hear you. I assume you want to congratulate your hero?' She gave a mock bow as she said it, knowing they would be watching in the flame dish. Nobody answered. She straightened up, frowning. 'What's wrong?'

'Captain, it's Abderos,' said Epizon, his voice grave. 'He's gone.'

THANK YOU

Thank you for reading Skies of Olympus, I hope you enjoyed it! It would mean so much to me if you could leave a review on Amazon, just a few words can help so much! You can do that here.

If you want to find out what happened when Lyssa and her crew went to Leo to pick up Tenebrae then you can read the exclusive short story, Winds of Olympus, by signing up for my newsletter here. You'll also be the first to know about new releases!

And you can carry straight on to book 2: Tides of Olympus!

Made in the USA
Las Vegas, NV
14 January 2021

15910793R10198